Luke may never have been close to his father, but he feels like he knew him. Jay was a frustrating parent – always urging Luke to go to mortuary school, disapproving of his Broadway aspirations, and favoring his other children. He even had the audacity to die mid-argument, forcing additional guilt on Luke for never meeting his expectations.

However, Luke's assumptions about Jay are thrown into turmoil at the funeral when an enigmatic stranger, Tom, expresses gratitude that Jay finally shared his past with his children. When Luke can't hide his confusion, Tom realizes his mistake and bolts. Riddled with questions, Luke confronts his family. He is shocked to discover that everyone guards the truth that Jay was a transgender man who'd been raised as a female. Practiced at keeping his father's secrets, they're unwilling to reveal anything further at Luke's demand. Devastated by Jay's lack of trust in him, Luke feels forced to abandon the family who deceived him although leaving them behind won't answer his questions.

To discover the reason his father hid his gender identity, Luke seeks the only other person with answers, Tom. In Luke's eyes, he is owed an explanation, even if it's a difficult one. However, Tom harbors a deep protective devotion to Jay, a loyalty he feels the truth would betray. Additionally, as a man suffering with terminal cancer, he has no desire to drudge up painful memories by playing Luke's Virgil. Luke must earn his trust before the secret past of both men dies with Tom.

I0544001

Published by
NineStar Press
PO Box 91792
Albuquerque, New Mexico, 87199
www.ninestarpress.com

Print ISBN #978-1-945952-25-8
Cover by Natasha Snow
Edited by BJ Toth

Warning
This book contains brief graphic depictions of death, terminal illness, and suicidal ideation.

Boy: A Journey

James Stryker

Dedication

For my grandmother and kindred spirit, Elaine.

Acknowledgements

My words first appeared in print when I wrote the obituary for my grandmother in 2003. She continues to influence elements of my writing, but in particular, *Boy: A Journey* honors her memory. Grandma, thank you for sharing fifteen years with me and impacting the person I am today. I love you and will always wish we'd had more time together.

Boy: A Journey couldn't have made it out of the "think tank" without my wife, Jayme. Thanks for encouraging my craziness and corralling kids and puglets so I could work on it.

I'm also grateful to the visionary team of NineStar Press for their support of this book and LGBTQ literature. I've been fortunate to work closely with BJ Toth, an editor with a brilliant left brain, who's probably scarred for life by my comma splices.

And as always, the most thanks to you, the reader, for investing your time on another adventure into my headspace.

Chapter One

Harrisburg International Airport, Pennsylvania
February 2038

Luke stepped off the escalator and searched the baggage claim area for Beau. Broadway had spurned him, but she never would. He'd wrap his arms around her, pick her up, and spin her around as if they were in a black-and-white movie. He anticipated the long ride home when he could confide to her how the year in New York had treated him. Rejection after rejection after rejection. Beau would understand. She'd be sympathetic, consoling, and wonderful. She was the only one who would be, and the only one to whom he planned on revealing the truth.

It took several scans of the room before Luke realized that *he* was standing by the luggage carousel. He might've been receptive if his father had looked remorseful. Like he regretted the actions that had driven his son away for a year. But Jay just stood there, and when they made eye contact, he smiled.

I'm going to kill Beau. Kill her. Now I'll be stuck with him for almost two hours in the car. Three hundred cubic feet of space. Goddamn it, why am I here?

He marched past his father to the revolving glass doors and stepped onto the sidewalk. It was February and freezing cold, but he'd stand there, rubbing his arms, and call a cab. Or he'd walk. Or he'd call his sister, scream at her, and then beg her to come get him.

"Luke." Jay appeared beside him and touched his arm. "I know I have a few more gray hairs, but surely you still recognize me?"

He glanced at his father's hair. There were more than a few, and he'd lost weight. A lot of weight. From worry? From guilt? Luke doubted it. Maybe with Luke out of the picture, Jay had done lots of classic, active father-son pastimes with Beau's husband, Jake—Luke's replacement. His father and Jake probably played basketball together, or catch. Maybe Jay had gone full measure: thrown on a Cosby sweater and taught that fucker to ride a bicycle without training wheels.

"Where's Beau?"

"She's at home. I wanted to pick you up."

"And she let you?"

"Why would she have prevented me?" Jay laughed. "I've missed you. You have two weeks to spend with her, but I want to hear your adventures first."

Luke scrutinized Jay's face, expecting to be mocked. Beau was aware of his lies about how he was doing in New York. Did she tell Dad? Was that why he came? To make the ride home one big, long, inescapable "told you so" lecture? More haranguing about a "real" career?

But there was no gleam in his eye, no knowing grin. His father just seemed happy to see him. Luke should've known Beau would never betray him. She'd broken her promise to come to the airport, but Jay had probably insisted. If she seemed too resistant, it might've aroused his suspicion. Luke could forgive her.

"You travel light, like Mom. I parked close, just in case." Jay clapped a hand on his back, nudging him toward the parking garage.

"How's Mom?"

"Fine. Wondering why you don't call us, but you call Beau. I can't say she's the only one who wonders that."

"I'm busy."

"Auditions?"

"Several."

It was true. He devoured *Backstage* magazine and never missed a casting call. Since he wasn't an Equity member, he had to come the second or third day and stand in lines with hundreds of actors waiting to be seen, but sometimes he made it through the doors. And occasionally he got to sing more than a line.

"Any roles?"

"Several."

This statement was somewhat less true. Part of choruses, as a backup if the preferred nobody was hurling behind the curtain. Expendable. Unseen background noise. He'd tried to view it as a "foot in the door." A start to "making the right connections," like people said. But fuck people. He didn't want to wave a palm frond in *Aida*. Luke wanted the center stage spotlight.

"Major ones?"

"Most likely."

This time he spoke a blatant lie. Last week it might've been a supremely overconfident assumption, but not a "no."

He saw the white van, and the journey home loomed ahead. He hoped his father would drop it. But he didn't. He was interested. Or faking interest. It was probably faking. Definitely faking.

"Oh, yes? What?"

Luke named a role and got into the car. He folded his arms and stared through the windshield. He heard the other door shut and the engine start. It wasn't enough. It was never enough. And this game was proof of the curiosity not being genuine. Jay was trying to tease out more information, only to catch Luke in the lie.

"Now I could see that. You'd be perfect for that role. Very suave. Very cool." Jay backed the van from the spot. "But I hope you didn't limit yourself. I could picture you in either lead. You're more on the high side, so they might think your voice is better suited elsewhere."

Luke would've accepted anything. *Aida* palm frond holder included. But the casting director hadn't agreed he was a fit. He received word there'd be no callback. Absolutely nothing.

"I'd love to see you in that. To see you in anything. Mom and I can come to New York."

Believe me, when I get a lead, you'll be the first one I'll call.

That was part of the plan. He'd land a lead role in a huge production. Carnegie Hall. A big, classic Broadway show with his name on a marquee in huge letters. And then he'd call his father to rub the success in his face.

Unfortunately, it'd been a year, and that glorifying redemption was still a dream. After the disappointment from the last audition, he'd given in to Beau's pleas to come home. He needed her to soothe his bruised ego.

"I was watching the video of your last stock performance the other night. That was something. I mean *really* something."

You thought it was something all right. Luke's back stiffened as he crossed his arms tighter.

The fight had happened after his final show at the local theater. His father had gotten on his case about him wasting time at "this shit." Sure, he'd watched the video. Watched it with his arm around Jake while they drank beer from frosted mugs and laughed about the waste of matter Luke was.

"I was thinking how we watched that recording of Robert Cuccioli a hundred times. We stayed up all night the day you got offered the show, watching his every move because you wanted to nail that part." Jay drove past the onramp to the highway, and Luke groaned inwardly. He was going to take the long way. "And you absolutely did. Absolutely! You were meant for that role. It was like a second skin on you."

Well, I did do it justice. Despite his sour mood, Luke grinned. *Justice as in slaughter. I slaughtered it. It was fantastic. I was fantastic.* But then he remembered the fresh rejection. *If those bastards knew what I could do!*

"I was so proud of you." His father reached over and patted his arm. "I *am* proud of you."

Luke shrugged off the touch and said nothing.

You'd be proud of me if I went to mortuary school. If I were Jake. You haven't missed me. You have your perfect son-in-law married to your perfect daughter. You don't need me. Watching my video? I bet you trashed it.

Jay sighed and returned both hands to the wheel as he pulled into the gas station.

Thank God. We aren't taking the long way, we just need gas. Thank you, God, for cutting me a fucking break.

"I'll be right back. Do you want anything?"

"Not from you."

Luke wasn't sure he caught the comment. The car door shut, and Jay walked across the parking lot. And as if it were a dream, Luke watched the Honda Civic collide with his father.

The metal bumper hit Jay's calf and knocked his legs from under him. He flipped into the air, and his body crashed onto the car—torso slammed against the sleek hood and his head smashed into the windshield. The car swerved a little, and Luke heard the screech of brakes and smelled hot rubber. The speed and force of the stop ripped his father out of the windshield and sent him flying forward. His body skidded a few inches on the blacktop before he was at rest—a crumple of blood and glass in front of the car.

Luke shoved open the van door and ran to kneel beside his father's twisted body. Although he knew he could make the injuries worse, he pulled Jay's head into his lap. He smoothed the hair and glass from his face, trying to find him somewhere in the blood. When he called his name there was no response.

Then he felt a wet spot on his jeans and thought he'd pissed his pants. *You've got to be fucking kidding me!*

Luke curved his hand under Jay's head, his fingers moving through his matted hair, until they were stuck. Sunk in a crevice. And he felt something solid, like hard gelatin left open in the fridge for a couple of weeks. He ripped his hand out. Blood dribbled from the ends of his fingers. He hadn't pissed his pants. But he wanted to.

Oh, my God! Oh, my God! He looked at his father, who still hadn't opened his eyes or moved. What he could see of his skin through the blood was losing color. Luke pressed his hands to Jay's face, willing that living tinge not to fade. *No! Please stay! Stay with me, Dad, please!*

Luke heard sirens in the distance, but he knew they were too late. More of the syrupy blood saturated his jeans. No one could lose that much and pull through. No one could survive having their skull open, their brain exposed. He sat on the asphalt of the parking lot, caressing his father's hair, and watched him die.

Chapter Two

Salt Lake City, Utah
February 2038

Tom DuBelle knelt, puking out the sparse contents of his guts, when the phone in his pocket rang. At first, he resigned to let it ring. The caller would leave a message if it was important. He gripped the toilet bowl as he continued vomiting.

But when he heard no signal of a new message, and the phone rang for the fifth consecutive time, he decided he might as well see who it was. He only had the dry heaves anyway.

Tom brought his face from the toilet and turned against the side of the bathtub. His head spun, and he took his time stretching his legs out since the caller obviously wasn't going to stop. When he leaned back on the tub, his body shuddered from the exertion. He tilted his face to the ceiling and closed his eyes.

Why me, God? I should just put a bullet in my brain. It'd be a better way to go than this. Someone else would have to clean up the mess.

He smiled because this thought reminded him of Jay.

But chances are the person cleaning my mess wouldn't be like you. I'll be boring, but clean. I'll overdose on the meds. I'll take everything I've got and just go to sleep.

He took a breath, and his muscles relaxed as he expelled the air. A deep sleep was a delicious idea. Freedom from the weight of a broken body shutting down. Wherever one went after death, whether by suicide or letting time grind to a halt of its own accord—even if there was nowhere, and a person only rotted in the ground. To be still. To be finished.

I'm tired. So fucking tired.

Tom ran a hand over his face.

The phone rang again.

This wasn't the time to sweep into preparations. The excellent thing about suicide was that it had no expiration; it wasn't a limited-time offer. He could revisit the plans as often as he liked and act when he was ready.

That's real freedom, you motherfuckers. I'll go when I want and on my terms. There's nothing you bastards can do to stop me.

He wasn't sure who he directed the affirmation to. The cancer cells? The doctors? The parts of his body that persisted in functioning like good soldiers? Not that it mattered. They were all powerless when it came to taking his own life. And they were all motherfuckers.

The phone rang a seventh time, and Tom dug it from his pocket. When he saw the caller's name, he felt a flare of energy and was sorry to have taken his time. Jay wouldn't object to talking over the toilet bowl. Tom didn't have to keep up pretenses with him, though Jay wasn't yet aware of his current situation.

You've been trying to tell him for months. This is as good a time as any.

He imagined what Jay might say when he answered.

"'Ground control to Major Tom!' What took you so long? I thought you were dead."

Tom always answered when Jay called. Wherever he was, whoever he was with. It'd been that way for over thirty years. If Jay's name was on the screen, Tom picked up instantly. Three in the morning or three in the afternoon.

And this comment would give him the perfect segue.

"No, I'm not dead. Yet. Now, if you were to call five or six months from now..."

There wasn't much point in planning these talks. Depending on what news Jay had to report, their conversations turned a thousand ways. At the beginning of each call, Tom promised himself to tell the truth about his health, but once again the opportunity hadn't come up. He'd disconnect and realize he'd kept Jay in the dark another week. But he didn't feel guilty for long. It wasn't Tom's fault the right time hadn't presented itself. And there was always next week.

But you've been saying that for weeks now. And sooner rather than later, there won't be a next week. Do you want it to be a stranger telling him you're on the slab? You've got to do it.

Resolved to disclose his secret, Tom slid his finger across the screen to answer the persistent call and put the phone to his ear.

"Hey, buddy, how's it going?" Tom smiled.

"Is this Tom DuBelle?" Jay's voice sounded different. Perhaps he had a cold. Or maybe he was playing a joke, putting on a different voice. Yes, the usual Tom DuBelle would absolutely have taken his call the first time, not the eighth.

But current cancer husk, Tom DuBelle had happened to be hanging over a toilet bowl.

"Hilarious. I'm sorry I didn't pick you up immediately. I was busy."

"Mr. DuBelle, this isn't Jay."

He pulled the phone away and again read the name on the screen. No, he hadn't imagined Jay's number. But why would someone else call him from Jay's phone? And who would know to call him? Jay kept Tom's number under the phone contact "Memorial Hospital" so when Tom called, anyone who might pick up would think nothing of it. They'd pass the call along without interest in hearing details of a requested removal. And it gave Jay an excuse to escape the house to talk.

But who would know that? And why? Before his brain scrambled further for an answer, the caller's identity dawned on him. Confusion turned to nerves. This call was definitely unexpected.

"Hello? Are you still there? Mr. DuBelle? Hello?"

"Yes, I'm here." Tom swallowed. "And you can drop the Mister. It's not necessary."

"You know who this is?"

"Of course, I know who this is."

Tom had seen Luke a handful of times in the past twenty-six years. The most recent had been a year ago from the farthest seat to the right in the dress circle of the Community Theater of the Arts. Tom had been the weird douche bag who wore a baseball cap in the theater, hid the lower half of his face with a red-and-black scarf whenever the houselights came up, and had the audacity to snap a picture during the show. But the peculiar looks and the nimrod seated to his left elbowing him in the side had been worth it. For two and a half hours, he'd watched Luke move around the stage and listened to him sing. It'd been the longest span of time he'd been in the same room with the boy.

When the performance had ended, Tom had hidden in the corner of the vestibule. He'd pulled his trench coat around himself and tried to melt into the wall as he'd waited for the performers to file out of the theater.

"You look like a suicide bomber."

Jay found him first. He clapped a hand on Tom's shoulder, making him jump.

"Or like I have the plague." Tom's smile had been masked by the scarf. He'd known something was wrong with him at that stage, but they'd only started digging into the issue. It'd been too early to confirm anything other than he wasn't contagious.

"You can breathe unfiltered air. There's no one else here but me."

"At the final show? Really?"

"If you'd let me know you were coming, I could've told you that. I would have arranged for you to sit with me, instead of alone."

"I don't mind being alone."

"But you look God-awful in hats, Tom." Jay pulled the cap from his head and handed it to him with a grin. When Tom took it, Jay again put his hand to his shoulder. "Do you want to meet him?"

"No."

"Isn't that why you came? Why you're waiting?"

"I just wanted to watch." Tom turned from his friend as he heard the double doors of the auditorium open. "There's nothing to be gained by meeting him."

Actors and actresses emerged in clumps. The other members of the audience who had waited for them began to clap as if they were taking another curtain call. Jay's reply was lost in the eruption of applause when Luke came through the door, the leading actress on his arm.

Luke had been unable to hide the pleasure in his eyes at having all attention on him, and he'd put up his hand to acknowledge their praise. Although the boy had tried to remain dignified and calm, Tom could tell from the way he lifted the heels of his shoes and tapped his fingers on the actress's arm that he wanted to jump out of his skin with pride.

This was how I felt after that last performance at the Rudolfinum. Swarms of people cheering. It's a drug. It's mainlining heroin. There's never enough. Veneration and unbridled acclaim for your talent—it's the most fantastic feeling there is.

"You've got to get him out of here. It's time." Tom had nudged Jay without looking from Luke. "He can't keep doing stock theater shit. He has enough experience in his portfolio that he can apply for school or go to a larger venue. He could start earning his Equity card."

"I'm talking to him about it tonight. How long will you be around?"

"I fly back tomorrow."

"You always make these trips short. Unexpected and short. I spent over a year with you, but you can't spare me a couple days?"

"I'm a very busy man," Tom lied. He tucked the baseball cap in his coat and shoved his hands in his pockets. Luke had put his arm around the actress and given her a kiss on the cheek. He wondered if that was for show. Did Luke like this girl? Wouldn't Jay have mentioned the boy having a girlfriend? Maybe he did though, and they were in love. Perhaps he'd marry her, and Tom could secretly attend another wedding. That would be nice.

You're not dying, Tom. Don't be stupid, he'd assured himself. *You're sick, but you're not dying. You have plenty of time to watch them. And someday you'll meet them, under the right circumstance. But not right now.*

"I'll call you after I talk to him. We'll have a drink, yes?"

He abruptly turned his face and brought the scarf over his mouth as Luke's eyes centered on Jay and he waved. Tom took two quick steps away before realizing how conspicuous the action was. Thankfully, Luke's attention had been diverted as a member of the cast started to belt a bubblegum song a cappella.

"Yes?" Jay's hand squeezed his shoulder again.

"Yes, but go."

"You're not a leper."

"That you're aware of."

Tom had exited quickly, once again leaving, having not spoken a word to Luke. He'd only observed, silent in the background. Only listened. Regardless of what went on. Until now.

☆

His heart froze.

Your phone voice is different than your voice in person. Or your singing voice. All this advanced technology, and people still don't sound the same over the phone.

"Then you probably also know the purpose of my call." Luke ended the sentence with a cough.

"That, I'm completely unaware of," Tom replied. "Do tell."

What might it be? And what had prompted Jay to finally tell Luke the truth? Jay had always been adamant about not revealing anything to Luke or his sister. If Tom had accepted the offer to "meet him" a year ago, he knew it would have been meaningless. Jay would introduce Tom as a friend; Tom would shake the boy's hand, and that would be it. But if Luke was now aware of his existence, something must've been disclosed.

Perhaps Jay really knew how sick he was. When they talked last week, had the weariness come across in his voice? Had Jay guessed? And having guessed, had he decided it would be nice for Tom to know the boy through more than stories, photographs, and the occasional stalking? Maybe Jay's conscience had driven him to take the chance that his children would understand.

But I'm not sure I want that. And it's fucked-up that you'd do this without talking to me first. Not that it's out of your character to do some pretty fucked-up things.

He wished he had time to think the proposition over. If he accepted, he wanted to plan how to proceed and how much to invest with the amount of time he had left.

It's a kind offer, but it's too late to forge relationships. I don't give a fuck. Tom grimaced and ran his hand through his hair. *I'm dying, Jay. You don't know how that is. It's burden enough without having this thrown at me spur of the moment, jackass. Besides contact with you, I just want to be left alone.*

On the other end of the line, Luke answered Tom's question with his voice crackling.

"I'm sorry to tell you this, Mr. DuBelle, but he's gone."

"He's gone? Who's gone?"

"Dad. He passed away this afternoon."

Tom's stomach dropped, and a chill shot through his core. Of all the ways he'd imagined his first conversation with Luke, this wasn't one of them.

"There must be some mistake."

"Believe me, sir, we wish there was."

"He can't be dead! He wasn't in bad health. I just talked to him last week. He's not an old man. He's only fifty years old!"

But you're only forty-eight, Tom. Tears burned his eyes, and his breathing became heavy. The density of the air seemed to grow. His chest hammered as if he were bench pressing while being compressed in a strait jacket. *And you're not going to make it to forty-nine.*

"It was sudden."

Luke choked, the emotion apparent in his voice. A strong feeling of compassion for the boy eased the pressure of the laces and pushed back Tom's grief. As hard as Jay's death was for Tom, how much more difficult it must be for Luke? Especially since it was unexpected. Things could be easier if they were anticipated and planned for. Luke would've become accustomed to not having his father anymore. But to have him ripped away? And it was so soon after Luke had returned from New York after being away for a year. Presumably, the boy had patched things with Jay prior to his death.

"How are you holding up? And Beau?"

"As well as could be expected." Luke sounded surprised by Tom's question. "I was asked to call and let you know."

"Asked by whom?"

"By him."

Not that it could've been anyone else. No one had been aware they'd kept in close communication, even Jay's wife. The revelation of his past must've been a deathbed confession made at the brink of the abyss. It didn't matter what Luke thought after he was dead. Jay wouldn't be around to worry about it. At his death, Jay's ideal world was forever crystallized.

More likely, after twenty-six years of keeping his children in the dark, the admission had been in a moment of desperation. Tom knew Jay only would've ended the silence under extreme duress. What could be more pressure than dying? And it wasn't Tom's imminent death that had pulled the trigger.

Pretend you're one of those bright-side, blue-sky bastards, Tom. He gritted his teeth. *There are two things to be grateful for: he didn't carry that secret to the grave, and I'm off the hook. I don't have to tell him I'm dying. Concentrate on that. I can evaporate, and no one will miss me.*

But he knew that wasn't true. With Jay telling the truth, Tom's presence had been revealed. He still had unfinished business. *God-fucking-damn it.*

"Do you know when the funeral is yet?"

"Don't worry. I just promised I'd let you know."

"I'm coming. Don't be ridiculous."

Tom would do whatever necessary in order to travel. He'd stop the meds that prolonged his pathetic existence, but had the cute, fluffy bonus of nausea. He'd force his doctor to give him a stronger pain prescription. He had to see his friend one last time. He had to say good-bye to Jay.

It was a lesser priority, but he could also build a fakey-fakey bond with Luke, if that's what the boy wanted. He wouldn't permit either of them to get too close. Small talk. He'd ask Luke what he'd been up to in New York over the past year and offer whatever advice he could on performing and auditioning. Or if Luke had decided to go to school, Tom could help him compile his application.

I wonder where he'll try to go. Now that it's in the open, I could pull strings. There's nothing preventing me anymore.

And, yes, Tom would listen to Luke express his sorrow about the loss of his father. The same went for Beau. He wouldn't tell them he was dying, and he'd let them think he'd wanted to be nothing more than an aloof shadow in their lives. Warm, but not too warm. One-armed, crisp hug. Three-second handshake. And he'd desperately try not to focus on how much the boy resembled Jay. Their likeness would suck him into a black hole from which he'd never be able to emerge.

The children wouldn't be told anything about him and Jay beyond what they might already know. Which he doubted was much. No amount of dying could've driven that information from Jay.

Afterward, he'd fly home, all parties satisfied. And he'd overdose on the meds. That would be the perfect time to do it. He'd be dead before an emotional investment could develop into any profound connection.

"No, really. Don't."

"Why not?"

"Mr. DuBelle—"

"Tom."

"I was only to call and advise you. I don't think you should come. It would upset people." Luke took a breath. "Dad wanted me to tell you, and I've done that. I can't see what good could come of any contact."

"You're specifically asking me not to come for the funeral?"

"Yes. I am." Luke stumbled in hesitation, and Tom waited to reply. "I'm sorry it has to be this way, Tom."

"Are you really?"

"Yes. I don't agree with all his actions, or the secrecy, but I will honor his wishes. He asked for you to be notified. That's all."

Tom considered giving a cocky response. If Jay hadn't explicitly prohibited his attendance, there was no violation of his request. And he knew Jay wouldn't have forbidden him. He'd never technically barred Tom from visiting. They'd just come to the consensus that it wasn't the best arrangement. Tom kept his distance except on rare occasions when he was able to blend into the crowd. He contemplated telling Luke this fact as well.

I've already been there, and neither of you knew. I saw you graduate. I watched Beau get married. I was in the dress circle of your final performance the night you had that fight with your dad. And I saw more than you may think.

But he said nothing. He heard the quaver in the boy's voice and could almost read Luke's thoughts, pleading for him to not push. Let him off the line to proceed with the grueling task of burying his father.

Tom also felt the underlying emotion behind the words. It was the ultimate tempering factor—loyalty. Luke was misinterpreting Jay's direction, and his excuses were bullshit, but the sentiment came from faithfulness and love. Two emotions Tom felt strongly in regards to Jay.

Tom decided to say, "You're a good son."

He heard Luke suck in several quick gasps at a distance from the phone. When the boy spoke again, the tightness in Luke's throat brought his voice an octave higher. "Thank you. He was the only father I've ever known."

There was silence until Luke continued in a stronger tone. "Anyway, it was nice talking with you. I'm sorry for your loss; I know how close you were."

"You could call again sometime, if you like."

"I don't think so. But take care of yourself. Good-bye, Mr. DuBelle."

"Tom."

"Good-bye, Tom."

"Good-bye, Luke." By the time Tom said it, the call had already disconnected.

Tom dropped the phone, and the back panel popped off, the battery skidding across the bathroom floor. He took steady breaths to lessen his queasiness.

Jay was dead, and he might as well not have revealed the secret to Luke. Yes, the boy had cared enough to call and notify Tom; however, he didn't want anything to do with him. Not that Tom was convinced he could've reciprocated, but a part of him was hurt that their first and only contact had been nothing more than a chore. And now Luke had washed his hands of him. He was a devoted son who'd done his duty.

Tom had been right; he had no unfinished business. The only person who cared if he lived was gone. The only person who *he* cared if *they* were alive was dead. Jay was the most crushing loss. Again. But Jay wasn't moving two thousand miles away and disappearing into a new life. That had been difficult, but knowing he was out there—in a place where Tom could occasionally visit—made it tolerable, if he kept busy. Jay had still been within reach. Now Tom was unequivocally alone.

I should do it right fucking now. Walk into the kitchen and take every pill I have. Tears streamed down his cheeks. *Do it before all the pain sinks in, and it becomes real that he's gone. You have to. If you don't, you'll die alone, Tom. Alone, caked in your own shit, with some hospice bitch hoping you kick it quick so she can leave early. You don't want that.*

Tom drew himself onto his knees and placed his palms on the cold tiles. He tried to summon the strength to get to his feet, but putting his weight on one leg to rise made his head spin. He picked up the phone and its battery, tucking them into his pocket. Pushing aside the shame of his degradation, he crawled from the bathroom like an animal.

His living room was only yards down the hall, but he wheezed as he reached the doorframe. He held his breath when the pinpricks went up the back of his neck.

I'm not going to throw up on the floor.

The vertical blinds covering the windows were rotated open. Afternoon sun poured in through the sheer fabric attached to the vanes; the light cascaded over an ebony grand piano, the room's centerpiece. The lid was closed, and several frames rested on its surface. Across the room, another hallway led to the kitchen. He could make it there once he caught his breath. And after enough time lying on the floor, he'd be able to retrieve the pills from the cupboard.

He turned cautiously on his side and curled his arm under his head. As he waited for his heart to stop pounding, he squinted at the pictures adorning the piano. His vision blurred the finer details, but he saw the faces.

I forgot to ask what happened. I hope it was quick. And if you were aware of it, I hope you weren't alone.

In whatever context or circumstance though, Jay's death wasn't fair.

Not just to Tom, but to Jay himself, and to his now-fatherless children.

I know, I know, life isn't fair. But you weren't ready to die. And those kids weren't ready to lose you. Beau will be okay, she has her husband. But Luke needed you. I told you that you should've trusted them and been honest. That's a fairness you could've controlled but chose not to.

He thought of what Luke had said on the phone—"I don't agree with all his actions, or the secrecy."

Did you really mean what you said after that?

Tom picked over the conversation in his head. It was possible Luke meant every word literally, but it also seemed plausible that more could've been implied. He'd said he was "sorry it had to be this way." Wasn't that the same as saying "I wish it could be another way?" How did Luke want it? Tom was no longer curious, but the boy might be. Perhaps Luke wanted him to come, but he was wary of a scene with his mother. If Luke didn't know of the times Tom had been there, he might not understand how he could be invisible—and he had no intention of starting a fight with anyone. Maybe Luke was being reasonably careful about a man he didn't know.

But I'm the one who's dying. I need to think of what I want to do. It's not whether I should or shouldn't go. And it's not about him. It's a free country. I'll do whatever I want.

Tom ran through the times he'd been there over the past twenty-six years. He remembered again Luke's final show and seeing the grin on the boy's face. He thought of sitting at the corner table, while Jay had the father-daughter dance with Beau at her wedding reception. Watching both children receive their diplomas at the podium as he lurked in the back row. At every opportunity, he'd chickened out on sharing even innocent words with them. Random people shook their hands, but Tom couldn't. There was something sacred, something pristine and golden about Jay's children that he'd soil by infiltrating any more than he had.

But that was okay, he told himself. *I didn't feel bad. I liked watching them. To see success, to pretend things had been different made me happy. And I did mean to someday break the silence. Even if they didn't know who I was, I'd look them in the eye. "Hello, I'm Tom."*

Perhaps that was another reason why Jay had asked Luke to call him. The funeral would be Tom's last chance. Jay had been his only connection to what happened in their lives. He'd never again be apprised of any important events, including those he was already aware of on the horizon.

This is your way of forcing me to accomplish my bucket list. Tom turned on his back. *It's true, now that they know, I'll regret it. Unless I kill myself right now. You don't want them to see you like this anyway, Tom. You're barely human anymore. If I can get into that kitchen before thinking any further—*

But when he braced his hands to the floor and tried to raise his torso, his head swam. It took great effort for him to lower his head and not let it crash to the hardwood. Tom covered his eyes with his arm.

And there's you. I want to see you one more time, Jay. You son of a bitch.

Tom moved his hand to his pocket and picked out the phone and its separated battery. He pieced the two together, and a few screen swipes later, the phone rang. His oncologist's office answered, and he explained to the receptionist his need to travel for a funeral on the East Coast. With little need for persuasion, he was prescribed a stronger pain medication, another pill for the nausea, and she pushed his next appointment back a week.

Someone will be glad for that slot. Tom ended the call and stared at the ceiling. The oncologist was in high demand, and it hadn't been easy to secure him. There'd been a time when Tom hadn't wanted or expected to die. When, although the prognosis was grim, he truly believed he could be the exception that made it. Instead of dying before he was fifty, he'd be back on the road. Or on a plane. Country hopping to concert halls and doing what he loved.

He looked at the piano, centering on it rather than the pictures. *What will they do with you when I'm dead, baby? Sell you to a family with a snot-nosed kid who'll run greasy fingers across your keys?* He sighed. *Can you be cremated with a piano? I could only let them burn you if you were whole. They can't break you apart like a bunch of firewood. But we could go together. You're the only thing that never left me. And when they'd open the door after we disintegrated and collapsed together, there'd just be my bone fragments and your beautiful, blackened strings to rake out. Now, that is a great scheme. Is there a crematory big enough? Jay would know. He'd find one for me.*

But Jay was dead. And it was a stupid idea. His piano would be sold to the highest bidder. His photographs would go in the trash. And his ashes would be tossed behind the crematory for a dog to shit on. Who gave a damn? When Tom was dead, he wouldn't care.

And that's where I'll focus. The end of the caring. About the piano, about Jay, about Jay's children. And the new silver lining: now I have more choices. I can go by way of the old pain meds, the OxyContin, or we could do a nice mix and leave no fun for any junkies that might go through my medicine cabinet. It will be pleasant to mentally mix my death cocktail on an eight-hour flight to Pennsylvania and back.

Chapter Three

Williamsport, Pennsylvania
February 2038

As Luke looked at his father's body in the casket, he was keenly aware of the skill his brother-in-law had demonstrated in putting Jay's face back together. He preferred not to think about Jake having talent or purpose on the planet, but it kept him from contemplating the fact that his father's face had needed to be put back together.

There's a reason why Jake does this, he thought. *I couldn't have done it.*

But Luke knew how much work had been involved.

There were two problems with the repetitive statements people incessantly spewed at him. Not only did they not have a clue how it'd been to be there, but the death was far from a "passing." His grandmothers had "passed" in quiet submission. Jay's mother, Meecie, had had a coveted death—after living with them for several years, she'd died silently in her bed, her son holding her hand. That was passing. Jay had been partially digested by a Civic and thrown up to die in a mass of mangled gore. Luke had barely been able to distinguish his features amid the embedded glass.

Now he found no evidence of the contorted face he'd last seen. It was just Dad. Asleep. His head turned at that fifteen-degree angle. How many heads had Jay turned in this way? And how many hands had he joined and placed over the abdomen? Luke had always believed the pose was stupid. Who slept like this? With their hands clasped and legs together, the toes of their shoes in the air like a tin soldier that'd been knocked over? His father had, of course, answered this question for him years ago.

☆

"They're not supposed to be asleep," Jay said. He continued massaging the hands of an older man Luke had helped him place in a casket.

The removing was fine. The transporting. The lifting. But Luke refrained from technical details. They held no appeal. And he had no idea why his father had any interest either. All he could think was that someone had to do it. Someone had to change car filters and clean portable toilets too.

"But that's what they want. That's what they all say." Luke made a face, continuing in a nasal voice. "'He looks like he's asleep.'"

This comment made Jay stop what he was doing and face his son. "That's not funny, Luke."

"Well *that's* not sleeping. The way he slept, he wouldn't fit in that casket."

"I told you, they're not supposed to be asleep."

"So what are they supposed to be?"

"Not in pain anymore. At peace."

"People still don't look like that when they're at peace. I'm never at peace in a monkey suit. I wouldn't sleep in a monkey suit. He probably slept bare-ass naked."

Jay gave a heavy sigh, and there were several uncomfortable seconds with only the rise and fall of "Recondita Armonia" in the background.

"Come on, Dad. I'm stating the obvious."

"Death isn't a pleasant thing. Some of these poor people hang on for months, suffering. And it's not the movies. When they go, the horror they've faced doesn't just evaporate—"

"I've been on pickups."

It seemed since Luke had been old enough to walk, he'd been encouraged to accompany Jay on body removals. He wasn't able to be of actual help, but he remembered sitting in the front seat of the white van and feeling the back doors open. There'd be the sound of the bag sliding in, the gurney then folded and placed beside it. And he was a little boy, alone with a dead body until his father climbed into the driver's seat.

"Think about this. If something terrible happened to someone you loved, how would you want to see them? And how would you want your family to see you? What would bring them comfort?" Jay returned to loosening the tension in the dead man's hands. "Someday, this will be you."

"I know I'm going to die, Dad, I know that."

"No, I mean doing what I'm doing. You'll need to be more sensitive. And think of doing things for others without reciprocity. Even if you don't fully understand, caring for someone without an ulterior motive is—"

"A 'good deed of truth.'" Luke cut him off with an exaggerated nod.

"You should build your life with those. You won't always be the same person, in the same stage of life you are now. Eventually, you'll be where I am."

☆

His father had known Luke had goals that were infinitely more important than embalming and cremating bodies, but he still spent time trying to push his son into his footsteps. Luke had shown no interest and, after graduating high school, had remained at home, participating in only quick and unskilled tasks. But he knew Jay believed he'd "come to his senses."

The final straw had been their fight last year—Luke had declared he didn't intend to pursue a career in the mortuary industry. He'd continue acting.

And not just any acting—*anyone* could say words in front of people. He wanted more. Musical theater. Broadway. The Great White Way. *That* was a show. And he had a gift for it. He danced and sang, working the entire audience into wishing they were him or could be around him. He'd held prominent roles in every stock theater production for the past six years.

For the life of him, Luke hadn't understood why Jay was disappointed. Unlike other things, Luke went to the trouble of trying to solve this problem. He'd been attempting to make sense of it since that rat bastard Jake had come into the picture and supplanted him. Luke had assumed that with his father's love for music, his own musical aspirations would've pleased him. For certain, Luke's talent would make him more than just a failed hope. But it hadn't worked.

And now here Jay was. Scraped from the road. An empty shell, but a serene empty shell. Yes, all the reconstruction and cosmetics were a mask for death. But did he want that horrible sight to be his last image of his father? With the glass sticking out of his face and his skull cracked open? As Jay had once asked, how would Luke want to see him?

Alive. Luke clasped his trembling hands at the small of his back. *I want to see you alive. I was hurt and angry that you didn't believe in me. That you wanted things for me I didn't. That you replaced me. But I never wanted you to die, Dad. I wasn't ready.*

He could practically hear his father answering how no one is ever ready. "Even if they think they are. Even if the person you love is suffering, and it's for the best," Luke imagined he'd say. "There's always a part of you that thinks, 'Not yet.'"

If Jay had stayed alive, perhaps an apology would've followed. Luke hadn't intended to make it easy; he wanted to force his father to work for forgiveness. But he'd died at the beginning of this torturous, dramatic episode. Sans absolution. Without Luke telling him that he loved him, and that he'd missed him too.

During his time in New York, Luke fought missing Jay. He struggled passionately against the homesickness and to keep his anger hot. But sometimes, in the quiet of the night, when he was alone except for the roaches racing like greyhounds through the apartment, he remembered watching Robert Cuccioli with his father and wondered if he was wrong. But the memory of the fight came on the heels of any pleasant recollection, and Luke knew he was right. Still, the notion of his culpability surfaced from time to time.

Perhaps if I'd said that I remember being excited with you. But then you insulted what I'm trying to accomplish. You didn't force me to leave, but you wanted me to! You wanted your embarrassing son out of your life so you could have your collection of everything that does fit with what you want! How can I forgive you for that?

That speech would've thrown Jay a bone. And then when he'd gotten mown up by that Civic, Luke could've found solace in having tried.

But what had he said?

He'd pulled away from his father's touch.

"Do you want anything?"

"Not from you."

What if I'd asked for a candy bar? A fucking Milky Way. You can't stay angry with someone who gives you a fucking Milky Way.

Suppositions didn't matter though. It was done. Luke was a slug and felt he owed his dead father: to abandon his Broadway dream, come home, and be a good funeral director.

He wanted to blame Jay for the feelings of obligation, but it wasn't his father's doing. It was sick divine manipulation trying to pin him in a corner. Luke didn't believe in God usually, yet here He was.

It won't work. I don't care how many deities interfere. I won't give up my life for you. You have your fucking son.

As perfectly reconstructed as his father was, Luke expected Jay to open his eyes. To tell him he was being an idiot. People got hit by Honda Civics all the time. God wasn't trying to strategically maneuver individuals into different career choices. It hadn't been a specific attack. No one was out to get him.

"The world doesn't revolve around you, Luke," Jay would say.

Logically, he knew it didn't, but it felt that way a lot.

Despite whoever the center of the universe actually was though, Dad was still dead. And as contrary as it seemed, having grown up surrounded by death, Luke had never taken into account that eventually Jay would be on his own embalming table. His father had been a permanent fixture. He'd live forever.

There'd been no ticking clock. He could rush to New York, become successful, and be a son a father couldn't help but be proud of. In the short term, he could exact full control over the reconciliation. He'd prolong it until the dramatic good-bye at the airport where Luke would bestow forgiveness on Jay. And he'd had two weeks to plan. Until two weeks unraveled to less than an hour, and it had been figured out for him.

"You never did say what happened."

Luke didn't care to find the source of the voice. People had been approaching him during the viewing, vomiting hollow sympathies and questions that neither he nor they cared about. It was just moving through the expected motions of grief. Jay would've reminded him that people didn't always know what to say, and he should be considerate, not critical of their discomfort. He wouldn't have approved of Luke ignoring anyone, but his father wasn't in the position to do anything about it.

"Am I interrupting?"

Luke kept his eyes on Jay's face and said nothing. Let the visitor think he was in the darkest stages of mourning.

"Hello? Can you pause the keening for a minute?"

Now Luke turned, but only to shut the person up with a glare.

A man stood beside him, and as deep as Luke had been in thought, he might've been there for some time. His careworn face made him appear older than Jay, and he had an intimate, friendly feel.

He held Luke's gaze, and for a moment, something overtook the magnetic amusement that had first dominated the stranger's expression. It was a sudden shift, and what flashed through Luke's mind was a fragment of music. The thundering orchestra around him stopped, leaving behind a solitary woodwind. The look in the man's eyes—

"Ma in altr'uomo qui mi cangio—But here I become another person!"

As quickly as it came, the recognition vanished, and Luke wondered if he'd seen anything notable at all, or if he was just so nostalgic for Jay that pieces of his father's favorite opera were haunting him.

"I don't mean to be rude, but he's not going anywhere." The man tipped his head in the direction of Jay's body with a casualness that made the action vulgar. "I, however, am. I have a plane to catch tomorrow."

"You may not mean to be rude, but you are."

"Rude is ignoring someone who's asking you a question."

The rebuke twinged. "Go read it in the newspaper, old man."

"Old man? My God, you're cruel, boy." He put his hand to his chest. "Your dad wasn't an old man, and I'm two years younger. I was one grade behind him, only one! If I'm an old man, what is he?"

A dead man, Luke thought, but said nothing.

"A dead man, I suppose," said the stranger.

"Jackass," Luke muttered.

"You still haven't answered my question."

Luke glowered at him.

"It was a car accident, all right? He died in the street as if he were an animal! A Honda Civic mowed him down like a fucking dog!"

But Luke thought of how Jay's body had actually hung in the air a split second before crashing onto the front of the car.

It wasn't "mowed down." It was "mowed up." He scrunched his eyes closed, and tears spilled from the corners as he tried to eject the revolving image. He wiped his hand across his eyes and rolled his shoulders before glancing at the man.

"Are you happy now?"

His face was unreadable, but his gray eyes were probing as he contemplated Luke. Maybe that was why the man was familiar. His expression reminded Luke of the way Jay used to look at him. His stare moved like hands across a brick wall, feeling for a crack or a leak.

"No one's happy, Luke," he said. "It's fucked-up. Just fucked-up. A boy shouldn't have to bury his father."

"I thought it was that a parent shouldn't have to bury their child."

"No one should have to bury anyone, in my opinion, until they're so fucking sick of them, that they'd sooner kill them personally than have to spend another second sharing the same air. I know you were angry, but you didn't hate him." His glasses slipped an inch down the bridge of his nose, and he looked at Luke over the frames. "Please tell me you made things right before this happened."

The odd thing about the stranger's statement was that no one outside their immediate family had been aware of the rift between Luke and Jay. Everyone else assumed he was just ready to pursue his dream in New York, not that he'd been banished from the house and hadn't spoken to his parents in a year. Some people who'd approached him today hadn't been aware he'd left at all.

"Well, did you?" the man asked again.

Who was this person who'd infiltrated their circle?

"How do you know about that?"

"I know many things."

"Such as?"

"Jay didn't keep much, if anything, from me. Particularly concerning you and your sister." He motioned to where Beau stood across the room. "I doubt there's anything new you could tell me. Except New York. If you're feeling up to it, I'd like to hear how it's been."

Who are you? Luke felt his forehead wrinkle as he tried to place the man. Jay had been friendly but reserved. He hadn't confided to anyone other than his wife, or perhaps Beau.

"You need to learn to come out of your head, Luke, and pay attention to what's around you." He gave a gentle smile.

His father had often given him similar advice, so the chiding felt almost comfortable.

"Who are you?" Luke asked aloud this time.

The look on his face was one Luke was accustomed to seeing—disappointment. He felt that he could've discerned disappointment in a pitch black room. The stranger had expected to be known. Luckily, he made a speedy recovery.

"Your mom probably wouldn't have approved of any pictures of me. I live alone and can do as I please. Though, I'd know you anywhere." He again studied Luke over his glasses. The smile crept back onto his face, and he extended his hand. "Tom DuBelle. People sound different over the phone, so I'll forgive the faux pas in not recognizing me."

The name didn't help.

Tom removed his hand after a single shake as if he was afraid to be in physical contact for too long. He looped his thumbs in the front pockets of his slacks, and more color came into his cheeks.

"So, how about it? Would you care to humor an 'old man'? I'm only here until tomorrow night, and it'd be nice to know you more through your own words."

"How do you mean?"

"You could regale me with your tales of New York. I lived there once, but I didn't have time for anything that'd be of consequence to anyone beyond myself. Ergo, your stories would be highly amusing to me." Tom shrugged. "You wouldn't refuse a humble offer from an 'old man.'"

"What offer?"

"Breakfast tomorrow. An hour from your day would be sufficient."

"I'm burying my father tomorrow." Luke raised an eyebrow.

"All the more fitting, wouldn't you say? You're not burying him in the morning, and you have to eat. And..." Tom looked at Beau again. "Invite your sister, if she'll come. You could also, if you were feeling generous, persuade her to bring a picture of the sonogram. Jay had promised send me a copy, but I don't think he got it in the mail."

Luke wasn't sure if anything Tom said could've unsettled him more. An intuitive person might've picked up on the split between him and his father, but Beau was only eight weeks along. She'd said she wasn't planning on even telling them, only she couldn't bear to keep it from her parents. And she told Luke everything. She'd need their support if the worst happened. No one else was to know until it was necessary. But this man expected a picture of a sonogram that'd taken place only a few days before.

"I told you, your dad didn't keep anything from me." Tom seemed to read the shock on Luke's face. "I know about the last one too."

"Everyone knows that. No one is supposed to know about this."

"I'd prefer to listen to you talk, but I guess I could continue to dazzle you with my knowledge of your life, if that will secure a slot in your busy schedule."

Luke felt more than mild curiosity. The intrigue provided a welcome distraction from his current situation.

"Six."

"Jesus Christ. Proof that I'm not an 'old man.' Only old men get up at that hour. Seven thirty. Not a minute earlier. I'm staying at the Virginian. Meet me at the restaurant across the street. And if Beau doesn't want to come, don't try to force her. But do bring the picture, if you can." Tom surveyed the room. "We'll talk more tomorrow. I need to leave, while I still can." He again flipped out his hand. "Luke."

"Mr. DuBelle." Luke couldn't determine what or who Tom was looking for. He took his hand and again received one shake.

"Please, call me Tom."

Tom DuBelle moved toward the door with a pace and precision that confirmed he wasn't as old as he appeared. In order to bring him to Beau's attention, Luke sprinted across the room. She was talking with two other people, and he tugged on the sleeve of her blouse to break her from the conversation.

"What is it?" Luke wrapped his arm around his sister's shoulders and steered her away.

"Do you know that man?" He pointed at Tom, who was pulling a long coat from a hanger.

Luke waited for any recognition to come into Beau's expression as she followed the direction of his finger. The man slid on his coat in one fluid motion and cast a glance at the open casket before striding out the door.

"No. Why? Who is he?"

"His name is Tom DuBelle."

"Tom DuBelle?" He caught the lilt in her voice.

"Yes! You do know him?"

"No."

"He seemed to know a lot. He knew about my fight with Dad. He even knew about you."

Beau stared at the floor and ran her fingertips along a silver necklace she wore.

"I know. It was surreal. He said Dad told him everything."

"What did he tell you, Luke? Did he say anything about Dad?"

"No, he seemed more interested in me."

He considered revealing the breakfast appointment. Not necessarily to invite her, as Tom had bidden him to. He was still deciding if he'd go himself, and it'd be nice to get her opinion. But with the nervous way she was acting, he settled against it. He wanted to see if she'd disclose any other information, however subtle, if he tugged the right threads.

"I think he came from Utah."

"Why? What makes you say that?"

"He said he's got a plane to catch and that he was one grade behind Dad. The way he insinuated they were close. I think they went to school together."

Luke could hear the gears turning in her head.

"How did he find out?" She asked at such a low volume that he imagined she was too deep in the machine to be aware she'd posed the question aloud.

"I don't know. He commented that 'people sound different over the phone.'"

"Did you call him?"

"No. I don't know who he is to have called him. I didn't think Dad had friends he kept in contact with from Utah."

"Neither did I, but someone must've called." Beau's voice trailed off when a spark came into her eyes. She blinked a couple of times before returning her full attention to him. And she smiled much too sweetly.

"I wouldn't give it another thought." She took his arm. "Dad knew a lot of people."

"But how did he know about the fight?"

"You've been away for a year. Dad tried to keep it under wraps, but it was bound to slip."

"How did he know about you?"

"Maybe I'm showing."

"You're not," Luke said.

"I could be."

"You're not, Beau."

"Maybe he's a psychic." She tried to laugh.

"That's stupid. He started by asking me what happened to Dad."

"Let it go, okay? You'll never see that man again. Who cares what he knows and how?" Beau put her hand to his cheek. "If you start worrying about things, you'll get too many lines around your eyes to play all those handsome young men on stage. Take care of your moneymaker."

Luke smiled. She was trying to manipulate him. Let her think she was succeeding. He'd seen the inspiration come onto her face. She knew more than she was telling, and he was glad he hadn't said anything about breakfast. Now they each had a secret.

"You're not worried?"

"Why would I be? Everyone will know sooner or later, won't they? Just chock it up to being one of Dad's crazy friends and forget it." Beau swiveled her view around the room. "Have you seen Ginger? I should put an ear tag on him."

Luke saw that outside the vestibule door a flower truck had parked, and his brother-in-law was on the sidewalk. But he'd been irritated even prior to spotting him. Jay had started that pet name. Everyone had a quirky, affectionate name but Luke, and Luke was the only one who called Jake by his real name.

There is no affection between us, motherfucker.

"He's directing more nasty fucking flowers in here."

"You're such a vulgar boy."

His sister's casual walk to the door accelerated to a near run. She pushed the door open with the flat of her hand, the other drawn in a fist. She stomped toward her husband, and Luke briefly felt sorry for Jake.

But the pity was swept away by confidence. Karma was a bitch, and Jake deserved whatever he was going to get.

Chapter Four

"Jacob."

Ginger knew he was in trouble. He felt Beau's stare boring through the back of his head. Nothing foreshadowed more evil than his *full* first name.

"I need you. Now."

He chewed the corner of his lower lip. *If you could just be cool. You don't know what the issue is, and you're already acting guilty.*

"Just hold tight, Beau." Ginger accepted the clipboard the delivery man offered. He could also tell by the man's pinched face that it was bad. She wasn't shouting. yet but she was already at a level six.

"No. Now."

"You can take these into the main room. There's a space by—"

"For the sake of your own body, tell me you're not ignoring me."

Level eight.

He turned to her. Her eyes were cold, and color rose into her cheeks. *Maybe eight and a half.*

"I'm not ignoring you, love, just working."

"It's flowers. He seems like an intelligent person." Beau glared at the delivery man. "Do you think you can find a place to put these without him holding your hand? It doesn't need to be feng shui. Put the damn flowers in the room! Think you can handle that?"

"Si."

"Crisis solved." She met Ginger's eyes again. "I'll be in your office. I will wait for two minutes. If I have to come and find you, you'd better hope I can't."

Beau rushed inside. Ginger looked back at the clipboard and read each word slowly in his head, trying not to think of the tornado that awaited him.

"Don't get too comfortable, jefe." The delivery man scratched his chin. "Your clock is ticking."

"Believe me, I'm aware of that. You can put them anywhere." Ginger signed with his last name and first initial, crafting the letter to pass for either a "G" or a "J".

"A little advice to you, if you live much longer, the next time she comes at you, you say only two words, 'Yes, dear.'" He snapped his fingers and slapped his thigh. "You heel like the dog you are!"

Ginger returned the clipboard with a smile.

"Wiser words were never spoken. Gracias, and grab Luke if you need help with this. He's in there someplace."

"Si, I did hear he was going to be coming home."

"The prodigal son has returned."

"No comprendo."

"Yes, he's home." Ginger checked his wristwatch. He pictured Beau pacing the office, steam trailing from her ears. "I need to scoot, buddy. Take it easy."

He clapped the laughing delivery man on the back before walking toward the building.

"Good luck, jefe! See you soon! Maybe!"

Maybe is right.

Ginger had worked for Jay at the funeral home since he'd been eighteen. Had any of the family ever called him by his first full name? Maybe "Jake" before "Ginger" became the norm. Beau had called him "Jake" three years ago when they'd spoken their wedding vows. And he'd used her first name, although it felt odd. But he was sure she'd never referred to him as "Jacob." He couldn't remember the last person who had. High school? It was unnerving. Even Luke called him "Jake."

What did I do? Ginger prepared to dodge a lamp or a stapler as he pushed open the door to his office.

"You're lucky. Another fifteen seconds, and Dad would've had you for company."

Beau leaned against his desk, her hands curled under its side, and her lips pressed in a stern line.

Level nine.

"Aside from the obvious, what's wrong, sweetheart?" He reached to pet her hair but stopped as she put up her hand.

"If you touch me, I'll break your arm. Don't 'sweetheart' me."

"Jesus Christ, what's the problem?"

"Yes, you'll need to invoke every deity you know! Ganesh, Zeus, Muhammad, Odin, the fucking Buddha!"

Nine and one quarter.

"Beau, calm down."

"Don't tell me to calm down!"

Nine and a half.

"There is only one thing I want to hear from you!"

"Name it! What do you want?"

"Tell me that you didn't call Tom DuBelle and invite him here! Tell me you're not the reason he came!"

Oh. Fuck. Ginger felt his throat closing. *Fuck, fuck, fuck. What to say, what to say?*

Beau's finger hovered in his face, demanding an answer. As he repeated her question in his spinning head, relief flooded him. She'd left an out.

"I did not invite Tom DuBelle."

"Are you saying you called him?"

"You asked if I called him and invited him here. I didn't invite him."

"But you called him? Don't try to wriggle free of this, Jacob. Did you call that man?"

Ginger could lie. Anyone could have called. How did she know other people weren't aware of Tom DuBelle? Perhaps her mother had called him, or another friend. But was there much sense in lying? The sage words of the flower delivery man came to mind. He closed his eyes and visualized crossing himself. He did need every available deity.

"Yes, dear."

He saw Beau's hands shaking to strike him across the face. A level ten of fury, boiling over, and he was ready for the sting. He flinched.

But instead of violence, she turned and folded her arms tightly. He heard her labored breaths. Her shoulders were so tense that if he touched her, she might shatter. Or spin around and claw his eyes out. Either way, he stayed silent and stationary. He had nothing to say. He hated seeing her upset, but he'd only kept a promise he'd made three years ago to her father.

☆

"There's one other thing I need from you, Ginger," Jay smiled as he pushed a folder across the table.

Pressure eked from the room, and Ginger felt a sense of release. He hadn't realized how uncomfortable it was to be called anything but

"Ginger" until the sobering topics had pushed Jay to use his first name. "*Jake*, I need to tell you... *Jake*, this is what happened... *Jake*, I am..." In the end, what Jay had said didn't change anything, but he disliked conversations where he became downgraded to "Jake."

"It's more important than everything else, since Jackie isn't aware of this request."

"Oh?"

Jay's wife had been present for half of the two-hour conversation. Jackie hadn't done much in the way of talking. Her function appeared to be supporting her husband and evaluating every move her future son-in-law made.

"Yes. I apologize for pulling you into yet another level of secrecy."

There were things that no one outside the family of four knew. There were things only Jackie knew. Things that Beau knew, but Jackie didn't know that she knew. Luke didn't know anything. Each disclosure was accompanied by a synopsis of who knew and who was not to know. It was complex enough to understand, and here he was on the threshold of another room within the inner sanctum.

Jay looked to the door—there was no face in the window. He reached into his pocket and retrieved his wallet. From a space behind his driver's license, he removed a white business card and held it out.

Ginger took the card.

"Leopold Harland, LLC. Attorney-at-law—"

"The back."

He turned it and read a single name and phone number that hadn't been written in Jay's careful hand.

"Tom DuBelle."

"I want you to call him if anything happens to me."

"Who is he?"

"An old friend I went to school with," Jay said.

"And Jackie can't call him?"

"Oh, she can. She just won't. But I know you will." Wow, this really was a new degree. For Ginger to be tasked with what *could* be given to Jackie. "I trust you implicitly, and I need you to do two things for me—keep what I've told you tonight in confidence, and call Tom if anything happens, and I'm unable to call him myself."

The first night he'd spent under Jay's roof, Ginger had promised himself that he'd never let this man down. Jay had not only opened his home and paved the way for him to pursue a meaningful career, but he filled a previously unknown role—that of a mentor and father. He'd always endeavored to honor his pledge and repay Jay's faith in him. He wanted to question but let it drop.

"I will. You can count on me."

☆

Ginger hadn't given the request much more attention until two days ago.

He closed the rear doors of the white van and slipped into the driver's seat. It struck him that three hours prior, Jay had been in the same place. It was his set of keys hanging from the ignition. There was still his opera music pouring from the stereo. But now Jay had been permanently relegated to the back. A mutilated body gathered in a black bag.

Ginger glimpsed around the loading area at the side of the hospital. No one was around. He folded his arms on the steering wheel and let himself cry.

Why did you have to die, Dad? I'm not ready to handle this alone. How can I take care of everyone? What do I do?

"Keep your promise." He heard Jay's voice in his head and turned to the passenger side. It was empty. But Ginger imagined him there, perhaps looking out the window.

"What promise?"

"To call Tom DuBelle."

"But I can't. I know who he is; I remember when Beau put it together. Mom will kill me. Beau will kill me."

"I gave you everything. And all I asked was for your confidence and for you to call Tom DuBelle when the time came."

Ginger's skin had tingled. He could feel Jay's hand on his shoulder.

"Don't let me down, Son. You've never disappointed me."

He kept his promise. It took eight tries to finally reach him, but he got through to deliver the news. Tom DuBelle seemed a nice enough man, and it was too bad things had to be the way they were.

☆

Back in the office Beau's breathing grew balanced, and while she still didn't turn around, Ginger saw that her grip on her own arms had loosened.

"I'll give you the opportunity to explain yourself. Why did you call that man?"

"Dad asked me to."

"He was DOA. He couldn't have asked you to do anything."

"Three years ago. When he told me about his situation. After your mom left, he requested me to call Tom DuBelle if anything happened and he couldn't himself. That's why I asked you who he was."

"Didn't my suspicion make it abundantly clear that he's not wanted here?"

"I only called and told him Dad had passed."

"You didn't think he'd come?" She faced him, some of the exasperation having left her eyes. "Are you *really* that naive?"

"I gave him only basic info and told him several times not to come. I didn't even say who I was."

"I know you didn't say who you were. You know how I'm aware of that? He thought Luke had called him."

Ginger felt the heat rush from his face. Jay had specified that Luke wasn't to know anything and extensive effort had been expended to keep the secret from him. What had Tom said? What had he done?

"Oh, my God."

"'Oh, my God' is right. Fortunately, there's no harm done, aside from rousing his curiosity, which isn't hard to divert." She unfolded her arms.

"He didn't give it away?"

"Apparently not. He told Luke he had a plane to catch."

"That's good. We're all good, right?" Ginger relaxed when she moved closer and allowed herself to be wrapped in his arms.

"I don't know how you could be that foolish," Beau said. "I hope the baby has my brains, not yours."

"Not giving my name was foolish. Calling was keeping my word."

He was nothing if not an honest man. Without question, he was sorry for causing mischief and almost demolishing the carefully constructed house of cards. But he didn't regret following Jay's wishes in the slightest.

"Ginger, I know Dad meant a lot to you." She pulled back and straightened his tie, tracing her slender fingers along its edges. "But he's gone, baby. And your first loyalty is to me and your child." She looked at him. "If he made you promise anything else in reference to Tom DuBelle, I release you from it. I never want to lay eyes on that man or hear his name again. It's an insult to Dad that he was here and that he even spoke to Luke. If there's anything else he asked you to do regarding Tom DuBelle, forget it. Right now."

Ginger was glad his task had only been the phone call. As much as he loved and wanted to please her, if Jay had requested more, he would've carried it out. But his burden was over, and he could commit to having no involvement with Tom DuBelle, his integrity intact.

"I understand." He took her hand from his tie and brought it to his lips. "Don't worry."

"Good, since I don't know where I'd hide your body. I'm sure I'd find someplace, but I have other things to think about at present." She smiled and brought back her hand. "You can go back to your work. If I need you again, I'll find you."

"Hopefully it'd be under better circumstances."

"It depends if you've done anything else naughty, though you'd be hard-pressed to top this one. Let it be the first and last time you upset me this much, Ging." Beau walked to the door. "And I won't tell Mom, since I don't want to be a single mother."

Ginger watched her leave and sank into one of his office chairs. He was a lucky man. Even if he had the immense pressure of operating the business alone, he'd been trying to convince himself that it'd be okay. Luke was back, and the boy did help some. Jay had always wanted more for him, but Ginger didn't feel the need to push him to further achievements.

If he wants to hang around doing his shows and help on removals, I don't care. He's just a boy. An amusing concept occurred to him—Luke and Beau were the same age. *Twenty-six. But everyone still thinks of him as a little boy. I can't remember ever thinking of Beau as a little girl.*

☆

She'd been twelve when they first met. She wore her long, dark hair in a braid down her back and sported scratches and scrapes on her sun-baked legs and arms from climbing trees. But Beau had an air about her; her eyes didn't contain the impetuosity of youth. She was measured and in control of herself.

"This is my daughter, Beau. Beau, this is Ginger. He'll be working with me," Jay said.

She extended her hand. "Is that your middle name? Ginger?"

"No, it's the hair." Her hand was delicate on the outside, but he felt the coarseness of her fingertips. He shook it, glancing at Jay to ensure he'd done well.

"What's your real name? Is it stupid? My first name is stupid, so I'm lucky my middle name is better."

"Jacob."

"And you're lucky you have red hair."

He and Jay laughed, and the left side of Beau's mouth tilted in amusement.

And then Luke skirted around the corner.

Ginger remembered how rumpled his appearance had been. He had the same battle scars as his sister, but Luke seemed more wild. More agitated. More something. He hadn't immediately noticed there was a guest in the room. When he did, his hand rested on Beau's shoulder, and he looked stunned, like a wide-eyed rabbit with a rifle trained on him.

"This is my brother, Luke. He has a ridiculous middle name and no other notable features."

"Beau." Jay shook his head before turning to his son. Ginger noticed how a different gentleness entered his eyes and voice. "Luke, this is Ginger. He'll be working with us. You're not going anywhere, but we could use extra help."

The boy said nothing, but Ginger offered his hand.

"It's nice to meet you, Luke."

Luke shifted, positioning himself behind his sister.

"Don't mind him, Ging. He's weird when meeting new people. I'll shake your hand again so you don't feel like an idiot." Beau gave his hand two strong pumps.

Out of the corner of his eye, he saw Jay cover his mouth and cough, possibly to hide another laugh. Ginger only smiled. He felt initially about Beau as he had about Jay—she had the blend of eagerness to please and self-confidence that yielded sincerity. Jay possessed an additional layer of warmth, but they both were easily likeable.

Luke, however, didn't share these characteristics. His similarity to Jay seemed to end at appearance. But perhaps it just took him a while to get used to a person. Ginger was sure the boy would come around once he became a familiar face. And maybe Luke could be like his brother. He'd always wanted a brother.

☆

Unfortunately, their relationship hadn't moved much past that first encounter. He'd developed a fierce loyalty and love for Jay and Jackie, who'd treated him as another son. And, of course, he'd gone from liking Beau to absolutely adoring her. But time hadn't brought him closer to Luke.

Ginger felt he'd gone out of his way to be Luke's friend. Maybe it was because he'd married Beau; Luke's hostility had escalated around the wedding. He'd never been violent, but he didn't try to hide his dislike anymore. And Luke had stopped calling him Ginger after the engagement had been announced.

Did you think she'd stay with you forever? She was going to get married. Whether to me or someone else. And it's been three years. Get over it. Ginger shook his head. *He's just a selfish little boy. That's his biggest problem.*

He left his office and returned to the viewing room, grateful that Beau had been spared this immature quality. Even if she wanted to kill him sometimes.

Chapter Five

Once everyone left, Luke stood in front of the open casket flanked by his mother and sister.

Of course, Jake was there too. He was always there, like a fly buzzing in a person's ear and then landing on their food and shitting all over it. Jake had his arm around Beau, and her head leaned against his shoulder.

"Thank you," Beau said. Luke knew she was referring to Jake's restoration of Jay's body. She hadn't witnessed the state it had been in, but she too had seen things and must've intuited how bad the condition was.

"It was the least I could do."

The verbalized appreciation for Jake's skills was as irritating as his brother-in-law's response. There was nothing Luke could've done, nothing he might've contributed that required thanks.

While he'd latched onto the Tom DuBelle intrigue, the excitement blasting away the refuse that'd been collecting in his brain, his attention strayed as the guilt returned.

If I'd just come home earlier. If there'd been more time. If New York had been better, he started to think. *But if you'd landed every role you wanted, your dad would still be dead. Or would he? Maybe if I'd had success in New York, I would've come home sooner. As a triumph! And that fucking car could've mowed up someone else's dad.*

"He looks like he's sleeping." Beau exhaled, her voice breaking. "I'm almost afraid to talk too loud, or we'll wake him."

Luke deliberated telling Beau what Jay had said about how the bodies weren't supposed to look asleep, but anxiety enveloped the four of them, and he stayed quiet.

After several seconds of anticipation with the only noise being Beau's attempts to breathe easily, his mother removed a handkerchief from her purse.

"Take them, please." Jackie folded the fabric and held it pinched near her chin.

Jake unwrapped his arm from Beau and kissed her hair, shushing her away with the tips of his fingers. She fled to Luke and hugged his neck, pressing her face into his shirt collar. But Jake had to ruin that feeling too. Nothing could be pure and good with his pollution. Luke looked between his mother and brother-in-law.

Another hidden plan, another members-only agreement. Who knew there were so many secrets in this family?

Jake leaned over the casket, positioning his body to obstruct Jackie's view. He raised each of Jay's hands and slid two rings from his fingers.

Luke remembered how his father had removed his rings by twisting them slowly to the right. Now there was no longer any friction to dissuade them from leaving. Jay had dead hands now, and when Jake moved them, there was no pliability in the wrist; it was like picking up a severed tree branch. Luke shivered and pulled Beau closer.

When Jake placed the rings in Jackie's hand, she seized a fist around them and pulled the handkerchief to her mouth. Her frame trembled, and her tight shoulders strained against the fabric of her black jacket. He thought about letting his sister go or shuffling together over—

Jake touched Jackie's arm first.

Aren't we lucky to have you? Someone has to comfort my mother. Someone had to be the son Dad always wanted. To complete his perfect family.

He often wondered if Jay had planned it. If he'd had a gut feeling from the beginning that Luke would be a disappointment. So he'd located Jake, a nice enough young man with no definitive career plans or place to go. And Jay pushed him to pursue Beau, offered her as a bribe, as bait.

You'd sell your daughter to have him as your son. Luke thought, even though he knew it wasn't true. As unfortunate as it was, no one had forced Jake and Beau together—it just happened. Jake hadn't taken Beau on a date until she was eighteen. Luke even remembered Jake asking his opinion.

☆

"Will your dad be upset, do you think?" Jake had been driving the van, Luke in the passenger seat, and a partially decomposed body in the back.

"Why are you going to ask him? It's not the eighteenth century, Ging.

It's fucked-up that you're more worried about Dad saying yes than her."

With the vapor rub under his nose, Luke still felt queasy. He was glad it was summer and he could lean his head out the window, but also sorry that the hot air made the smell worse. As weak as it was, he didn't know how Jake and his father did without a menthol shield.

"But I *know* she'll say yes."

"She might not want a man who smells like putrefaction and embalming fluid. She might choose to leave this place. She might be like 'Fuck. No.'"

"It's only a date. She'll say yes to that."

Luke knew she would, though he hoped otherwise. He'd seen the way Beau had been looking at Jake. But though he was a moderately okay guy and kept the heat off Luke by helping his father, Luke hated the way his sister looked at Jake. Like she wanted to go away with him. Away without Luke.

It wasn't that he had any unnatural desires for Beau. But she was more than a sister. She was his first friend. His best friend. Sometimes he'd felt she was his *only* friend. There was no one he'd ever been closer to. He was terrified of her favoring someone above him and then being taken away.

"Leave Dad out. He doesn't own her. He doesn't own me. He doesn't own *you*, even if you like being his bitch."

"I'm not his bitch. I have respect for him. For both your parents. You could try that."

"I'll respect them when they respect me. Especially Dad. When he accepts that I'm an individual, and I'm striking out on my own path."

"Maybe when you actually do it, you'll get the respect you want." Jake kept one hand on the wheel, but he reached over and ruffled Luke's hair. "You little pioneer."

"Shut up, asshole." Luke scowled and concentrated on not breathing through his nose. "Furthermore, when were you planning to ask my permission to date my twin? I'm the closest to her. She's more mine than anyone else's. And I didn't give you permission to even *like* her at all."

And though Jake laughed, Luke hadn't joined him.

"I'm not kidding, you fucker. You should really ask me."

"All right, all right. Luke, may I please invite your sister out for dinner? May I have your authorization, your expressed permission, your endorsement, your seal of approval to *like* your sister?"

"No."

Jake had laughed, but again it was unaccompanied.

"And how will you stop me? Sing a ballad? Do a dance? Convince me in catchy verse that I don't love everything about her? That I don't hang on her every word? That I don't get butterflies when I think of her? Go on. Burst into song. I'll stop the van, and you can tap dance on the roof."

"You're a douche bag. A fucking douche bag."

"Come on." Jake punched his arm playfully. "It's dinner. No drinking and driving. No drugs. No PG-13 movies. I'll bring her back by ten. I promise."

"One dinner. *One.* I'll grant you that since I'm a generous person. Even to dickheads."

"Relax. She's not going anywhere. I'm not asking her to marry me, Luke."

"You should promise me you'll never do that either."

"That I cannot do, my friend."

"I'm not your friend. And why not?"

Luke stared at Jake and forgot to breathe through his mouth. The stench of decomposing flesh crept over the menthol and, combined with the horrific notion, made him sick to his stomach. He hadn't thought that far ahead. If Beau went with him, she might keep liking him. The bastard was likeable—only Luke had been immune to his conniving tricks. Jake could take her away. Not temporarily. Forever. And he'd be all alone. Luke felt alone now except for Beau. If Jake asked her to be his wife, she'd say "yes" and would belong to him instead.

"I keep my promises." Jake turned and winked at him—a wink of pure evil.

☆

As they stood beside the casket, Luke patted his sister's hair.

I'm not a sicko. I just don't want anyone to have her. I want her to be mine again. We're a team.

He liked pretending Jake was still only Jay's apprentice, not his brother-in-law. One of the good things about his father's death had been that Beau had come home. Down the hall, in her old room. He could walk only five steps if he wanted to talk to her in the middle of the night. It was a nice daydream.

To be sixteen again.

That'd been perfect. When there was Jake, but he had yet to metastasize through the family. He'd been useful in deflecting his father's attention, and Luke hadn't had to go on many removals. Beau hadn't been interested in him and had been Luke's only companion. Jake had liked Beau, but he'd been too shy, too gentlemanly, too much of a fucking pussy to do anything. And that was the age when he'd had that first role in the high school production. He'd felt on the threshold of a great and promising future. The realization of his gift. Sixteen.

Luke tried to block out the viewing room and imagined being drawn back into that flawless past with Beau.

How long will you stay with me? I can get over Dad's death and failing in New York. As long as I can keep you one room away. You may be hiding something about Tom DuBelle, but you'd never lie about anything important. We can ignore everyone else. You'll stay with me if I ask. You'll do anything I need you to do. You love me, and you're the only one who understands me.

As if she heard his thoughts, Beau hugged his neck. It was wonderful, and he felt reassured. But when he looked at his mother being comforted by Jake, the reality returned.

Beau couldn't stay. She was pregnant. And his father was dead. And he was a failure. And his mother didn't need him. She had Jake, the good son. No one needed him. He might as well not exist.

Why do you like him? Why do you have to have his baby and tie yourself to him forever? You'll have even less time for me with his baby fastened to you. Why can't you lose it like the last one? Just fucking lose it!

Luke felt a cold sweat break across his shoulder blades. He hardly heard Jackie clear her throat, shocked that such a despicable wish could come into his head.

You're one sick motherfucker. How could you have a thought that evil? You'd hate me if you knew me as well as you think you do, Beau.

His mother coughed loudly again, and Luke finally turned. She gave him a stern look, gesturing him forward with a slight motion of her closed hand.

He released Beau, who didn't waste any time returning to Jake's waiting arms.

That's all I am. A placeholder for that dickwad.

But Luke went to his mother and tried to forget it.

"This is yours." Jackie held out her fist. She dropped Jay's gold high school class ring into his palm.

His fingers curled around it, and his hand shook. Jay had worn this ring every day, but now it was cold. As Luke worked it onto the first knuckle of his middle finger he felt the engraved lettering of the date his father had bought the ring etched into its undersurface.

"And you—" Jackie interrupted herself with a choke and offered Jay's wedding band to Beau. Her voice was coarse and craggy. "This is for you."

"I don't want it, Mom." She wiped a sleeve across her face and looped her arms tight around Jake.

"He wanted both of you to have them."

"They're his. Let them go with him. What are we going to do but cry over them?"

"I—I don't care what you do. This is what he wanted. You'll take them and not bother me about it. I have enough to handle without you fighting me over stupid shit."

Jackie hid her face with the handkerchief again and turned away. But as she appeared ready to buckle in tears, she whipped her neck back with sudden venom. "Take them! Just fucking take them! What does he need them for? To fucking rot around them? Take them and shut up!" She threw the ring on the ground at Beau's feet. It bounced beneath a flower arrangement.

His sister began to cry, and his heart ached for her. But there was also his mother.

Alone.

Luke felt alone in most things. Particularly as of late, since no one seemed to feel what he did. But amid all the "I'm sorry"-ers and "He's in a better place"-ers, Jackie was like him. Tom DuBelle had helped by recognizing and acknowledging his fury at the unfairness of it all; however, he hadn't appeared to share it. Jackie's anger made him feel better.

He went to his mother and hugged her.

"Thanks, Mom." Luke was glad he'd already pushed the ring onto his finger as he patted her shoulder with his open hand. Her chest heaved, but she didn't pull away. He put his cheek on her hair, and when he inhaled, she smelled warm and alive. "I'm so glad you're still here."

The simple statement seemed to ease his mother, and she slipped into easy breaths. He wondered if this was what she'd wanted someone to say to her. With all the attention on her husband's death, did she feel as forgotten as Luke often did?

Maybe I'm really not as fucked-up. I'm a support. An important *support.*

He peered around Jackie's head at Jake.

That ass licker wasn't watching. Jake was wiping the side of his fingertip under Beau's eyes. He kissed his sister's forehead, completely missing what a comfort Luke was to Jackie.

But consoling his mother was still good despite Jake not observing it. Jackie wasn't overly affectionate, and Luke had always suspected that, like his father, she preferred Beau.

Mom didn't bring Jake in though. And she wasn't the one who cast me away.

During the fight, Jay had said he spoke for them both, but Jackie hadn't been present. Who was to say she hadn't taken Luke's side? Perhaps with Jay gone, Luke could now carve a space for himself. She clung to him as if she needed and wanted him. She hadn't hugged Jake in the same way. She—

"We should go. Everyone's waiting."

Luke flirted with the idea of biting Jake's hand as it appeared on Jackie's shoulder. Jake ruined everything.

Always. And again.

His mother pulled back and pushed a piece of Luke's dark hair behind his ear. The biting inclination somewhat dissipated.

"I know you told Ging you were tired, but come with us."

Luke had immediately declined the dinner invitation when it'd been made. Who wanted to sit around at his grandparents' house and listen to everyone spew how great Jake was? Besides, he had work to do. He needed to research Tom DuBelle, and the optimum sleuthing environment consisted of him being alone.

"Please." Jackie smiled at him through her tears, her hand still at his temple.

He hesitated. The chance to publicly lounge in his newfound importance gave "after-viewing meatloaf party at Grandma's" an attractive veneer.

Maybe they won't spend all night jerking off to the sound of Jake's voice. Everyone will see how I'm the good son now. Luke looked away from Jackie and began to fidget with the class ring as he considered his options. *What more was I planning to do anyway? Google Tom's name? There are no other leads. He's just some random guy Dad probably went to school with and—*

His thoughts broke off as he smoothed his finger over the indentations of his father's name on one side and graduation year on the other.

"I'm sorry. I'm really tired, Mom. You understand, right?"

There was a lead. Jay had more than a class ring. He also had a yearbook.

☆

In the two hours he'd been sole master of the house, Luke had managed to smoke half a pack of cigarettes on the porch, change and wash his clothes to hide the aforementioned deed, and Google Tom DuBelle.

As anticipated, the Internet hadn't yielded much. It confirmed that Tom was from the same state his father had grown up in, but he couldn't locate an address or telephone number. There didn't appear to be a social media profile, and Tom's name had only been mentioned in older, random articles without a picture to confirm the pianist was the same man. Even if he was, who cared? Tom could play a Viennese waltz with a Goddamn kazoo up his ass—it wasn't relevant to Luke's purpose, which he'd realized was even greater than mere curiosity now.

After closing the computer, he went to the bookshelf in his parents' library to search for the yearbook. As he knelt and ran his finger along the spines, he imagined Jake's smug face. While it was true that Beau was also hiding something from him—

That shit hole is hoarding secrets about my father. And no matter how much Mom wants me now, he'll still think he's better than me. Sure, he's probably let Beau in on some of it, but I know he's kept the majority to himself. I'm doing us both a favor.

He was hot on the trail, his fingertips tingling with anticipation.

There we go.

Luke pulled the volume from the shelf, its top covered in dust. Vaguely, he recalled Jay showing it to him several years ago for whatever reason. The book only stood out in his memory because of how ugly it was. Unlike his own dignified, black-bound senior yearbook, his father's was wrapped in a corny red plaid.

He tucked the book under his arm and walked to his room.

I am powerful. I am the one in control. And I'll have the satisfaction of riddling this out myself. I'll discover what Beau knows and more.

Luke fished a bottle of bourbon from under his bed, already feeling the accomplishment and internal applause. He sat the half-full liquor bottle on his desk beside the yearbook and opened the cover.

The 2005 senior photos were a juxtaposition from the rest of the book's overblown graphics. Unlike the other students' black-and-white photos, senior pictures were broadcast in full color, with names in elegant script below each image. The paper of their section also had a distinct, shiny texture. The teenagers all wore identical dowdy gowns—girls in red, boys in blue—and were positioned in the same pose—left arm folded on the table, right in a relaxed fist under the chin. It was a hall of Rodin's *Thinkers*. Luke wondered how many of them flipped burgers and shoveled garbage.

Leafing to the subsequent sections of dismal teenagers, it was clear that their poses were irrelevant as long as no one gave the finger. Here his cleverness was rewarded as he recognized Tom's face. Thirty-three years had left their mark on the man, but there was no mistaking Tom. If his name hadn't been listed on the side, the same sarcastic grin would've given him away.

Luke marked Tom's page with his thumb and moved forward to the colorful senior photos. Jay was in the second row on the fourth page.

Pinching the pages that separated the two pictures, he turned them back and forth. Tom looked older now, whereas his father hadn't changed much from his senior portrait. Jay's hair had been streaked with gray when he died, and there were wrinkles around his eyes, but otherwise he was himself. Luke let go of the senior section and faced only Tom.

So, you definitely went to school with Dad. And you were close even after he moved.

Luke wasn't exactly sure when Jay had left his home state. His father had been a private person, and he hadn't said much about his life before meeting Jackie and moving to Pennsylvania. It was like he'd decided that was where his life started.

Luke drained another glass of bourbon.

He could name all the schools his mother had attended, the activities she'd been involved in, and boring bits of trivia on both. All he knew about his father was that he'd attended a high school with an ugly yearbook.

He could retell many of Jackie's adventures with her siblings, family, and various friends through the years. Jay had only had one brother. But Uncle Gordon had died when he and Beau were in grade school, before Luke met him. He remembered that his father hadn't seemed upset, but that wasn't remarkable. Jay's father had also died without knowing his grandchildren. The man had gone to war when Jay was in high school and hadn't returned. Jay called him a war hero, but hadn't been inclined to talk about him. He'd never mentioned having a friend.

Luke returned to his father's picture and looked into his unblinking eyes.

I don't feel you understood or knew me. But I didn't know you either. This interpretation scared him to an extent. *You had this whole life you didn't share with us. Why the secrecy? Maybe if you'd told me your experiences—if you'd shared your knowledge, I wouldn't have made so many mistakes, and I could be a better person.*

Further guilt heaped itself onto Luke's already-large pile. Jay had never given him a chance, but had Luke ever given his father one? Jay hadn't been cagey. Information had come easily from him, when he was asked direct questions. He'd never purposefully hidden anything. His father just recognized that no one cared to hear anyone else's past. People only loved to talk about themselves. Luke was only twenty-six. Why would he have given a shit about Jay's childhood? He still wouldn't be thinking of it if he hadn't met Tom DuBelle and fallen down a bourbon-assisted rabbit hole.

Maybe this is my fault. The whole thing. Whatever my career, the fight aside, I never gave a fuck about you. How could I expect you to love me as much as you love Beau or Jake?

"I'm sorry," Luke whispered. "But it's too late, and now you're lost to me."

He touched his father's photograph with the tip of his finger. Jay's cheerful smile blurred under tears that Luke blinked away. He snapped his hand to the glass of alcohol. The high school class ring, which he'd placed on his ring finger, clinked sharply. He swigged the drink, refilled the glass, and twisted the ring from his hand.

He was glad his mother had chosen to not have Jay buried with the only jewelry he ever wore. He had memories of playing with his parents' class rings when he was a child. With their large gaudy jewels, they made perfect pirate treasure or status symbols for a great king.

Luke ran his thumb over the red garnet in the center, its cuts dulled by everyday wear. He peered at the inside; the date Jay had received it was inscribed in calligraphic script: February 18, 2007. He slid the ring back on his left hand and thought of himself as a little boy, thrusting a bedazzled hand to anyone, commanding his rings to be kissed. No one but the dog had complied, but he'd imagined them quaking at his power.

Along with the happy memory, hope rushed back to replace the sorrow. Didn't Luke have a breakfast engagement with someone who'd known Jay as a young man? Surely he could coax Tom to reveal enough to satisfy his desire to recapture what was missing. He could bring the yearbook to refresh Tom's memory and get the stories flowing.

Luke drained another glass and looked at his father's picture with renewed cheerfulness. His gaze trailed over the dark hair and light eyes they shared. Jay seemed to stand out in a friendly way, the garnet of the ring appearing dull in the poor school lighting—

Luke dropped his glass. It shattered on the floor as his mother's key turned in the front door lock.

Chapter Six

Years of practice enabled Luke to pass off being asleep when Jackie opened his bedroom door minutes later. The glass and spilled bourbon hid under the bed in a soggy T-shirt mess, and the yearbook lay under the blanket.

He kept any tension from his face when the pads of her fingers touched his cheek, and she sniffed the air. There was no way to help the room's smell with so little time available. Anything he might've dribbled around to cloak the alcohol would've been equally suspicious.

But a harsh wake-up and rebuke didn't come. He pictured her surveying the room and released a long sleep sigh in case she was uncertain if he was alive. Her hand came away, and he hoped he hadn't overplayed it.

The ruse appeared effective. When he heard footsteps descend the stairs, Luke opened his eyes to the room's blackness. Rather than relief, anxiety churned in his stomach, along with a sense of vertigo. His calf burned where it lay across the yearbook, and he twisted the ring on his middle finger.

His father had graduated in 2005. The ring was engraved with the year 2007, not in itself a big deal—class rings could be purchased after the fact. When Beau had asked about the date, Jay had freely told them it'd been an unnecessary expense in 2005.

"Dad died a couple years before that." Jay had said. Luke was hopping from one foot to the other. One of his eyes had been covered by a plastic patch, and the other shot between Beau and the ring his father held. He'd devised the perfect place to hide it. "These things are expensive, and we were barely making ends meet. I bought my own later."

"In 2007?" His sister had asked.

"Yes."

"That's the date on the inside? The date you bought it?" Beau tilted her head.

"Sure." Jay had turned to Luke, his eyebrows drawn together. "Are you okay?"

"Yeeessss. I know right where I'm gonna bury it."

"Mom and Meecie have their full names inside theirs." Beau had drawn their father's attention to her.

"I'm not them, am I? I let you bury my valuable objects all over the yard." At last he'd dropped the ring into Luke's small cupped hands. "Don't make it too hard for your sister to find."

"I always make maps."

"They aren't very good ones," Beau added.

"Yet you always manage to uncover what he's squirreled away." Jay had petted a lock of hair behind Beau's ear, but he'd been focused on Luke. "If a secret is important, you leave clues for someone to figure it out. If they really want to."

In the present, Luke's heart raced. It was as if Jay spoke beyond the grave.

Twenty years ago you set me up for this. Told me you were leaving something for me to find. He stared at the dark ceiling and worried the ring around his finger while he felt the yearbook under his leg. *You lied about this ring, or that yearbook photo is fake. But why would either matter? What are you hiding?*

Before Luke could waste all night delving into various conspiracy theories, the furnace kicked on. The push of tepid air into the room brought with it the smell of coffee. He threw off the covers and got out of bed, his head only mildly cloudy from alcohol.

This isn't some Illuminati shit, Luke. There's a simple solution. Go ask Mom.

He left the yearbook in his room and crept downstairs. He rubbed his eyes, making a conscious attempt to keep the lids only at half-mast as if he'd just woken.

When Luke entered the kitchen, he was relieved to see only his mother at the table. Jackie stared into a mug, but she looked up as he entered the doorway. She didn't try to hide the tears on her cheeks, yet she smiled at him. "Did I wake you? I'm sorry if I did."

"No, I haven't been able to sleep well since—" Luke dropped into the chair opposite her and took the filled cup in front of him. Her puffy face and the redness around her eyes were too evident to discount. He'd have to be careful broaching the subject. "I haven't slept well for a while."

"Me either." Jackie leaned across the table. She pressed her hand to his forehead and patted his cheeks. "Do you have a fever? Or is your temperature because of the alcohol?"

"I just woke up, Mom."

"You look flushed, and it's not worth lying to me. If there was a liquor store open, believe me, I wouldn't be having coffee."

"Yes, you would." His mother always had coffee. If she could, she'd have a constant drip flowing into her veins. It wouldn't surprise him if she drained two more pots that night.

"But I'd have it with a side of vodka. No glass, right from the bottle. I could be hungover tomorrow." She took Luke's hand and rolled her thumb over Jay's class ring. "But, Luke, if you drop your dad's casket because you're wasted, I don't think I'll be able to forgive you."

"That's why there are six of us. The five Puritans can pick up the slack when I go down."

"Or you can be a good boy and stay sober."

Jackie still looked at the ring, and she drew in a ragged breath. It was as good a bridge as any.

"Mom, thank you for the ring. It means a lot to me."

"Don't thank me. It's what he wanted. He said you were to have the class ring, and Beau was to have the wedding band."

"Do you know why?"

"Sentimentality?" She tilted her eyes up to him. "I don't know why your dad did a lot of things. I felt I was only along for the ride sometimes. It was a good ride." Luke felt guilty for saying anything as her lower lip quivered. But she forced past the emotion and retrieved another smile. "For the record, I don't care what you do with my things."

"We won't have to think about that for a long time."

"You shouldn't have had to think about your dad for a long time." She looked past him as if he were invisible. "We assumed I'd go first. I'm older, and he's always been in better health. He was hardly ever sick."

"It doesn't matter how healthy you are when you get mowed up by a Honda Civic."

Jackie focused back on him. "I'm not saying right now. I'm not saying tomorrow, a week from now, a month, a year, so on. But someday, you'll need to get over that."

"I don't have a problem forgiving the driver," Luke said. "He was a careless douche bag, and he didn't do it on purpose."

"I could give a shit if you forgive him. Accident or not, the result is the same—he killed someone. You can stay upset with the driver for the rest of your life. I'm going to. I meant you'll have to get over yourself. Dad loved you. It broke his heart when you ran away from us and—"

"I didn't run—" His anger started to boil.

"Shh." Jackie continued in a calm voice. "We won't be arguing that tonight. Your interpretation of events isn't relevant when we're talking about what your absence did to him. He was devastated when you left like that, Luke. And you ignored us. For a year—"

"He forced me to—"

"No one forced you to do anything. You don't know how difficult it was for him to say what needed to be said. Now, should he have done things better? For one thing, he should've waited for me to be there. You both needed a referee. But what's done is done. Or, you know what he'd say?" His mother smiled into her coffee mug. "He'd say, 'You can't repeat the past.'"

Luke's temper ratcheted down. His questions hadn't been answered yet; it wasn't a good idea to get into a fight.

"I don't care what you think." Jackie looked at him again. "You put him through hell the past year, but he forgave you. You need to pull your head out of your ass and forgive your dad and yourself. For the fight, for the misunderstandings, and for his death. I know you have it in your head that it's your fault. As nonsensical as it is, you think he was to blame for that argument, but you're responsible for his death."

When he said nothing in response, she seemed satisfied. "I know how your brain works, Luke. You think you're deep. I won't say what you really are, but it's not deep. Not so deep that your mother can't see through you."

Luke wasn't hurt by the statement. This was her way, and she was actually holding back. Ordinarily, she wasn't one to spare people's feelings and would've just said he was being a dick. Maybe that was yet another level of his distress about the fight with his father. The harshness had never come from Jay. Of either parent, the most likely to tell him to leave would've been Jackie.

"We don't all get stupider as we age. I know you more than you think. You imagine you're a misunderstood black sheep, but I like black sheep, and you're my favorite."

"Your favorite child?"

"No. My favorite black sheep. I love my children the same. Or I try to. When you're good, I love you equally. I won't lie and say you all don't piss me off in various ways because you do."

"Yeah, Beau pisses you off. Being perfect pisses you off?"

"It does. But she's not perfect. Both your sister and Ginger do plenty of things I don't agree with. When the three of you are obnoxious, I hate you all as equally as I love you. I have no rankings. And your dad didn't either." Astonishment must've crossed Luke's face, and she laughed. "Honestly, how wrapped up in yourself are you? I know you've felt you were displaced. That Dad favored Ginger over you."

"Then why didn't you do anything?" he snapped. Would putting her on the spot catch her off guard? It was true. She could've stepped in at any time. Any fucking time. But she had an answer for everything.

"First, it wasn't my place." Jackie rose and walked to the counter for the coffee pot. "Next, it wasn't true. And most importantly, you need to find your own value. We all have to do that, Luke. It doesn't matter how important or unimportant someone else thinks you are. And who am I to stand in the way of you learning a life lesson? Even if it seems to take you longer than everyone else. You'll get it eventually."

Luke felt his mother insinuated that he had a mental handicap, but again, brutal criticism wasn't atypical.

"However, since you haven't learned it yet, and we're burying your father in twelve hours, I'll indulge you by saying this." She sat, and her cruel implications disappeared. "Whatever you believe, you were not unimportant to him. He never thought of Ginger as more of his son than you. Believe me when I tell you, Luke, Dad was incredibly proud of you."

He wasn't sure at first how to respond. He averted his eyes from Jackie's as tears cascaded down her cheeks. Instead, he stared at the table and tried to remember why he'd come downstairs in the first place. It hadn't been to have a heartfelt conversation.

"Why wouldn't I believe you?" Luke said. "The things you say could scar a child."

"Sometimes you need to be told when you belong on an emotional short bus, sweetheart. When you get off the bus, I'll stop scarring you."

"I'm glad you don't lie to me, Mom. You don't treat me like a boy. You tell me things."

"Go ahead. This sounds promising." Jackie placed her mug on the table. "I knew you didn't venture down here to keep me company."

Luke felt his cheeks grow hot. How did she do it? How did she know it all? He tried to rid his face of the visible embarrassment and slipped Jay's ring from his finger.

"I was wondering—why does Dad's class ring have February 18th 2007 engraved inside it? Didn't he graduate in 2005?"

"That he did, Sherlock. I believe the 2007 date is when he got the ring."

"And he didn't have another one, before?"

"No. Your grandmother couldn't afford it when he was in high school. Why the sudden concern?" Her lips pressed flat.

"I was thinking it seems funny to have a date of purchase engraved on it. There's no other significance to the date?"

"That's what he told me, and I have no reason to doubt it's true."

"But why would he have the date he bought it engraved? Isn't that weird?"

"It wasn't weird to him." Jackie shrugged. "Maybe it had significance in that it was something he always wanted to have. He purchased it on his own. Like a status symbol."

"Didn't he have other status symbols by then? A first car? A first apartment?" He had no idea when Jay had gotten his first car, or when he'd left Meecie's house.

"How do you know he didn't carve his move-in date into the floorboards of that first apartment?" His mother winked. "He had many peculiarities. Always kept things exciting." Her smile diminished. "Now I'll be the boring, old widow who drinks a ton of coffee."

Luke considered retrieving the yearbook, folding it open, and demanding she answer how Jay was wearing a ring in a photograph taken two years before he had it. What could she possibly say?

But her sorrow stopped him. She folded her arms on the table and buried her face in them. He couldn't hear her crying, but he knew she was. He wasn't going to get more information from his mother.

"You won't be the boring, old widow for long." Luke touched her arm. "Soon, you'll be the boring, old grandma. You'll be so busy scarring Beau's baby, you won't have time to be sad."

Jackie's face was red when she raised it, but she chuckled and placed her hand over his.

"You're a good boy, Luke."

When he realized she knew no more than he did, he crafted a plan. He needed time to think through how he'd proceed with Tom DuBelle.

It occurred to him that he could mention the name to Jackie, to see if she knew him. However, her current state gave him pause. As did remembering Tom's scan of the viewing room before leaving "while he still could." Luke didn't know the identity of the threatening person, or why they were a danger. It could be anyone, including Jackie.

He said nothing of Tom and let out a lengthy yawn.

"Poor baby." She patted his hand. "You won't be any good to us tomorrow, wasted or exhausted. Get some rest; you don't need to stay with me."

Luke stood and pushed his shoulders back, yawning again.

"I'll go because I'm terrified of what you'll do to me if I drop the casket."

"You should be. I'll throw you in the hole with him."

"Good to know the admonishments for forgiveness aren't given by a hypocrite." He turned to leave the kitchen.

"Luke."

He looked over his shoulder.

"I know I can be harsh sometimes." Jackie swallowed. "But since your father is gone, I'll try to be softer, like he was. If you need a little smoke blown up your ass sometimes, I'll get out a blanket and build a fire."

"You don't have to do that." Luke smiled. "Sometimes people need to know when they belong on the emotional short bus."

"Whatever your mode of transportation, I do love you. You're *my* son."

"I love you too, Mom," he rattled off.

"Don't leave this room without kissing me good night."

Luke spun on his heels and returned to her chair where he gave the obligatory kiss on the cheek.

"Anything else?" He crossed his arms.

"I knew you weren't asleep." Jackie gave a sly grin. "Why did you think there was an extra cup on the table? You sing beautifully, sweetheart. But that's not enough. You have no hope making it in New York if you can't act well enough to fool your own mother." She smiled again, outwardly pleased at having eroded his sense of security. "Yes, I know that too, and not from Beau. We knew you were struggling."

"How?" He wasn't sure whether to feel relief that he didn't have to admit failure, or humiliation that it'd been apparent.

"Your own idiotic silence. However angry you were at Dad, you would've been crowing at him if you were doing well, not ignoring him. You outsmarted yourself. Like you did upstairs. Think about that next time you do anything, Luke. Whether you're trying to pull one over on me or going for an audition—you're not as smart as *you* think *you* are, and your audience isn't as stupid as *you* think *they* are." Jackie brought the cup to her lips.

"Are you calling me stupid?"

"Let's just say you're more stupid than you give yourself credit for."

"That's cute. You should print it on a mug," Luke grumbled.

"Print this on the other side: 'You are your own biggest problem,'" she said to his back.

So much for softer. For building a fire and pulling out a fucking blanket, he thought as he walked down the hall.

Chapter Seven

Despite being terminally ill, having flown two thousand miles to attend his best friend's funeral, and being intent on committing suicide when he returned, Tom DuBelle felt pretty fantastic.

Pretty fan-fucking-tastic.

He attributed the rejuvenation to his new meds. The prescribed concoction to enable his travel was fabulous. There was nothing like Oxy and cancer drugs with THC. The cancer remained, and he was still dying, but the perception of it and the image of himself as a brittle, weak man loosened its stranglehold. He'd forgotten several times that he was sick, and when he remembered, it didn't trouble him.

THC pushed his appreciation for life full throttle. He hadn't been high in thirty years, and now he remembered why it was amazing.

Tom had been at the restaurant since six o'clock but awake for several hours. Not from nerves; he was low-key as ever. He'd woken up starving, similar to yesterday. He also had a bizarre request that had been nagging at him.

"Can I sit outside this morning?" he asked and gave his most charming smile to the waitress.

"The patio is closed."

"But you could open it for one crazy customer, couldn't you?"

"It's barely over forty degrees."

"I like the cold. I could do with some cold."

"The patio is closed, sir."

Tom leaned his elbow on the counter, the winning grin on his face. It exhilarated him to have this confidence back. To not feel like a wretched, diseased piece of shit. He could barely believe he'd had the courage to say more than two words to Luke yesterday. Then to ask him out to breakfast? And now he was badgering a waitress with the casual ease that'd been disappearing from him for months.

"The patio is closed, sir," she repeated, but he could tell from the curves at the corners of her mouth that his case wasn't lost.

"What if I told you I was dying? Would that change your mind?"

"If you told me you were dying, I wouldn't believe you. You don't look like you're dying. You don't act it."

What a marvelous compliment.

"I'm on these extraordinary meds. But I really am dying, I assure you."

"Of what?"

"The big C." Tom watched her amusement fade, and he almost regretted being a pest. "No, don't worry. There's nothing you can do, so why worry? And I mean about the cancer. I still want to have breakfast outside. You can worry about that."

"What type?" From her expression it was clear that she knew someone else who had it too. Or had had it. Everyone did. This common ground bode well for his request.

"Pancreatic. And I'm sorry for your loss. It's a shit-ass way to go." He covered his mouth with his hand and smirked. "I apologize. I'm just feeling really good this morning."

"It's okay."

The waitress pulled a set of keys from her apron and grabbed a spray bottle and towel from a shelf on her way to the patio doors. Since the sun was only beginning to creep over the horizon, she flipped on a bay of lights to illuminate the patio.

"It *is* a shit-ass way to go, but I'm glad you're feeling good this morning, sir." She held the door and waited.

The blast of cold air did nothing to erase his resolve. Tom walked to the stacked chairs alongside the wall and pulled one down, carrying it to the first table. After he sat, the waitress wiped the dusty surface.

"Thank you for indulging me, sweetheart." He took a deep breath; the fresh air was incredible. "I'll leave you a nice tip."

"Will you be alone this morning?"

"No. But I might move inside when my friend arrives. He's young and won't appreciate how great it is to bask in the cold." Tom smiled. The waitress shivered and uncapped her pen. "What you brought yesterday would be perfect. All of it. And coffee."

"Do you want that cold too?"

"Not necessary, but thank you."

Tom closed his eyes as she hurried inside the building. He tipped his head back, and the chilly air seeped through his jacket and into his bones. He was completely comfortable. It might've been seventy degrees.

Maybe you shouldn't kill yourself tomorrow, Tom. If it could be like this a few days, a few weeks, that wouldn't be bad. Living instead of just existing. You can still do it when the meds stop working.

The sun ascended and won over the exterior lights. He scanned the crusty brown field that stretched behind the patio.

This place is ugly in winter. Most places are. No, I'm going to do it when I get home. Why wait? I want to die when I'm feeling this spectacular. Well, not exactly. I'll eat first; I'm fucking starving.

Food had been a necessary evil the past several months. It wasn't just the nausea that'd destroyed eating for him. The radiation, the meds, and the pain made everything taste like particle board. He subsisted on the bare minimum. It was fuel only. Alkaline fuel. The doctor had been harping that he needed to eat, that cachexia would make his condition worse.

You should've given me the weed a long time ago, motherfucker.

Tom dove through the presented spread. When everything he'd eaten for the past few months tasted like bland garbage, this actual trash was more than tolerable.

I'd sell my soul for a steak. I swear to God. He pushed his empty plates aside, glad that Luke wasn't early. He didn't want the boy to think he had an eating disorder. But he did want the steak. Terribly.

He tilted his head back and closed his eyes again.

That season Leo and I spent in Spain. I was able to tolerate him because of all the performances, and it was so beautiful. The performance in the Auditoria de Tenerife: gorgeous. But the best food was when I played the León Auditorium. That place in Castilla y León where I got that entrecôte. Jesus. Fucking. Christ. I would sell my soul for that right now. Sign it right the fuck over.

The idea crossed Tom's mind that he didn't have any pressing appointments. Nothing awaited him at home except death.

Fuck it.

He could fly to Spain that afternoon. He could go wherever he liked, do whatever he wanted.

But your passport has expired, Tom. And you'll be dead before you can get it renewed.

Perhaps he could charter a private plane. Did he need a passport then? Could he stow away?

Maybe they'd make an exception for a dying man who only wants one more steak.

But the government wouldn't be as obliging as his waitress. It'd take more than a smile and the cancer card to open international borders. He sighed.

Moral of the story: Always keep your passport valid in case you get pancreatic cancer and suddenly want to fly to Castilla y León for an entrecôte. God, the closer I get to death, the wiser I am. Look out Confucius, Tom DuBelle is creating pearls of wisdom that will knock you on your fat fucking ass.

"Maybe you can talk some sense into your friend, and get him to come inside."

Tom opened one eye as the waitress held the door for Luke. The boy stared at him, using his left hand to rub his right arm from the cold. He looked like he would've been patting both arms if he didn't have a book tucked under his right, the cover hidden beneath his jacket.

"It's gotten warmer." Tom made no sign of getting up.

"Maybe two whole degrees," said the waitress as she removed his plates.

"And we mustn't be ungrateful for small blessings." He watched Luke take a chair from the wall stack.

The boy placed the chair on the opposite side of the table and sat. He plunged his hands into his jacket pockets and gave his order to the waitress from between chattering teeth.

Luke ducked his chin into the jacket's high collar. "It's freezing, Tom. Fucking freezing. Don't you want to go inside?"

"Not really. I may not be this cold again until I'm dead."

"Most people would prefer it that way."

"I'm not most people."

Tom had doubted Beau would come, so he hadn't been too disappointed that Luke arrived alone. He hoped the boy had remembered the sonogram picture though. Maybe he had it in the book under his jacket. But since it was just the two of them, Tom wasn't inclined to relocate, despite Luke shivering like a mad man.

Sometimes it's good to be uncomfortable. You have the rest of your life ahead of you, and I don't feel I should have to accommodate anyone. Not even you.

"Zip your jacket, spunky. Give it a few minutes, and you'll be fine."

"I *am* fine." Luke gritted his teeth and fidgeted on the cold metal of the chair.

"Put more conviction into your acting. Make me believe you're not freezing your ass off."

"That's hard to do when I'm freezing my ass off."

"Which may be why The Great White Way didn't work for you. Not that it wasn't always a one-in-a-million shot, but if you can't even pretend you're not cold for fifteen seconds, how can you make me believe that you could be anything else?"

Luke huddled around his coffee cup like a campfire until his body stopped shaking. Except his shoulders, which made Tom smile.

Jay was always cold in the shoulders too. You're so like him. You have his eyes, his hair, his posture. I could squint and swear you're him. It stunned me for a second when I stood face-to-face with you yesterday.

He deliberated telling Luke this, but decided not to. The boy had likely been reminded a hundred times during the viewing how much he resembled his father. And he'd hear the same thing a hundred more times today.

"Tell me about New York?" Tom offered, curious as to what lies Luke might create.

"Actually, I have questions I was hoping you could answer." Luke met his eyes.

"With pleasure."

He should've anticipated that Luke would have questions. Whatever Jay had told him, there must not have been time to address any confusion. And depending on what he wanted to know, Tom knew he was the only resource for certain details. As much as Jackie was aware, there were gaps that could be filled by Tom alone—he'd been there.

It was moderately entertaining when Luke unzipped his jacket and revealed the red plaid book. The boy pushed it forward on the table.

"This fucking thing?" Tom ran his hand across the cover—the motley Scottish terrier playing bagpipes under a gold-emblazoned year. "It's an ugly son of a bitch, isn't it?"

"Yes," Luke replied.

Tom opened the book and flipped through the pages. As he turned them, he let the forgotten memories return. He hadn't seen this book in years. A copy was at home, alongside three other editions, but he hadn't taken it down since putting it on the shelf when he moved into the high-rise. And it'd been even longer since he'd gone through the photos. It seemed an old-man thing to do. Yet here he was at the end of his life, sifting through his youth and enjoying it more than he might've had he not been on cancer medication spiked with THC.

"There's me. Orchestra." Tom pointed to a photo of two dozen teenagers crowded onto three rows of bleachers. He was in the last row, the walnut-colored scroll of an instrument visible behind the shoulder in front of him. "I was first chair in violin my junior and senior year."

"Were you?" Luke leaned forward, moving his chair closer.

Tom nodded, continuing to comb through the pages. "It was good, but not great. I prefer the piano. I auditioned for both programs at Julliard to double my chances. But thank God I made it with piano. I don't think I would've been happy with anything else." He wondered if this might catch the boy's attention. Luke would be a special kind of idiot to not realize that Tom's connections in the music world might benefit him.

If you ask me, I'll do it. I can't guarantee you a place there, or wherever you want to go, but I can ensure you get a callback. Jay wanted you to make it of your own merit; but I don't have a problem giving you a leg up.

But that Luke didn't ask pleased Tom, and he knew would've satisfied Jay as well. Maybe he didn't want the help; he wanted to make it himself. It was an attitude Tom respected.

"Is my dad anywhere else in that book?"

"No." Tom pinched several sports pages together and passed over them. "Jay didn't do extracurriculars his senior year."

"What was he like?"

"What do you mean?"

"Well, what type of person was he?"

Tom looked up from the book as he was about to flip by the sophomore photos and into his own year. Luke fiddled with a red class ring that was as recognizable as the ugly yearbook.

No, he wouldn't have told you how it was for him. If he'd had an infinite amount of time, it was still a sensitive subject. But it's touching that you intuited how hard it was for him and want to know. Perhaps you're less selfish than everyone thinks.

"Before or after?" Tom returned to paging through faces. He wondered how many of his classmates were dead.

"Before or after what?"

"Before or after he came out. He was a different person before the spring of 2004, when he decided everyone could go fuck themselves, and he was going to concentrate on escaping alive. To most people, it was a complete changeover when he came clean and stopped being as the person everyone else thought he was." Tom located his junior photo and laughed again. "Was I ever this young?" He brought the book close to his face, tilting it to the side. "Or this awkward?"

"What do you mean he 'came out'? 'Came clean'?"

Tom's gut seized sharply as he lowered the yearbook. His stomach had that tight feeling it did when he'd been vomiting for hours.

For the love of God, please tell me you didn't, Jay. Or rather that you did—that you told him.

"Was my father gay? Is that what this is?"

"Not that I've been aware." Tom swiped through the first half of the senior class of 2005. When he reached the correct page, he read the elegantly scripted names in his head. He looked at each face on both pages. He turned the page and analyzed the faces behind it. And then he read all the names again.

"He's gone."

"You're not back far enough, Tom." Luke reached across and leafed four or five pages farther.

"That son of a bitch."

Somehow, there Jay was. In the same blue gown as the rest of the class. His name in the same font. In front of the same motherfucking slate background. How had he done it?

Tom moved the pages between his thumb and first finger. They were a different texture. It could be missed, but they were lighter, glossier. And the pages preceding and following Jay's page were of the same higher-quality paper. He turned the book on its spine and examined the binding. The yearbook was comprised of fifteen sections of folded paper, all professionally glued and stitched at their crease into the cover's spine. It was subtle, but the eighth section was out of alignment. Tom set the yearbook back on the table.

"I know it's fake." Luke's gaze slowly ping-ponged from him to the book, and his shoulders stopped shaking. "I want to know why."

Tom cleared his throat. "What did he tell you?" Luke's look of confusion said it all. "How did you know to call me? Why did you call me?"

"I didn't call you. My brother-in-law did."

"Oh, my God." Tom put his hands to his forehead, digging the heels of his hands into his eyes until they ached. This was why the voice on the phone had been different. But please say he knew something, even if he hadn't made the call. Tom took down his hands. "Do you know who I am? Did Jay tell you anything about me at all? Anything?"

"Your name is Tom DuBelle. You went to school with my dad. You were his friend."

"All things *I* told you. What did *he* tell you?"

"Nothing."

"Nothing," Tom chuckled to keep from yelling. He rubbed his temples as he pushed back his chair and stood. "I have to go."

"Where? Why?"

"Home and because I don't belong here."

"But you can't go. I need you to tell me what he's been hiding from me!" Luke caught the sleeve of his jacket. "Please, Tom."

Tom stopped but pulled away his sleeve.

"It's not my responsibility to tell you. Your dad should've told you. But since he didn't see fit to, if you have questions, go to your mom."

"What if she doesn't know?"

"She does."

"What if she won't tell me?" Luke grabbed his sleeve once more.

Tom turned fully and looked him up and down. Again, he was struck by the resemblance, and his chest ached. Luke could've been the young man in the yearbook. He could've been Jay, standing there and asking another favor. Years later, now *Jay* asking *him* to stay. Begging *him* to stay. Tom blinked several times and pushed aside his inclination to give in to the specter. He glared, and his eyebrows furrowed.

How could you do this? Put me in this position? I'm dying, Jay! It's not fair to me! You've never been fair to me! And it's too late for you to demand anything else!

"How will I find you if she won't tell me?" Luke pulled his sleeve timidly.

"If she won't tell you, you don't need to know." Tom jerked away and stormed to the door. "And don't try to find me. I don't exist."

As he left the restaurant, he placed a large enough bill on the counter to amply compensate the waitress. She was across the room, but he responded to her nod with a wink, notwithstanding his fury.

This is where the boy gets his selfishness from. You could've told him at any fucking time. But no, you go die a quick, painless death and leave your good friend Tom to clean up your mess! Time and time again, you fucking screw me over!

Luke came through the patio doors, the yearbook under his arm, and Tom wanted to spit on the floor. He might've, if the waitress hadn't been so kind to him. He slammed the door and left before Luke could approach.

Chapter Eight

Ginger woke that morning for the first funeral he'd handle without his father-in-law in the wings for assistance. Instead of standing at his side, Jay was center stage in the box. Ginger felt multiple roles weigh heavily on him.

First he was the collected professional, capable of wading through the most difficult situations and solving every crisis. A businessman used to the gore and unassailable anguish of death, he could detach and manage it all. He was a conductor, a drum major. He'd lead everyone with ease.

Ginger had carried out this part hundreds of times, with rare exceptions. And for those extenuating circumstances, there'd been Jay to depend on. With him gone, Ginger had no backup. There was no one to pick up the pieces if he fell apart. Luke could remove bodies, be an extra pallbearer, play the piano if the audio system went haywire. But for the most important tasks, he was of no use.

What if we lose the baby?

It'd been this possibility which startled Ginger from his half sleep at four in the morning. He took several full breaths to subdue his panic.

Every single body that comes in is mine now. I can't pass anything. What if it happens again? I can't do it. I can't! I couldn't even hold him.

He cupped his hand over his mouth and pretended to breathe into a paper bag. Nice and steady. No reason for alarm.

Beau hadn't been able to hold the baby either, though they said she should. The doctors said they both should hold him. And rock him. And sing to him. And take pictures of him. Bond. As if they were going to bring him home and place him in the crib, dress him in the tiny clothes. As if they were going to see him smile and watch his eyes sparkle when they entered the room. Hold him. Rock him. Sing to him. As if he were alive. As if he'd ever lived. As if he weren't a lump of flesh. They were told that performing these actions with the dead infant was normal.

But they'd been too upset to play fantasyland. Beau had turned her head and folded her arms. She hadn't wanted to see him at all.

After they'd pressed the still bundle into his arms, Ginger pulled back the blanket and immediately wished he hadn't. The sight of the swollen, red face remained branded into his consciousness. It was really more purple than red. A dark shade of plum that was too ripe, and the skin had appeared thin enough to rupture at the lightest touch.

"Here."

Jay had swept in to rescue him as Ginger was about to drop it. He'd taken the bundle and cradled it in the crook of his arm like it wasn't ugly and dead. He'd looked at it without disgust and smoothed his hand over the baby's forehead. It was the only loving touch the dead child had received.

"He has red hair." Jay had tucked the blanket around the head. It might've been a loaf of bread.

Ginger had shoved his hands in his pockets and stared at the floor in shame. He hadn't noticed hair. There'd just been purple. The God-awful purple. He'd seen a dead baby. Many of them. He embalmed them. He cremated them. He placed their contorted bodies in Styrofoam containers. But he'd never seen any like this. Or maybe he had. He couldn't remember. Nothing he'd been confronted with had paralyzed him in this way.

"One of you." Beau's voice had come thin and uneven from the other side of the room where Jackie sat at her bedside. "Get it out of here. Now."

"Are you sure—"

"Yes, Dad. Get it out of here."

"What do you want us to do with—"

"I don't care! Just get it out!" Beau had cut him off, yelling through her tears. "All of you! Get out!"

Ginger hadn't known if "all of you" included him. He hadn't wanted to go or be part of the "us" who'd be taking care of the dead infant. His dead infant. His dead son. He hadn't wanted to see it again. He couldn't touch it.

"Stay." His father-in-law had provided the answer he'd needed. "I'll take care of him, Ginger, unless you want to."

The compassion in Jay's eyes told him it was okay, and he wouldn't be regarded as weak for not handling the body. His expression said he'd already known how Ginger felt.

He'd mouthed "thank you" and gone to Beau's side. As Ginger held his wife, Jay left the room with the dead baby in his arms.

Ginger knew the body had been placed in the refrigeration unit. Jay wouldn't do anything until he was given unambiguous direction, and it took Beau a week to decide she wanted the baby cremated. There'd be no ceremony of any kind. What was there to remember? Enduring constant discomfort for nine months in the anticipation of his arrival? The excitement of collecting toys and decorating the nursery? The playful debates over names or who the sonograms resembled?

"Or how about being told he was healthy? Hearing his heartbeat, feeling him fucking move? That's a *great* memory. Let's build a funeral around that. One minute he's fine, and then he's dead."

That's how it was with all death—one minute you were fine, and then you died. But Ginger had known she was aware of that. It was comparable to how he couldn't bear seeing the baby regardless of having handled hundreds of disturbing bodies. Old hat took on a new light when it became personal. Or rather, it brought new darkness.

"If you want to have a fucking ceremony over it, Ging, I don't care. Build a shrine. Get a Goddamn jazz band to march through the streets. Send it to sea in a Viking ship. I don't want any part. Burn it. Don't embalm it. And if there's anything left, use one of those white Chinese-food boxes in the stockroom. Shove it in a casket with whoever goes next. Don't waste a burial plot. Or a name. Just get rid of it, and forget it happened."

And Jay had been a Godsend not only due to physically handling the body, but he hadn't been immune to Beau's callousness. He showed no hurt or disapproval, assuring Beau her instructions would be carried out. But later that day, when Ginger was alone, Jay sent him a text message requesting his help at the funeral home.

When Ginger had arrived, he followed Jay's opera music and found him leaning against the crematorium. The machine wasn't on, but the door was raised. And before the open door stood the gurney upon which rested a standard, full-length box. But Ginger knew the box wasn't completely filled.

"She'd tell you not to waste a good box. To use a shoe box. Or a paper grocery bag. Or to stuff it in a burlap sack and toss it in like drowning a bunch of cats." Ginger had tried to chuckle.

"I know it's hard, but try not to judge her too harshly. It's devastating to want something desperately, and have it taken or kept from you," Jay said. "I speak from personal experience when I say that." He'd pushed himself away from the crematorium. "No one knows how fiercely I wanted my children. And how angry I was at everyone around me who had what I wanted. Trust me; be glad she's sniping and angry. There are worse things one could feel."

Ginger would've asked more, but his father-in-law had continued. "However, there's no reason you shouldn't have a say in what happens. Beau said she didn't care. Tell me what you want to do."

What did he want? Did it matter if the body was cremated without ceremony, any remains stored in a cardboard box under an inventory number? He hadn't been able to hold the baby, but did he want to pretend it hadn't happened? No, these elements were all important to him.

But Beau is more important.

"I want you to do what she asked. Take care of him as she said."

Jay hadn't seemed dissatisfied with the answer. Had the man ever been disappointed in anything?

"Do you want to see him one more time?"

"No," Ginger answered quickly, images of the purple face skidding through his brain.

"Do you want to put him in?"

"No."

"Do you want to close the door?"

"No."

"Do you—"

"Dad." He'd touched Jay's arm. "I know what you're doing. It's appreciated. But please, you handle it, and let me stand here. That's all I feel I can do."

Ginger had watched him push the cardboard box inside the crematorium and place the metal chip with the number on its inner ledge.

Just a number.

The door lowered, and Jay adjusted the machine's dials before he looked to Ginger. His finger hovered over the button. Waiting.

Ginger nodded and the machine rumbled to life. Jay stood by his side in silence, his hand on his shoulder as they listened to the breathing dragon.

I could've stood shoulder to shoulder with him someday. Instead, he's in there. Burning. And I don't know what's wrong with me. I can't be nonchalant and fake like I don't care. He felt the heat behind his eyes. *He didn't live. He didn't breathe. He might as well have never been. How can you be attached to what was only a fucking figment of your imagination?*

"You can love something sooner than it exists. Even when it doesn't exist anymore. And it's okay if people don't understand that. Fuck people," Jay said.

Ginger remembered that Jay had embraced him. And he'd felt better that someone had understood, and given him the empathy he hadn't received from Beau. Thanks to Jay, the last time Ginger had seen his unnamed son had been in the arms of his grandfather.

And what will I do now that you're not here? Ginger bit the knuckle of his first finger. *If it happens again, and I have to do it myself? I could barely take care of you.*

Of everything Ginger had experienced as Jay's apprentice and his partner, only two would haunt him for the rest of his life—the glimpse of his dead son's head, and the act of putting Jay's body back together. Just unzipping the black bag and seeing Jay awash with his own blood, unrecognizable from the bruising and lacerations on his face; it was all Ginger could do to pretend it wasn't Jay.

You were so broken, Dad. You must've been in so much pain.

Ginger had to get up, although it was still hours to sunrise, and the business professional part of him didn't need to take action until eleven. He slipped from bed quietly to avoid waking Beau and left the room.

I'm glad we came home. I didn't want to stumble downstairs at four thirty to have a fit in front of Mom. I want to be alone.

It was the only time he'd have all day to crash and burn by himself. There'd be spare instances when he could reflect in the silence of his mind, but he couldn't fall apart like he needed to. Jay had taught him it did no good to put up a strong front when you were torn inside. To help anyone else, you had to take care of yourself and be okay with you. In order to reach that solid foundation, he had to ready himself for the day.

Ginger planned on being at the funeral home first. He'd open the casket to check Jay's body and make any necessary repairs.

Next, he'd hide a small white cardboard container near Jay's shoulder beneath a casket insert flower arrangement. Beau was under the impression the box had been placed with her great aunt a year ago, but Ginger hadn't felt right "shoving it in with whoever went next."

Today, he'd retrieve the real box from the other containers of unclaimed ashes. It had a number on the outside. And on the spreadsheet that contained data for the boxes, there was also a number. He'd check it out like a library book or a piece of inventory. But he wouldn't just mark the number off as if the ashes had been retrieved. He'd put a name on the line. A name he would then cross out.

Ginger moved down the stairs one at a time, his back to the wall as if he were a burglar. The stairs creaked if they were used normally, and he couldn't imagine Beau was that deeply asleep.

I love you, but I have to be the pillar all day.

The family pillar had become his other position. The death was personal, but he was the mast they could lean upon. Whoever needed an embrace, a pep talk, or to vent. He was the glue. Wasn't he the new patriarch? Luke could hardly care for himself.

Though I'm too young for that. Way too young.

But Ginger felt himself slipping into it. He'd always been Beau's personal shoulder to cry on. Now Jackie needed him. Luke would also need him, though he fought it. They'd all be looking to Ginger for strength. Two days ago their perception of him had changed. And he felt like an asshole, but he was drained from their tears and problems. But they'd need him more than ever today. They would be at their most vulnerable. The pillar. It was easier when he wasn't the main support—when Jay was beside him, carrying most of the weight.

He took his jacket and coat from the hooks by the door and slipped outside. He pulled the coat on as he walked to the white van in the driveway. Tossing the jacket over his shoulder, he put his hands to the ladder attached to the rear door and climbed onto the frost-covered roof. He deposited the jacket in a rumpled ball and lay down with his arms folded under his head.

Ginger stared at the stars and allowed himself to sink into the role he genuinely felt. He was a son who'd lost his father. His mentor. In many ways, his best friend.

Why'd you have to die, Dad? Why? He asked for the hundredth time. His eyes throbbed with tears, and he didn't fight them. *It's just not fair!*

It wasn't fair for anyone, but he called on Jay, on God, on whoever was listening, to hear that it was specifically not fair to him. Ginger had never known either of his biological parents. He'd been raised by his grandmother, who'd been well-intentioned but too old to parent a child. From a young age, he'd had to be responsible for himself, and by the time he was a teenager, he'd taken to caring for her.

She'd needed all his time. To the extent that he had almost left high school. They'd had no one but each other and lived shrouded in secrecy because social security checks only went so far. There'd been a constant fear that if the conditions in which they lived were noticed, the authorities would remove Ginger. And they'd shut his grandmother in a nursing home. She hadn't been the best caregiver, but he'd loved her and hadn't wanted to be taken away. When he turned eighteen, he'd felt somewhat secure for the first time.

But one day, he'd returned from school to find the apartment door broken in. Instead of his grandmother, the landlord had been there. The man reported that paramedics had been called, and she'd been taken to the emergency room. He drove Ginger to the hospital, where he'd learned that the medical crew hadn't been able to revive her.

"Where is she?" He'd asked the doctor who'd given him the news.

How will it work? Ginger had worried. He couldn't make it without her. Literally. Emotion aside, he couldn't financially support himself. He had no place to go. How would he finish school? And what would happen to his grandmother now?

"She's downstairs."

"What will you do with her?" What did people do? He'd seen funerals on television. He'd read about them. But that was all he knew.

"We can't do anything more, son," the doctor said.

"But what am *I* going to do with her? I don't know what to do." Ginger had felt like a baby for crying, but he hadn't been able to help it.

"We've called someone. Wait here."

Since his options hadn't been numerous, and the hospital was heated and safe, he sank into the chair behind him. He'd bent over to his knees and cried.

Shortly, the plastic chair creaked beside him, and a hand had touched his shoulder. It'd been nice of the doctor to sit with him and wait. He wasn't sure what they were waiting for, but he must have other patients to see. Live patients. But when he'd looked over, it hadn't been the doctor.

The stranger wore a suit with a white button-up shirt and black tie. He gave the impression of being inviting and solicitous—like comforting a crying young man was of no inconvenience. He'd pulled a handkerchief from his pocket, but Ginger had been reluctant to accept it.

"Go ahead. I have plenty."

He'd taken the handkerchief and pressed it to his nose, inhaling deeply. It'd been the cleanest smelling thing he could ever remember.

"My wife uses lavender fabric softener." The man had shrugged when seconds of silence had gone by with Ginger holding the fabric to his face. "I wouldn't know the first thing about it. I just pay the bills."

"Who are you?" He'd asked from behind the handkerchief.

"I'm the man who's going to take care of your grandmother."

"What does that mean? Take care of her?"

"I was advised it means whatever *you* would like it to. You're the person responsible for her. Is that true?"

"Yes." His voice had cracked. "We only had each other."

"I'm very sorry to hear that." The stranger's eyes were kind, and he'd given an understanding nod. "You have no one else?"

"No."

"Do you have anywhere to go?"

Ginger thought of the squalid apartment with the damaged door. It was being gutted as they spoke. The landlord wasn't a fool.

"No."

"Don't worry. It'll be okay." He'd squeezed his shoulder and stood. "Let's see after your grandmother first, and then we'll take care of you." He took a couple of steps near the door. "Come on."

"Where are we going?" Ginger lowered and folded the handkerchief. He'd placed it in his pocket as he'd followed.

"To the morgue. Are you afraid?"

He had been. He'd always been afraid of many things. Of not having a place to live. Of starving. Of being sick and not being able to afford medicine. Of being taken away from his grandmother. Scared was his first reaction.

But Ginger had met the stranger's eyes again, and his fear ebbed. "No. I'm not afraid."

Ginger could still feel Jay's arm around his shoulders leading him down the hospital hallway, and it made him cry harder as he lay on the van's roof.

I had absolutely nothing. You took me under your wing. You gave me so much, but you never made me feel I was indebted to you. That's why it's not fair. I never had anything. It was all taken away from me!

He stopped thinking and just felt the anger. The ache from having a piece of himself ripped out. He hadn't been this upset when his grandmother had died, or when the baby had been born dead. But they hadn't been part of him as Jay had. He'd never idolized them. He hadn't been able to rely on them, to trust them. After years of support, kindness, and love Jay had worked himself into Ginger's soul. It was as if he'd always been there. Jay had taught him to be the man he was.

But now he was gone. And there were no words to express Ginger's sorrow.

"But you still have Beau, Ging." He held an arm over his eyes and pretended it was Jay speaking to him. *"You need to pull yourself together to take care of her. And there's the baby. You have to be as good a father to it as I was to you."*

"Yes," he said aloud. No one else was there to hear anyway.

"And you're a good son. You did everything I asked. I know it was hard for you to call Tom since it would upset Beau. But you did it because you're a good son."

"I should've done more. I shouldn't have let you go alone. It would've been different if I'd been with you."

Ginger waited for the voice in his head to respond, but it didn't. Jay had never been one for the "it should've been me" diatribe. That wasn't what Ginger was thinking though. He didn't want to die in place of Jay. No one should die at all.

"I mean, maybe I could've done something." He bunched his hand into a fist. "I'm sorry, Dad, but Luke is useless. If I'd been there, I would've done more. He couldn't even pull his head out of his ass to apologize to you when you were dying in the parking lot."

He saw behind his closed eyelids the image of Jay's bloody, torn face when he'd unzipped the black bag. His brain oozing from the back of his skull like a pink slug.

"And he had to know you were dying with those injuries! What did he do? Did he tell you he loved you? Did he hold your hand? Did he comfort you? He was the worst possible person to be there!" Ginger's voice dropped to a whisper. "I would've done all those things. I would've tried to save you. I might've been able to save you."

"I did not want to be saved."

The voice returned from nowhere, and he pulled his coat tighter around himself. He wasn't sure if his grief had fueled it, like all the other consoling statements he wanted to hear from Jay. He wouldn't have wanted Jay to say that he didn't—

Something stiff brushed across his arm. He jumped, and his forehead bumped into a plastic broom.

"Goddamn it!" He thrust the broom away and rubbed his forehead. The adrenaline from the scare released as he leaned over the van's side. He saw the broom wielder's curious face in the light that had begun to fleck across the sky.

"Are you Snoopy now? You sleep on top of cars?" Beau poked his arm with the broom again.

"Snoopy sleeps on top of his doghouse. Why would he sleep on top of a car?"

"Why would he sleep on top of his doghouse? Why would a man with a perfectly good bed sleep on top of a car in the middle of February? Aside from it being freezing, isn't it slick up there with the frost? You'll fall and break your neck."

"It doesn't increase my level of safety to be startled by a broom across the face." Ginger took the bristled end and pulled it free of her hands. "Or to be continuously jabbed with one."

"How else should I get your attention? I'm not climbing up there." Beau folded her arms. "I needed to poke you awake before you threw yourself off. You're lucky we don't have neighbors close by. Come down and give me my broom."

He tossed the broom and jacket he'd been using as a pillow to the driveway. The bristles prodded him as he descended the ladder. When he was on the ground, he faced her and found the broom at his chest. He raised both hands in surrender.

"Good. Now get in the house." Beau's eyes twinkled, and she motioned to the open door with her weapon. She removed it to let him turn and then put it to his back again, nudging him forward. "March. Double time."

"Are you holding me hostage?"

"I wake up to find you've disappeared. After a frantic search, I find you on the van roof half sleeping, half talking to yourself. How do I know you haven't gone off the deep end, hmm? Have you finally cracked? Do I need to put you in a padded room?"

"I'm fine."

But Ginger worried as he crossed the threshold. Not that he'd "gone off the deep end." The house was frigid. He hadn't left the door open; she had. And for it to be this cold inside, how long had she been out? What had she heard?

The door closed, and the broom fell to the floor. As he turned, she stood on her tiptoes, brushing the sides of his face with her chilly hands.

"You can't blame yourself for this, Ginger. Any of it."

He felt the pressure around his eyes that meant the tear stores had been replenished. His hands shook when she took one and led him to the couch.

"And you don't know what he did for Dad, baby." Beau sat next to him.

"Do you?"

"Yes." She drew her feet up on the couch and ran her hand through his hair. "Luke held his head in his lap. He stayed right with him." Ginger's temple was numb, and he barely felt her kiss it. "Dad didn't go alone."

"He really was right there? He stayed with him?"

"Yes, he did." Her voice came near his ear. "I know he's a silly boy, Ging, and he does things that don't make sense. But he loved Dad. And that was all Dad felt when he went. I promise."

To his shame, a few tears escaped before he was able to bottle the emotion. The time to transform had come. He was still unnerved by the voice he'd heard on the van's roof, but knowing that Luke hadn't stayed in the car made him feel better. Someone had held Jay's head in their lap and been with him. Even if it hadn't been Ginger, that Jay hadn't been alone was good.

"That's enough." He coughed, and Beau raised her head from his shoulder. "I'm okay. I need to get moving."

Ginger left the room. He cracked his knuckles as he went and envisioned sliding on the black suit coat—that skin of the business professional.

"If you need to talk, Ginger. If you have a problem, you can come to me."

He was halfway up the stairs by the time she said this, and he chose not to reply. Neither the professional nor the pillar needed consolation. The grieving son? Potentially. But Ginger didn't plan on releasing him again anytime soon.

Chapter Nine

Ginger wondered how much Luke had been drinking over the past twelve hours. Something was off when he dropped by later that morning to check on his mother-in-law.

He'd just finished offering to drive Jackie over to the funeral home before he picked up Beau, instead of waiting for Luke to straggle out of bed last minute.

"Speak of the devil," Jackie interrupted Ginger. He'd been across the room refilling her coffee, and he looked over to see Luke slouch against the doorjamb. "Good morning, sleepyhead. I'm amazed you're awake. And that you're dressed. You've been industrious this morning."

"I've been up for hours. We need to talk."

Luke slumped into Ginger's chair. He was dressed, but his hair was uncombed, and his tie hung loose and askew. Ginger saw a spot on the white collar of Luke's partially unbuttoned shirt. And he wore a pair of sunglasses.

To hide the red eyes, or because it's too bright in here? Ginger scowled. How was it anything but disrespectful to be hungover and/or drunk on the day of his father's funeral? Or did Luke think he was being funny and looking cool? He looked like he'd stumbled out of a bar. Jackie wouldn't allow him to leave the house that way.

"'We need to talk?'" Jackie repeated, and he saw from the lines around her lips that she was trying not to laugh. "That sounds serious."

"Are you breaking up with her?" Ginger returned to the table and placed the cup before her.

"Let me guess. It's not me, it's you?" Jackie snickered. "You need some space?"

Luke flipped up the sunglasses and glared at Ginger.

"What's *he* doing here, Mom?"

Generally, Luke's aggression was more subdued in front of Jackie or Jay, and the malicious stares were thrown in private. However, Ginger knew he may be overly sensitive in his current state of mind. It'd already been a highly emotional day, and it wasn't past noon yet.

Though Ginger had promised himself he wouldn't become upset when he was alone with Jay's body that morning, he hadn't been able to contain it. He'd placed the white box in the casket, concealed it with the flower arrangement, and had lost all composure. After pulling into the driveway of his in-laws' house, he'd crashed again.

He thought of Jay. Of closing the casket. They'd only open the lid one more time that afternoon. Then he'd be lost in the darkness forever. He also thought of the white cardboard container—his shameful secret. And the name he'd written on its side prior to tucking it in.

No one will ever know, Dad. No one but you and I.

He knew he was primed to interpret things as being more caustic, but his brother-in-law could be a colossal dick sometimes. Demanding to know why Ginger was there? Being such a slob on the day of his father's funeral?

"He's here to usurp you. Steal your throne. Divorce Beau and marry me. Just to piss you off, Hamlet," Jackie said to Luke. She laughed as his face grew red and he stood. "Luke, sit down. What do you want to talk about?"

"I can't talk to you while *he* is here. I want to talk to you alone." The boy remained standing.

"Why? Are you talking smack about your only brother? Keeping secrets from me?" Ginger smiled.

"I don't keep secrets from people!" Luke tore the sunglasses from his face and banged them on the table, making the coffee mugs jump.

He fled without waiting for a response. His footsteps thudded up the stairs, and his bedroom door slammed. Jackie sighed.

"He had a lot to drink last night. And probably this morning."

"It appears that way." Ginger nodded.

"Don't worry; I'm not letting him wear that shirt."

"Good. We can't have him acting *and* looking ridiculous."

"Ginger." Jackie touched his hand. "Cut him some slack. He's just a boy. He's not put together to handle things as well as you."

It wasn't like his mother-in-law to make excuses for anyone, especially her children. He decided not to question the sudden change though. It'd be a hard day for everyone, and she shouldn't have to justify the defense of her son. Ginger just patted her hand in return.

"Okay. I'm sorry, Mom."

But Jackie's justification of Luke's behavior nagged Ginger throughout the day. Luke wasn't "put together to handle things." What did that mean? Ginger didn't necessarily believe that he himself was "put together to handle things." Hadn't he spent part of the night sleeping on the roof of a van? He could fall apart, like anyone else. But Luke was *constantly* breaking down. Luke had always been able to unravel, which was the difference between them. Ginger hadn't been "put together to handle things." Luke just had never been given anything to handle in the first place. He didn't *know* how to handle things. He'd been too protected, too sheltered.

It's a chicken and egg thing. Was he protected because he couldn't deal, or he can't deal because he was protected?

Ginger was inclined to believe the issue was innate with Luke. After all, he and Beau had the same childhood, had been raised by the same parents; but, he'd always been different. He had this sense of being ill-equipped. Ginger wouldn't trust him to keep a plant alive for more than a day or two.

He also remained curious about the topic Luke wanted to discuss with Jackie. Ginger really didn't think it was in reference to him, but it was evident Luke was bothered. And Ginger sensed the issue was more than Jay's death as the antagonism continued.

"I only want to play the piano." Luke argued with him outside the chapel.

"You practiced this. You were practicing yesterday. Why the change?" Ginger tried to be kind, as he'd promised Jackie.

"Why not?"

"This is what Dad wanted. He wanted you to sing, Luke. He didn't want you to just play the piano."

"I don't care what he wanted. I'll do it only on the piano, or I won't do it at all." Luke gave Ginger a black glare. "And don't call him 'Dad.' He's *my* dad. Not yours."

There's something wrong in your fucking head. Ginger clasped his fists until his knuckles were white. *It's like you fly off the hinges. You need medication. Strong medication.*

"Fine. But don't make a scene. Stick to the song he wanted. Nothing else. And put those fucking sunglasses away."

"I don't make scenes." Luke skulked from the room.

Ginger also questioned if his brother-in-law was being difficult with everyone, or if the boy had singled him out. Not an hour later, when Ginger gathered him with their four cousins to plan how they'd proceed in carrying the casket, Luke folded his arms, and that look crawled over his face.

Goddamn it. What's wrong now?

"Why do I have to be in the middle? I don't want to be in the middle."

"Does it matter where you are?" Ginger attempted to cloak his exasperation.

"Of course, it does! He's *my* father. You don't think I'm important enough to have a corner? You don't *trust* me with a corner? I want a corner."

"I didn't assign positions based on rank, or amount of trust, Luke."

"How did you decide then? Dad didn't draw a fucking map of where he wanted the pallbearers positioned. You get a corner. I want one."

"I'm leading. *Leading.* Can you stop acting like a little boy?"

"I want a corner. I want a front corner. I *deserve* to have a front corner."

"Will you just let him have a corner?" One of the cousins whispered and elbowed Ginger in the side. "It's not important."

But it was important. That's what no one understood. No one but Luke, who'd spotted it right off.

No. I don't trust you. You're drunk, hungover, or God knows what, but you're not acting sane. I'd gladly give you a corner. Gladly. If I could trust that you wouldn't drop him, accidentally or purposefully.

Ginger stared Luke down in silence, until a different cousin nudged him with another plea for peace. "Give him what he wants."

That's what it always comes back to. "Give him what he wants." "He's not put together for handling things." Ginger covered his eyes with his hand. *For you, Dad. I can't trust him, but I have to believe he wouldn't do that to you.*

"Fine. You take the front right hand—"

"I want the left."

Oh, the pain. The ulcers Ginger knew were beginning to fester from holding back knocking Luke to the ground. Especially when he caught that smirk.

If I'd offered left, you would've wanted right. You're going to fight me on everything. For whatever reason, you really have singled me out, asshole.

"Luke, you take any corner your heart desires." He managed to release only the words, keeping the desire to punch him in reserve.

"I want the front left-hand corner."

"So be it."

Ginger made a hand-washing motion and walked away. He went to his office, miraculously refraining from slamming the door. After he'd locked it, he picked a pillow from the couch, held it over his face, and shouted all the things that his respect for Jay prevented him from yelling at Luke.

Why do you care about songs and corners? He's dead! It doesn't matter which fucking place you are around his casket! He's in there, and he's still dead! And all you can think about is baiting me? Embarrassing me and making me seem unreasonable?

When he reentered the viewing room, Ginger felt better. He toyed with pulling Luke aside and threatening to kill him if he dropped Jay's casket, or if he caused further problems. Instead he locked eyes with his brother-in-law across the crowd filling the chapel and shot him an unmistakably hostile look. Luke knew Ginger would kill him.

And Beau will kill you. And Mom. We'll each take one of your limbs and pull you apart. Slowly. Painfully. And I'll take both corners of your fucking casket and push you into the Goddamn creek, you piece of shit.

Chapter Ten

Earlier that morning, during their breakfast engagement, Luke had approached Tom the best way he could. In addition to uncovering Jay's secret, the desire to slake his guilt by picking Tom's brain motivated him to be indulgent and polite in exchange for his answers.

Though valuable minutes ticked by, he waited while Tom thumbed through the yearbook. His attention had only been mildly piqued that Tom had been first chair in violin and attended Julliard. Tom's connection to his father and any of their shared adventures could be of interest, but if playing the piano had nothing to do with Jay, it was as inconsequential as the rest of Tom's memories.

When it looked like Tom could spend the entire morning sorting through the faces of his past, Luke had been forced to maneuver the conversation. By playing his cards wisely, he kept Tom from discovering that he hadn't been the caller until too much had been revealed.

Even though Tom hadn't divulged the actual secret, validating there *was* a secret and Luke wasn't obsessing over what didn't exist had been a keystone. And while Tom had been angry at Luke's deception, there'd been other things swimming behind Tom's eyes. Was he upset with Jay for not revealing the information? Luke felt a sense of camaraderie with him on recognizing that Tom too was placed in a difficult position.

If Jake could know, I deserved to know. It shouldn't fall to a stranger to be the equalizer.

He'd watched Tom storm out of the restaurant with disappointment, but at least he'd been pointed in the direction of who to ask. Jackie couldn't withhold any truth she might know when he was aware of this much. If she knew anything, she'd tell him. In a sarcastic, deprecating way, but she'd tell him.

And if he needed to find Tom, he could.

Not that I should have to crawl to that bastard, but Jake has his number.

As Luke drove home, the unfairness pushed his thoughts down a spiral of hatred for his brother-in-law.

This is your fault! You swooped in and stole my parents and sister from me! It's not good enough that they love you most, but then you build this secret world with them. You've been walling me out of my own family, brick by brick for years, you motherfucker!

Luke crept into the house as silently as he'd left it. Jackie had likely been awake all night slugging coffee, and everything was still quiet. He'd started to ascend the stairs, but the kitchen light made him stop.

Get it over now. But I can't be angry with her. Calm down, Luke. It's not her fault. She's your mother. Save it for that douche bag. She could be as innocent as you and Beau.

When he entered the kitchen Jackie was asleep at the table with her face hidden in her arms and her shoulders moving in an easy motion.

You cried yourself to sleep.

Sympathy for his mother dismantled the urgency. He wanted to touch her hair, to kiss her cheek and hold her like he had the night before when she'd been upset at Beau's reaction to the rings. He wanted to be of comfort to her.

But you should rest. I'll be here when you wake up.

Luke went upstairs to his room, his resentment for Jake blunted to some extent. Yesterday Jackie hadn't seemed opposed to Luke being the consoling son. And *he* was her son. Not Jake. No matter how the maggot had tried to worm his way in. And she may not be as warm as Jay, but her criticisms were given out of love for him.

Maybe I should take her advice. Perhaps I am "more stupid than I give myself credit for."

He relaxed onto his bed and folded his arms under his pillow.

Here's what I'm going to do: I will give her a couple of hours to rest. I'll go downstairs and press her shoulder to wake her. I'll listen to her woes and sit beside her, petting her arm and letting her cry. Nodding my head for her to go on. I could have a handkerchief in my pocket and pull it out with a flourish. I'll offer it to dry her eyes like a knight in shining armor.

And after she expelled all her sorrow—

There'll be nothing to say to Jake. He'll have no purpose. I handled it.

Luke would ask his questions about Tom DuBelle and what Jay had been hiding. Either she'd know as Tom claimed and tell him. Or she'd be vindicated. Whichever it was, he'd get what he wanted, whether from her or Jake.

If she doesn't know, however fucked-up it may be, I'll go to him. Jake would love to see me grovel. But once I have what I want, I'm going to exterminate him.

Luke had no intention of literally killing his brother-in-law, but he'd create a plan to get Jake out. Push him away from his mother and his sister if he could.

Of course, it'll be difficult with him now controlling the business. I want to be the good son, but I'm not filling Dad's role. I can't lose sight of Broadway.

And Mom and Beau still like him. They'll like him even more when she has the baby. I just need to convince them they don't need him, and they can rely on me. His days are numbered.

But that scheme had to wait. He rewound to the plan.

Ideally, Jackie would tell him. That would mean she'd been a party to keeping him in the dark; however, he'd forgive her when she apologized.

Then I'll tell Beau.

By telling her, once again Luke would be the star. The hero. A bringer of news. He'd be in control, and she'd be grateful. Impressed that he'd solved everything and been unselfish enough to share his knowledge. Jake wouldn't have told her as much as he was willing to share.

Maybe the initial step in revealing what you really are is to expose how you've kept secrets from her. Your lies will be the first of your underpinnings to come loose.

Luke gave a crisp nod. It was a decent start. Considering they'd bury his father that afternoon, he felt good.

But then he heard the car engine.

A feeling of irritated dread came over him as he went to his bedroom window. The engine cut, and he pulled aside the curtain. His fantasy disintegrated when he recognized the white van in the driveway with Jake in the driver's seat.

The left side of Luke's face twitched, and his aggravation resurfaced. Jackie was still asleep, and Jake was about to saunter in and wake her up. He pictured his brother-in-law goading her into releasing her unhappiness to *him* without giving Luke a chance. He'd steal the spotlight like always.

I hate you so much. I wish I had a crossbow. A spear. Or one of those fucking African straws to shoot a dart into your neck. You'd drop like a rock. That'd be hilarious.

He waited for Jake to leave the car.

Come on in! You practically own the place!

But instead of trouncing in to ruin everything right away, Jake folded over the steering wheel, his body shaking.

Luke held his breath, frames of Jay's death flickering in his mind.

He's having a seizure. I should get help. I should do something. Anything.

But he clenched the side of the curtain and stared. He'd faced death previously—only days before—and lost. What made him think his intervention would yield any different result from last time?

Last time. It felt like a tight fist grasped the center of his chest. Seconds ago he'd wished for his brother-in-law to "drop like a rock." *That will live with me forever. Just like Dad. Just—*

Jake's convulsions stopped. He brought his head up and rubbed his suitcoat's arm across his eyes.

You were crying? Crying? A near spontaneous combustion of the guilt that had been building. In its place remained the fury. *What do you have to be upset about? He was my father! Not yours! Mine! They're all mine! You have no reason to be that upset!*

Except to spite Luke.

You dredged up tears to put on a show for Mom! To establish common ground so she'll talk to you instead of me!

Under Luke's glowering eyes, Jake stepped out of the van. He leaned down to the side mirror to adjust his tie, dust his suit coat, and pat his hair.

Believe me, I know prepping for a performance when I see it. Must be perfect, mustn't we? Just red around the eyes to get her sympathy.

Luke let the curtain fall, clenching and unclenching his fists as he imagined Jake rehearsing lines, practicing precisely timed sniffles.

It's always all about you!

He felt the shift in the house from its front door being opened, and heard the footsteps approach the kitchen.

And the master manipulator begins. Get your tickets, folks! It's going to be a great fucking show!

He began to pace his room, trying to work down the anger.

Relax. Relax and think. Why shouldn't my plan work? He's forgetting that I still have an advantage.

The coup being staged was on Luke's territory. No matter what Jake wanted to pretend, Jackie was *Luke's* mother. Jay was *his* father. And this was *Luke's* motherfucking house, *his* stage. Jackie knew that. With Jay gone, everyone else would realize it too.

I'll uncover whatever piece of info you know and then make sure you're kicked to the curb. This is my Goddamn show!

He slammed the door to his room and started down the stairs.

Also, you don't even realize who you're up against. Sure, the plan now has to be impromptu, but I know ad lib. I'm a professional. You just pump rotting bodies full of chemicals. I'm an artist. I can easily outplot and outact you whether I have ten hours or ten seconds to put it together.

He pulled a pair of sunglasses from the basket in the hall to hide any rage that might unintentionally reveal itself in his eyes, and entered the spotlight.

But somehow, despite the careful application of his skills, Jake had known. While Luke had merely made the reasonable request to speak with Jackie alone, he'd been shot down. Jake rallied Jackie to his cause, sitting beside her with a nasty sneer as he baited Luke. Repeatedly. He presided over the kitchen table like he'd already won.

You think today is about you, don't you? Luke thought, staring Jake down from behind the dark lenses. *You think this is your finish line. It's my turf for now, but you'll send Dad off today with perfection, and your performance will seal you in.*

He realized there was nothing he could do about this aspect. As the funeral director, Jake was in charge. He was going to ensure everything went off without a hitch, and thereby "prove" how valuable he was, and how much of a jackass he wasn't. And words aside, with that beady look in his fake grief-stricken eyes—was he daring Luke to wreck the funeral?

I know you want me to make a scene. There'd be more pieces for you to pick up. Think of how good it'd make you look, you self-seeking dick hole.

"Are you talking smack about your only brother? Keeping secrets from me?"

The comment was a push too hard. And not just because it was actually Jake keeping secrets, but to call himself Luke's brother? It was an insult that couldn't be born. Bile gathered at the back of his mouth from Jake's insinuation that they were equal. He left the termite burrowed into his mother. Once again his questions would have to wait.

I am not your friend. I'm not your brother. But I will be the burr in your side. You've been a festering blister on my ass for ten years, and I'm ready to return the favor. You'll have your triumph, for now, but you're going to be miserable.

A litany of things could be done to not *destroy* his father's funeral, but undermine Jake's purported control of the situation.

Whenever he walked by the funeral home's front doors, Luke casually turned the lock. He waited in the nearby hallway to hear the glass pane shuddering as the keyed door lever was tried repeatedly. Someone, he wasn't sure who, eventually let the mourners in after they resorted to ringing the bell, but he was always careful to have fled the scene by that point.

He felt only a little guilty when he swiped Jay's "Celebration of Life" guest book from its podium the first time.

It's just a collection of signatures. Who cares? He wedged the book in between two couch cushions and grinned. *Jake will care. That's who.*

But he needn't have even attempted to rationalize the action, since the damn book kept reappearing no matter where he hid it—under a potted plant, behind a lamp, inside a desk drawer.

You can try to best me, try. Luke checked behind his shoulder to ensure the entryway was deserted. Quickly, he unscrewed the nib from the ballpoint pen that rested beside the recovered guest book. Plucking out the full ink refill, he inserted a dry tube and refastened the nib. *Keep the fucking guest book.*

And it wouldn't just be the funeral's beginning that would be fraught with "mishaps" that any *competent* person wouldn't have allowed to happen. Luke imagined the chaos that would ensue when people went to the front closet to retrieve their coats and found them all missing. He chuckled as he transported another jacket and a pea coat to the rear closet and shoved them in.

And, imagine this: right as Jake is up at the pulpit wrenching out more fake tears and—

"Meow." He crouched and held an open can of tuna fish out the side door. "Meow. Meow. Come on you dumb little fuck. Meow."

The feral gray cat didn't answer back. It eyed Luke suspiciously as he waggled the can toward it.

Jake will be at his prime, gushing about how much he loved Dad and bullshit, bullshit, bullshit and then suddenly, this cat will streak across the room. It'll climb up the curtains, or maybe even tear apart a flower arrangement. Seriously, Jake? You can't even keep a wild animal out of the funeral home?

"Meow. Meow." The cat shifted nearer to the tuna can, and Luke dumped a little on the concrete, trailing the rest inside. "That's right, boy. You'll like it in here. It's nice and warm. There's lots of things to shred and piss on. You can even invite all your mangy friends."

He got to his feet and took a couple steps back, smiling as the cat edged closer.

"I'll leave your tuna right here. Good kitty."

To his irritation though, he didn't hear anyone talking about his disruptions. Someone, presumably that fucker himself, kept "fixing" things. Not only had the guest book continued to reappear, but Jake caught on to his dry pen trick and kept replacing those as well. He'd transported the same fucking pea coat to the back closet three times. And on returning to the side room where he'd tried to lure in the cat, the door was closed, the tuna gone, and his would-be minion gaped at him hungrily outside the window.

A bolder approach in provoking Jake was necessary.

Yes, Luke knew Jay had outlined that he was to sing a specific song, not just play the piano. But what kept him from feeling any remorse for refusing his father's request—

"This is what Dad wanted. He wanted you to sing, Luke. He didn't want you to just play the piano."

"I don't care what he wanted. I'll do it only on the piano, or I won't do it at all. And don't call him 'Dad.' He's *my* dad. Not yours."

The audacity that ass rammer had. However, there was success. He could tell from Jake's expression that he'd hit a mark in frustrating him.

"Fine. But don't make a scene. Stick to the song he wanted. Nothing else. And put those fucking sunglasses away."

"I don't make scenes." Luke pushed the bridge of the sunglasses, firmly sliding them tight to his face.

This is the way to go then. You need more than pranks. Fine. I have no problem in blatantly challenging you for what's rightfully mine.

Whether it was Luke's contribution to the funeral, or having a designated place carrying his father's casket.

Luke had pitched in to be a pallbearer hundreds of times when families were short on them. Typically, he hated having a front corner. It was too much responsibility. If the front went down, everyone followed. One false step on a curb and he pictured there'd be a corpse splayed out over the side of a casket. It'd never happened, but if it did, he didn't want the finger pointed at him.

You think I'm going to drop it on purpose. You think I'm not trustworthy enough to carry a corner of my own father's casket.

"Will you just let him have a corner? It's not important."

His cousins saw right through Jake's treachery.

You see, I have a family. It was difficult to not smile and just keep locked on Jake's glare without expression. *This is my family. Not yours.*

"Give him what he wants."

I know I froze up earlier and considered showing you mercy when I thought you were dying. But not anymore. I changed my mind. And it's more than a fucking corner.

"Fine. You take the front right hand—"

"I want the left."

Jake met his stare again, and Luke found he couldn't keep the grin hidden any longer.

I want back what's mine. I want you out.

Even if Luke hadn't known he was winning, his brother-in-law's immediate acquiesce to his demands and retreat proved it.

Go punch your couch cushions, douche bag.

With Jake throwing a pussy tantrum, Luke was free again to continue planting his tricks without them being "corrected."

After reopening the side door for his feline friend, he snuck into the empty chapel. He took the microphone wire that curled from the podium and held it as he crawled under the stage's platform to find the jack connection.

So, even before Mr. Kitty wrecks Jake's crap-ass speech, he discovers that no one can even hear his stupid fucking—

A sharp kick to his leg.

Luke sat up and smacked his head on the low ceiling. "Fuck!"

"What do you think you're doing?" His mother's voice made him drop the black wire.

"Nothing."

"Nothing, my ass! Get out of there!" She kicked him again.

Luke scooted out from under the stage. He ducked his head and met her eyes expecting to find curiosity.

What's the big deal, Mom? I'm fixing the microphone. Someone disconnected it. Yeah, that sounds—

"Stop acting like a petulant child! I've spent more time in the last hour cleaning up your pranks than I have with the people who came to see us! To honor and remember your father!" Jackie's arms were folded tightly across her abdomen. "Do you think this shit is funny?"

"No," he said, and his stomach somewhat sank. He hadn't meant for his mother to cover for Jake.

But why should you be rescuing him? He's not your son. I am.

"Then why are you doing it?"

Luke hadn't been sure what to say, but she saw through him.

"Damn it, this is not about you and Ginger! Stop taking everything as a personal attack. No one, not a single soul, is thinking of you, Luke! You're not the center of attention!"

"But Jake always gets to be the center of attention. Always." He stood and swept the dust from his slacks. *It's the same old shit.*

"Jesus Christ! You know who's the center of attention right now? The man in the casket. Do you want me to throw you in there with him? If it's that important for you to upstage every event and try to undermine the good work your brother is doing, I'll toss you right in!"

"He's not my fucking—"

"Listen to me." Jackie cut him off. "You will fix whatever you broke under that stage. And you will stop this juvenile bullshit and act like a civilized human being."

Luke hated always being spoken to like he was a child. Was that why Jake felt he could be run over? Because his family labeled him as only a boy? It was as unjust as Jake being the favorite. As unfair as him spoiling the magic Luke could've had with his mother that morning. As ludicrous as keeping a secret from him about his own father.

"Mom, I need to talk to you. Alone."

"Whatever it is, it can wait."

"It can't."

"I don't have the time or energy to argue through any of your paranoid delusions right now. Fix what you broke and leave Ginger and everything else alone. If you can act like a good boy, I'll talk to you tonight."

Jackie didn't even give him the opportunity to respond. She turned on her heels and strutted out of the chapel, slamming the door behind her. Again, Luke's anger hit the ceiling.

You don't have to bribe me to be good! I am good! I'm just sick of his shit! Of all your shit! And it isn't a "paranoid delusion!" I'm not crazy! You people are the ones hiding something from me!

He hated to consider it, but maybe Jackie was an active conspirator.

Just look at how quick she is to defend Jake. And it's one thing for him to call himself my brother. I know he'd give his nut sack to be an actual part of our family. But for her to say it. He wanted to gag. Yes, based on her actions she probably was among the pit of snakes.

But I need her information about Tom DuBelle. And not just for me.

Luke walked down the hallway toward the viewing room.

He couldn't forget that he wasn't alone in being deceived. Manipulated. Conspired against.

There's Beau. She's my only ally. For both of us, I need Mom to answer my questions and tell the truth.

So, when the gray cat bounded past him toward the chapel like a good little accomplice, Luke chased him back outside and tucked the sunglasses in his pocket. If he had to let Jake have his way to get a private audience with his mother, the asshole could take his moment.

Chapter Eleven

To Ginger's relief, once everything started, it turned out as okay as a funeral could go. Luke didn't make more trouble. He played the music Jay had wanted on the piano. He carried the front left corner of the casket without stumbling. He kept his sunglasses off and tie straight. He didn't say anything civil to Ginger; however, he also didn't go out of his way to be difficult.

With Luke behaving, Ginger was able to concentrate his energy and attention on being the business professional. He detached himself just enough, and the distraction even made him forget the private conversation Luke had requested with Jackie. Until it resurfaced that night.

The three sat silently in the living room. Jackie lounged in her recliner, pretending to read but not faking it well. Beau lay on the couch, with her head in his lap, pretending to sleep but not faking it very well either. Ginger stared into space.

He thought about Jay, as he assumed they all did. Only he reflected on where he now was. One of the warmest people he'd ever known, who formed lasting connections instantly and was only by himself when he opted to be; now he was below the earth. Cold and alone. Ginger couldn't break away from that image.

Though not quite alone. The thought of the white box comforted him.

"It smells like a bunch of fucking flowers in here."

Luke appeared in the doorway. Once again he wore the sunglasses, and he had a book tucked under his arm.

"There is a bunch of fucking flowers in here, Einstein."

Ginger smirked at Beau's comment. She hadn't been asked to give Luke a break, or if she had, she didn't care to.

"Mom, I need to talk to you." Luke ignored Beau; he never took swipes at her.

"Talk. I'm listening," Jackie said, but she didn't lower her book.

"Alone."

"Whatever you have to say to me, you can say in front of them."

"Beau can stay. But make *him* leave."

Again? What kind of conspiracy is this?

Beau propped herself on her elbow and looked back at her brother still standing by the door.

"What's wrong with you, Luke? And will you take off those stupid glasses?"

"I want to talk to *my* mom. And *my* sister. *My* family. *Alone.*" He removed the sunglasses, and after jamming them in his pocket, focused on Jackie. "Mom, make him leave."

"I absolutely will not!" She slammed her book on the side table. "After how you treated him today? After you were an asshole to him and made things more difficult for everyone? You should be ashamed of yourself! You're lucky I don't make *you* leave!"

Ginger felt glad. Not because Luke was being reprimanded, though he had to admit her rebukes had a sweetness. Jackie was sticking up for him. He'd always had a more special relationship with Jay, but Jackie had been the mother he also never had. It felt nice that she was as willing to champion him now as she'd been to defend Luke that morning.

"Yeah, you'll make me leave. Just like Dad. Kick me out. Go ahead. You don't need me when you have *him.*"

"You're bringing this up on the day we bury your father? But how am I *not* surprised?" Jackie laughed, but then her lips formed an unsympathetic line. "You can't throw an ace that doesn't exist."

"It does exist! He kicked me out!"

"Is this what you wanted to discuss? You want to disturb a semipeaceful evening to argue over arbitrary bullshit?"

"I didn't want to talk about it! *You* brought it up!"

Jackie closed her eyes and dragged in several breaths.

"Luke, just say what you want to say." Ginger knew he should keep quiet. It would be wise to lay low, but he could see his mother-in-law struggling to hold her temper. Buying her extra time would help, and if he said it in a kind—

"Shut up, Jake. Nobody asked you."

"Don't tell him to shut up! He didn't do anything to you!" Beau stood. "You were a total dick today! If it hadn't been for him—"

"No," Jackie cut her off. "Don't make it worse." She took one more breath and paraphrased Ginger's words. "Say what you want to say. What is it?"

The boy's body language reminded Ginger of the initial tremors preceding an earthquake or volcanic eruption. He stood in the doorway, his frame subtly shaking as he wound himself up for a fantastic explosion. When he finally snapped, he threw the book he'd been pinching under his arm to the floor.

"I want you to tell me what you're hiding! What I'm not good enough to know about *my* dad, but *he* is!" Luke jabbed a finger in Ginger's direction. "Tell me why Dad forged that yearbook! Why did a stranger show up yesterday thinking *I* called him? Why did he tell me Dad was a different person *before* and *after* he 'came out'! Came out of what? He wouldn't say! Tell me who Tom DuBelle is, and stop lying to me!"

He kicked the yearbook, and it slid beneath his mother's chair.

Ginger's heart pounded. *It's all coming out, including my part. Mom will never forgive me.*

But instead of launching into a fury, Jackie sat there. At first her expression just read confusion until she laughed. "What are you talking about? My God, boy, how much have you had to drink?"

"You know damn well what I'm talking about! And stop calling me 'boy'! All of you!" Luke turned to his sister and Ginger. "I'm not a boy! I'm a man!"

"Act like one!"

"Then treat me like one, and tell me the truth!"

Jackie didn't respond. She examined her fingernails, idly allowing time to tick on until it was unbearable. Ginger watched the outrage build in Luke the longer she kept him waiting, her detachment pitching him to a higher intensity. Finally, as he was on the verge of exploding again, his mother spoke.

"Your father didn't want you to know. Either of you." She tilted her head to Beau. "Neither of you had or have a reason to know. So he didn't tell you. Jake had a reason to know, so Jay told him." She stared at Luke, her mouth in a snide smile. "Get over it."

"Get over it? Get over it!"

"That's right. Repetition will cool you down." Jackie leaned back in her chair. "Like a mantra: 'Get over it. Get over it. Get over it.' That's what you'll have to do."

Luke stepped forward and put out his arm. And although Ginger moved to insert himself between Beau and her brother, he was too late.

Thankfully, all Luke did was take her hand. Still, Ginger remained wary, primed to throw him across the room if the mood changed.

"See, Beau? Did you hear how they are against us? It's not fair!" Luke petted her arm. "And I know you're aware of things I'm not. But there's something else we don't know that they do! They're trying to keep it from us. We have a right to know everything!"

The tightness in Beau's eyes relaxed.

"Luke, I do know everything."

"What?" The disclosure brought Jackie to her feet. For the first time, astonishment marred her face as she realized she wasn't holding all the cards.

The unwinding of layers. The demolition of the inner sanctum.

"I've known for a while." Beau looked from Luke to her mother. "Before Meecie went into the coma, she was hallucinating. There was a night when you were away, and she came into my room. She thought I was—so Dad had to tell me. I—"

"But, we were a team," Luke interrupted. "You knew, and you kept it from me for years? For *years*, Beau? How could you..."

Luke's crushed look inspired sympathy from Ginger, notwithstanding his recent behavior. The boy really had counted on him and Beau being together in their ignorance; their solidarity strengthening his argument. As he'd pitifully protested, they'd always been a team.

"He asked me not to tell anyone."

"But you told Jake." Luke seemed on the verge of tears, more upset than he'd been at either the viewing or funeral.

"He's my husband. I tell him everything."

Ginger's thoughts drifted to himself momentarily. Beau's statement was a sharp pinch. He was unable to say that he told his wife everything. Maybe he should admit the truth about the white box and—

"But I'm your brother. I've known you longer. I knew you first. We're partners. Tell me now. You have to."

Beau turned to Jackie, who gave a sigh and shrugged. She then looked to Ginger. He didn't understand why his approval was necessary, but it made him feel good that it was requested. And what purpose was there in maintaining deception? He nodded.

And now *here it comes.*

Beau took Luke's hands and sat with him on the couch.

"Luke, Dad didn't grow up normal like we did. With everyone seeing him as who he was. That's why the yearbook photo is fake. Because until he turned eighteen and started treatment, the entire world saw him as a girl."

"What?" Luke's voice sounded rusted.

Ginger remembered having a similar reaction of disbelief.

"Jay was a transgender man." Jackie answered before Beau could.

"What does that mean?"

"It means his gender identity didn't match his body. His brain was that of a regular man, but his body didn't develop correctly. He was born with the physical characteristics of the opposite sex, and that's how he grew up," she said. "When he was legally able to, he changed his name, he began hormone therapy, he moved away, and he started a *normal* life."

"How is that possible?"

Ginger had asked this too. It seemed science-fiction crazy. But it wasn't. Or if it was real, weren't transgendered people only men who became women? Those sometimes unusual-looking women who were too tall, or had an Adam's apple, or spoke with a low voice, and therefore warranted closer examination. He knew *those* were there. But he'd been in close personal contact with Jay for years. There was nothing out of the ordinary about him, no indication that he was anything but typical. He had passed so fully that he'd lived in the same house with Luke for twenty-six years, and the boy had never guessed.

Beau wouldn't have known either if their grandmother hadn't stumbled into her room and terrorized her. In the woman's delusion, she had seen in Beau the daughter she thought she'd had four decades earlier. Meecie kept calling Beau another name and blocking her escape. Jay had been too late in securing his mother in a locked room. The old bat's raving had exposed it all.

Years later, after Ginger had been trusted with the secret, Beau had described how Jay had told her over the kitchen table when she was twelve.

"But it wasn't the collected him, like you've always seen. Like *I've* always seen," she said. "He was manic. He was so keyed up."

"Why?"

"He was terrified."

"Of what? That you'd tell?"

"No," Beau had answered. "That I wouldn't understand. That I'd think him less. Less a man, less a father, and just less of him overall. I've never seen him that scared. Not before and not since."

"He wasn't like that when he told me. He was collected."

"He'd been preparing to have that conversation with you, Ging. But with me, it was on the spot, entirely impromptu. He was stumbling over his words, and at times I could barely understand him."

Beau had been correct in what she'd said—this was a side of Jay that Ginger had never seen. Jay truly must've felt his fears were valid.

"And did you feel that way? Less? Even when he first told you?"

"No," she had said without hesitation. "Did you?"

"No." Jay was the same man. Still Jay. Still his father. He'd had a different upbringing. A difficult one. So had Ginger.

And that'd been the end of it. Ginger hadn't spoken about Jay's secret again with anyone, and he rarely thought about it. He always pictured the lack of attention made Jay happy—to neither be a freak, nor special. To just be ordinary and not have layers attributed to his circumstance. He imagined this was the reaction Jay would've wanted from Luke.

But although Jackie explained the situation to Luke first in detail and again in simple terms, the boy said what made the three of them cringe. "Are you telling me that the person I thought was my father was actually a woman?"

I hope you aren't listening, Dad. If you can listen, don't.

"No," Jackie snapped. "Absolutely not."

"That's what it sounds like you're saying." Luke took his hands from Beau and stood. "When you break it down, that's it. You're just putting a spin on reality."

"Watch your mouth."

"And who's Tom DuBelle? What does he have to do with this?"

"He's the *gentleman*," Jackie strained to get the word through her lips. "Who gave me the two of you."

"So Tom is my real father."

Ginger had believed it'd be Jackie to do it. But if she'd been planning to, she didn't get the chance.

There were no levels to the rage. No escalation to the brink of physical violence, remembrance of herself, and harnessing the willpower to refrain. Beau rose and, in a calculated move only Ginger caught, adjusted the jagged diamond of her wedding ring before she reeled back her left hand and struck her brother across the face.

At first, Luke only stared at her. Beau had a fierce temper, but she'd never hit anyone.

"Get out," she hissed.

Still bewildered, Luke touched his cheek and brought back his hand. The ring had sliced his cheek, and the blood on his fingers rekindled his passion.

"You have a lot of nerve! You betrayed me! You're just like them!" Luke yelled at her, but Beau didn't flinch. "And you defend them! The whole fucking nest of liars! You're one of them!" He turned next to Jackie. "And you! Whatever you are! A whore! Some kind of sick lesbian! What the—"

He stopped midsentence as his mother took three steps in his direction.

Jackie didn't need to touch him. The look she gave was one of total apathy. It said she wouldn't be the one to shred him in pieces, but she'd stand by and watch. She wouldn't speak a word in protest as he was pushed through a meat grinder—inch by flesh-tearing inch. Jackie's coldness suffused the room's heat; it happened with such speed that steam seemed to follow her footsteps as she advanced.

Luke stepped back too fast and lost his balance. He staggered and fell as if she'd really hit him. But no one laughed. Jackie gave the same command as Beau, "Get out."

The boy just sat there, and tears brimmed in his eyes. "I'll go! I'll never come back!"

"Good! Go!" Beau was crying too, but when Ginger moved to comfort her, she shoved him away and turned to face Luke. "If you hadn't come back in the first place, Dad would still be alive, you piece of shit!"

"You're the one who begged me to come home!" Luke stumbled to his feet. "And it's good that I did! If I hadn't come home, if he hadn't died, I would've never met my *real* father! I would never have known he existed!"

This time, Ginger caught Beau by both wrists. She screamed and fought him, but he refused to release her.

"Save your strength to push out your satanic spawn." Luke turned to Jackie. "Tell me how to find Tom DuBelle. He's the only person who hasn't lied to me."

"If you think he'll take you in, you're going to be sadly mistaken. He's a self-centered jackass. That's where you get it from; it's in that gene pool. And no amount of time around a good man can fix being a plain fucking asshole," his mother said.

"Having never been around a good *man*, we wouldn't know if that's true or not."

Ginger was relieved that Jackie folded her arms and kept her icy, cruel exterior. Beau had stopped struggling, but she was still tense, and he didn't dare let her go.

"You're stupid. A fucking, stupid little boy. And that's all you'll ever be. If you want to run to him, you find him. Idiot."

"I'm a regular son of a bitch, all right."

"For the final time, get out. I can't stand to look at you." Jackie walked back to her recliner.

Luke left the room, and his footsteps pounded on the stairs.

Ginger released Beau, and she sank to the couch. She seemed shaky and unsteady, as if the anger had drained from her with a velocity that stripped her energy. But before Ginger could panic, Jackie provided an additional directive.

"Jake, go up there," she ordered. "Make sure he doesn't take anything that isn't his. If he tries to fight you, or isn't out the door in ten minutes, I'll call the police."

He knew better than to disobey.

His worry was mitigated as he heard his mother-in-law's voice behind him. The couch creaked as she must've repositioned herself next to Beau. "Breathe, honey. You're fine."

Ginger climbed the staircase, his eyes fixed on the only open door. *And I'm not concerned at all about you. Mom is right. You're just a stupid little boy. And that's all you'll ever be.*

Chapter Twelve

With an immediacy that staggered him, Luke felt terrible about what he'd said to his mother and sister. His face stung where Beau hit him, but it paled in comparison to the shame he felt as he took the stairs three at a time. He had a right to be angry, but he'd let his temper get the better of him. He'd said cruel things he didn't mean because he was hurt and wanted them to hurt too.

First Jackie had rejected him. He'd kept his end of the bargain and just followed the expected motions throughout the rest of the funeral. But when he tried to claim the prize he'd earned, he hadn't gotten two words out, and she'd started ridiculing him.

And dragging in that fucking bastard! When all I did was ask him to be quiet!

It'd been Beau who yelled at Luke for that, but he couldn't fault her. She was under Jake's evil influence. Both of them were. That's why Jackie had persisted in trying to lie after he'd presented the overwhelming evidence. She was further under Jake's control than he'd imagined.

And Jake had stood when he went to Beau, as if he planned to block her from him. Luke had been prepared to punch Jake in the throat if he'd tried to intervene. But he'd reached Beau and taken her hand, trying to rally her.

It'd been obvious they were alone against those liars. He'd pleaded with his eyes: *Please, Beau. I'm the only one you can trust. All we have to depend on is each other. We're a team. Partners. We'll go away. You can divorce that sack of shit. You're going to lose the baby anyway.*

It was an awful thought, but it was better for the situation. If she lost the baby, it would be much easier to cut ties. She could find a better husband who didn't steal other people's families.

But the plan had crashed in flames.

Beau had admitted to having known everything for years. And if she'd found out before Meecie died, she'd known even before Jake. She'd kept the guarded secret about their father for over a decade.

I'm your brother; you don't keep secrets from me. We have the same DNA. We're almost the same person. I've always trusted you. I confided in you.

Beau's treachery dominated the actual secret. He'd heard the sought-after answer under water. Jay had been a transgender man. He connected the description to individuals he'd been acquainted with in New York. He knew transgendered people and had no difficulty with the concept. It was more unorthodox than being a homosexual, but Luke still didn't care. The shadow of Beau's deceit hung over everything.

You betrayed me. You betrayed me, Beau.

Luke had stared at her, disengaged from his surroundings. She'd looked back in earnest, willing him to breathe a sigh of relief now that he knew. They could move on. The silence was over.

But what matters is that the secret was there to begin with.

Not only had Jay not trusted him, or Jackie, or Jake, but Beau didn't trust him. His twin sister. His first and best friend.

And you're not sorry you lied to me. You're not asking for forgiveness. You're expecting me to roll over like it was nothing for you to lie to me for years!

The ultimate disloyalty hadn't been Jake carrying off his family. It wasn't his parents consenting to be led astray. True, they couldn't be absolved from drinking the Kool-Aid, but what had topped it was Beau. However, he knew what to say to peel back the skin of all three of them, as they deserved; their pain being a small consolation prize. And he'd launched into pressing every weak spot he could think of.

And now I'm fucked. Fucked.

Even if he'd misinterpreted the fight where his father had asked him to leave, Jackie couldn't have been plainer.

Luke didn't know where he'd go. Saying he would go to Tom DuBelle had been primarily to cause them pain. They didn't know Tom had told Luke not to try to find him. Although he hadn't seemed the "self-centered jackass" Jackie had declared he was, Tom had been furious. If Luke was able to locate him, would Tom be willing to talk to him again?

But I have to leave now. I won't give them the satisfaction of staying or admitting I may have said things I didn't mean. Maybe I'll go to New York, or I'll find Tom somehow. But fuck all of them. Fuck—

"Mom wants you out in ten minutes, or she'll call the police."

Luke turned to see Jake in the doorway. What kept him from charging at his brother-in-law in rage, especially for referring to Jackie as "Mom," was that he could see Jake wasn't happy.

I thought you'd be fucking ecstatic.

Jake had that look people gave when they weren't thinking of themselves or how to screw someone over. It made Luke hesitate, before remembering he was still evil.

"Ten minutes? You've been wanting me out for more than ten years." Luke resumed packing. "Since the first time you saw me."

"That's not true. I've only ever wanted to be your friend, Luke."

"Lies atop more lies. Keep them coming."

"I didn't ask Dad to tell me and not you. I hate to say it, but if you're going to be angry at anyone, you should be angry with Dad. This was his game."

"It's not a fucking game. It's my life." Luke crammed several pages of sheet music into his bag's front pocket.

"I know. That's why he should've told you."

When Luke briefly regarded Jake again, the expected cynicism was absent.

"He should've told you," Jake repeated. "You shouldn't have had to hear it this way. You're right; it's not fair. And Beau shouldn't have hit you, but—"

Yeah, I knew you weren't on my side.

"You also shouldn't have been cruel. You can't have meant those things."

Keep telling me what I can and cannot mean. What I can and cannot do. Like you're in charge of me. Like you know me. No one knows me. I'm completely alone.

"And if I did mean them?" Luke slung the bag over his shoulder.

"I don't believe you did."

"I don't believe a fucking thing you say either. Get out of my way."

Luke didn't need to ask him to move. Jake stood against the doorframe, and there was plenty of space to step around. But Luke didn't so much as want to brush past him.

"Where will you go?" Jake positioned himself in the middle of the doorway, blocking Luke's escape.

"None of your damn business."

"Do you know how to find him?"

"I said it's none of your damn business."

Luke regretted the clipped response as soon as it left his mouth. If he'd answered "no", or said nothing, he'd have left the door open for any aid Jake might be able to provide. He'd fucked himself again.

Why can't you have a dress rehearsal in real life? Fuck.

Jake studied the floor, and when he raised his head, the tightness of indecision appeared in his eyes.

"You think I've never wanted to be your friend, and that's not true. It wasn't my intention to take anything from you, and I'm sorry if you feel I have. I only wanted to share your family. But you did have something taken from you." He scraped a hand through his hair. "I told Tom DuBelle when I called him that I didn't agree with Dad's actions or the secrecy, but I'd honor the request he made of me. I stand by that." Jake reached into his pocket and retrieved his wallet. "But Dad didn't ask me *not* to give you this."

He offered a business card, and Luke took it. On the front was the name and address of an attorney in Utah, but written on the back was Tom DuBelle's name and phone number.

Luke met Jake's eyes.

"Tom isn't your father, but he can tell you about him. I believe you can handle it. And I'm sure if he'd had the opportunity, eventually Dad would've told you. But he was taken from you," Jake's voice frayed. "He was taken from us. Not by me. By God."

Luke tucked the business card into his wallet and took a step closer to his brother-in-law.

"He had twenty-six years of opportunities to tell me, and *he* chose not to. And Beau had fourteen years of opportunities to share what she knew, and *she* chose not to. I find it difficult to give any of you the benefit of the doubt that you'd have told me of your own choice. However, thank you for being respectable enough to realize that you're all a bunch of assholes."

"Should I say 'you're welcome'?"

"No. You should get out of my way."

Jake moved aside to let him pass, and Luke pulled out his cell phone to call a cab. He felt himself watched from the landing as he descended the stairs. And it occurred to him, as he shut the door of his childhood home, that this was the second instance where he was leaving in a fiery tempest. Only this time, he had no plan of returning in triumph. He had no plan to return at all.

☆☆☆

In the cab en route to the airport, a new emotion tunneled under his skin. It lined up beside the guilt, needling him in a similar fashion.

Doubt.

Not that he'd done the wrong thing. But doubt regarding the course he was taking. What was he was seeking to accomplish by finding Tom DuBelle? He was hurt by Jay's lack of trust, but unlike what he was sure Jackie and Beau suspected, he couldn't replace his father.

Until you fought with me and drove me away, how you made me feel was real, even if nothing else was. And you may not have loved me as much as Beau or Jake, but I did feel loved. I can't forget that.

Tom couldn't be a substitute for him.

So why are you doing this? What is he going to be able to do for you? Jake thought I'd want to know more about Dad. Is that it? Luke stepped onto the airport curb and shut the cab door. *Do I have questions?*

When he'd gone through the yearbook at breakfast Tom had been enthusiastic to provide information, and especially animated in pointing out the orchestra picture. Luke knew so much about his mother and grandparents. They loved to rehash stories of their youth—lessons learned, experiences had. He was so bored with talk of gray days that had no relevance to him.

But Tom had revealed more in ten seconds than Jay had in twenty-six years regarding what were some of the most influential years in a person's life. He knew more of Tom growing up than he did about his father. And he'd only seen the man twice.

At the ticket counter, Luke paused. *If you can tell me about him, I want to know that.*

The airline representative extended her hand for his driver's license.

When did you become a man? When did you know? Why did you make the change?

"Sir, I need to see your identification."

And what happened afterward? What did you do?

He handed his license to the woman and scrutinized her face as she checked his information. She had smooth, creamy skin, and her black hair curled around her cheeks. If she hadn't been wearing makeup, she'd still be a woman. When he pictured Jay's face, he saw only a man. For twenty-six years, that'd been all he'd ever seen.

How did you do it? Did you look like this before? Did you have dozens of surgeries to change your appearance?

Luke read the woman's nametag.

You must've had a different name if you were born a girl. Why did you choose the name you did? Is it a masculine version of your original name? What was it? Jane? Janet?

He accepted the boarding pass with his driver's license and inspected his own name.

I like my name. If I chose a girl's name, I don't know what I'd call myself. Maybe I'd use my middle name. Is that why it's neutral? Beau's middle name is androgynous too.

Having always been a tomboy, Beau had favored her middle name. Her roughness didn't fit a name like "Lucy."

But you couldn't have predicted that. He tried to imagine his father going through school attached to a feminine name. It must've raked across his skin to hear it. *Just in case I didn't feel like "Luke," as many people do, I could go by my middle name. I could be "Andrea" instead.*

He'd never known where his first name came from, but guessed it derived from his sister's. Jay adored his 1961 recording of *Lucia di Lammermoor*, so "Luke" was a byproduct for Lucy's twin brother. But he'd assumed his middle name was an homage to Jay's favorite tenor. Or was it more than that? Had the possibility of his children needing to call upon a different name been accounted for? He wasn't sure how a person changed their name if it wasn't as a result of marriage. How difficult was it?

And after you changed your name and had God knows how many surgeries, you met Mom. Did you tell her right away? Did she care? Did you have problems getting married?

He slung his messenger bag onto the conveyor belt to be brought through the scanner.

And how did I get here? Mom said that Tom gave me and Beau to her. Did you let your friend sleep with your wife? Even if they artificially inseminated her, how could you be okay with that? How did you convince Mom to be okay? Is that why there aren't any pictures of her pregnant with us? She was embarrassed?

Luke checked the large blue board of departures and walked toward the terminal.

Perhaps Tom can answer why you didn't trust me. Maybe he can say why you excluded me, and I wasn't good enough to know your secrets.

He sunk into a plastic chair outside the departure gate. It was awful to admit, but Jake had been right. He did have questions, and that's why he was going to Tom.

Luke removed his phone and tried to call Tom for the third time. But once again, his call met a generic voicemail.

While an eight-hour flight provided ample opportunity to dig through the Internet, on his arrival to Salt Lake City Luke was left with the business card as his only lead.

At the late Attorney Harlan's office he'd been able to secure the last known address of the man's partner, without any confirmation that this person was Tom.

But it's something, he thought until the cab had pulled in front of an expensive contemporary high-rise. It looked like an office building, not a residential condominium. *Bitch most likely scratched down a random address to get rid of me.*

Still, he took the elevator to the building's tenth floor. But as he stood in front of the door, Luke hesitated.

He'd traveled over two thousand miles on an angry, desperate spur of the moment whim. In all likelihood, behind that door lived an unknown man who didn't know Tom or how to find him. Luke would be humiliated and at a dead end.

Why am I here? This is just stupid. Face it—all you'll ever know is that your father was a transgender man who didn't trust you with the truth. None of your questions will ever be answered because no one else trusts you either. You're alone, like always. Just walk away and save a scrap of your dignity.

But as Luke turned to leave, he stopped as he heard a familiar sound. And while piano music from within wasn't a guarantee that Tom was behind the door, it gave him the courage to ring the bell.

Chapter Thirteen

Salt Lake City, Utah
February 2038: Tom

As great as he'd felt the day before, Tom DuBelle was once again miserable. He'd stopped taking the cancer drugs that masked his sickness, made him want to eat again, and gave back his confidence. He had to.

I don't want to be tempted to hang in until they aren't effective. I'm tired of hanging. I'm tired of everything.

The morning he'd had breakfast with Luke had been the last time he'd taken them. And he'd decided to only keep on the Oxy until he got home. Sitting on a plane for eight hours would've been intolerable otherwise.

There's no purpose to suffering unnecessarily. I'm not a fucking martyr. I don't deserve any of this pain, Goddamn it.

He hadn't wanted to kill himself in Pennsylvania, though it might've been easier. He wanted to be at home, with his piano and photographs, where he could pretend nothing had happened.

The Oxy only has to get me home. Then I'm done with it and the other pain meds. I'll drive myself to do it.

As exhausted of life as Tom was, stopping the pain medication altogether intimidated him. His doctors had been ramping up his dosage as it became incapable of taking the edge off the pain. They'd probably been ready to move him to Oxy anyway. It was the first time in months he hadn't even felt the pressure in his abdomen that made every position uncomfortable.

He'd been careful to overlap the drugs during his trip. There'd only been a couple of times when he'd missed doses of the weaker pain meds, and it'd been agony.

Paying close attention to overlapping pain medication when your insides are being eaten is a priority. There's another nugget of wisdom for the next generation.

The pain and nausea would be horrible, but he'd wanted no excuse *not* to do it.

It will be so fucking terrible that I won't be able to think of anything else. Of Jay, of those fucking kids, of no one finding my body for a week after I've congealed onto the floor. Tom stepped inside his high-rise condo. He'd turned on the lights and regarded his floor, scuffing the hardwood with his shoe.

My poor floor. God, I hope they can get putrefaction out of you. I should set up a tarp. They can fold in my sludge like a hobo's knapsack and spare you.

He took a steady breath as he closed the door.

Be thoughtful of your hardwood floors and lay out a tarp if you plan on killing yourself. That's good. Really good. Spare the floor.

But Tom didn't have a tarp, and he didn't feel like going out to buy one. He wouldn't even unpack. He ran his hand along the black-lacquered frame of his piano in greeting and trudged down the hall to his bedroom. Against his better judgment, he took the Oxy from his carry-on for one last hit. He also dug out his cell phone, but only to power it off. The only person he'd enjoyed talking to was dead.

I'm pissed at you for being a dick, but I'd still talk to you if you were alive. I could never not talk to you. You'd make it up to me. And if you were here, you'd go get me a tarp. Fucking asshole.

Tom collapsed on his bed in a deep sleep.

This is the last time I will wake up, Tom thought when he opened his eyes the next afternoon. On checking his watch, he found he'd been asleep for fourteen hours. And this was the third dose of the cancer drugs he'd missed. He should've taken his pain medication four hours ago.

He already felt it. Lying in bed without moving, there was the uneasy fluttering of his stomach and that twisting pain in his back, like wringing a dishrag. The yellow warning to take the meds.

Fuck you. Fuck everyone.

Tom forced himself up.

He was going to pretend none of it had happened. He'd never received the phone call. The last time he'd traveled to Pennsylvania had been a year ago to see Luke's final performance. He'd never met Luke. Ever. They were a set of people two thousand miles away that he liked to watch sometimes. Jay wasn't dead. Someday he'd tell his children the truth, and Tom might meet them.

It's four days ago.

Or better yet, fuck semireality. It was his last day, wasn't it? He should be able to do anything he wanted. Have anything he wanted.

There is no two thousand miles. No Luke. No children. There's just you and I. As if you never left, and I'm waiting for you to get home from work.

Tom put on his favorite sweater and blue jeans. He sat in the cold sunshine on his balcony, surveying the Salt Lake City landscape while he made himself eat a granola bar. He pretended the granola bar was a steak and didn't taste like mouthfuls of nickels. He took his pain meds and arranged them on his coffee table with a couple water bottles.

And after he'd done all that, Tom pulled out his piano bench. He clasped his hands together as if he was about to pray, but he only cracked his wrists quickly. Moving the fall back from the keyboard, he placed his fingers on the keys. He let them rest a few moments as he daydreamed.

He'd play until he became too nauseated or was in too much pain. And then he'd stop. He'd take the pills. And he would *really* stop. It was a waiting game.

I'm at Symphony Hall. They've announced me, and I've walked onto the stage. I'm letting the drama build before I hit that first key to play Opus clavicembalisticum. *The lights go down over the seats, and I'm the only person in existence, except for you. You're there in the audience. You're listening, and you're waiting for me.*

Tom closed his eyes and began to play.

Hours later, as the feeling behind his stomach turned to a slow gnawing, Tom's doorbell rang. He continued to play his piano. It could be delirium setting in. He didn't think the pain was bad enough to cause hallucinations, but it could be. Maybe it was a side effect—withdrawals from the other meds.

A minute later, the doorbell rang again.

Fucking-A. He pictured Girl Scouts at his door. Or a vacuum salesman. Or Mormons. There were swarms of them everywhere, like adult flyer men on the Las Vegas strip. They always tried to convert him at the most inconvenient times. *You can pray over my body in an hour or so.*

There was a knock.

He had a feeling of déjà vu. Suddenly people were so anxious to talk to him. In another place and time, he might've been amused.

A second knock, followed by another press of the doorbell.

Persistent fuckers. Fine. Because your noise is destroying this movement. I'll listen to you prostitute yourselves for five minutes, which is quite generous of me, seeing as I don't have that many minutes remaining.

Tom placed his palms on the keyslip to push back his bench. It felt as if his organs were being shredded across a grater, but he bit the inside of his cheek and stood.

Three minutes. Assholes.

He walked stiffly to the door. Now that he was in motion, the nausea made itself known. He couldn't return to the piano, since he didn't want to chance being sick over it. This loss pained him as much as losing Jay.

I'll never see you or play my piano again. Two very good reasons to kill myself. His arm felt nearly too heavy to move to the doorknob. *After dealing with the Mormons.*

He turned the lock, pulled open the door, and nearly vomited on his threshold.

Luke stood outside his door.

"Tom." The boy's smile vanished. "You look sick. Are you all—"

Tom closed the door in his face and threw the deadbolt. He leaned against the door, his heart racing as his castles in the sky evaporated. Or possibly he really was hallucinating. It wasn't Luke on the other side of the door. It was Jay. A mirage created by heartache and pain. He could be dead already. Maybe he'd taken the pills and didn't remember.

He felt the knocking on the back of his head. Ghosts didn't knock.

"Tom, I need to talk to you."

It wasn't Jay's voice.

"Tom, please open the door."

How did he find me? Why did he find me?

"Why are you here?" Tom wanted to yell, but as his voice rose, the spike in his abdomen forced him to finish in a scathing tone. "I told you to leave me alone."

"I need to talk to you. They told me only a little, but they refused to tell me everything. I need to know."

"What do you need to know?"

"Please open the door."

Tom took a deep breath before he turned and drew the lock. He opened the door only a few inches.

"I was going to give the Mormons three minutes. I'll give them to you instead. What the fuck do you want?"

Luke appeared hurt by his reaction, and for a second Tom felt sorry. But he was in so much pain.

"I want to know why he did what he did," the boy said.

"That's a ridiculous question. If you woke up tomorrow in a woman's body, wouldn't you do something about it?"

"Not that. Why did he hide who he was from me?"

Tom didn't immediately respond. He could see how upset Luke had been and was becoming again. The boy was disheveled, and there was a cut on his cheek. Tom tried to respond with a softer inflection.

"He didn't hide who he was. You knew him."

"I didn't know him at all. Why didn't he trust me? I want to know everything."

Tears streamed down Luke's face. Tom almost opened the door. Almost.

But I can't. If I let him in, I won't be able to go through with my plan. And I want it to be over. The left side of his face flinched. *I don't want to think about you. You or Jay.*

"If he'd wanted you both to know everything, he would've told you. I respect that, even if you don't. Now leave me alone." Tom didn't slam the door this time. He just shut it.

As he stumbled away, Luke knocked again.

"But she does know!" Luke pounded the door with the flat of his hand. "He told Beau and not me! He told everyone but me! And she kept me in the dark too! They all lied to me!"

Tom had told Luke that Jay kept him informed, and he doubted anything could be disclosed that he wasn't already aware of. While Jay had flung bits and pieces to different people, Tom had honestly believed that he was the only one who knew it all.

You told her. When? In what context? Was it before I was at their graduation? Was it before I was at her wedding? Did you point me out to her? Does she know you've been telling me about her baby? That you promised me a sonogram picture?

"Please, Tom. Don't shut me out like everyone else."

Luke's voice sounded fainter. When Tom reopened the door, he was on his knees in the hall. Tom hesitated.

He looks so much like you, Jay. I could never refuse you.

"Wait here."

Tom closed the door and ground his teeth to move through the pain, to his bedroom. He removed the OxyContin from his carry-on, shook two pills out, and swallowed them dry before replacing the bottle. On his way back to the door, he stopped at the coffee table, took his other prescription bottles, and stuffed them under the couch cushion. Last, he walked to his piano and gathered the pictures on its top. He opened the lid itself and set the frames on the treble strings.

I'm sorry, baby. I don't know where else I can put them right now.

He returned to his door and opened it a fourth time, half expecting it to have been a dream. But Luke was still there. Standing now, his face red and a messenger bag slung over his shoulder. Tom held the door back.

"Come in."

"Thank you." Luke stepped inside.

Tom braced himself on the closed door briefly to regain his strength. He shut his eyes and took breaths through his nose, trying to quell the sickness.

God, I hope the pills disintegrate before I throw them up. It's too late to take the nausea meds.

"You have a beautiful home. The view is spectacular."

Luke stood before the floor-to-ceiling windows that comprised the two walls of Tom's living room. The windows were one of the reasons Tom had selected the condo. He could sit at his piano and feel he was playing to the entire city.

"Your dad always said Salt Lake was the most beautiful city to fly into at night."

"I got in this afternoon. It took me all day to find you."

"I don't consider myself easy to find." He'd used a stage name for thirty years. As much as he enjoyed the spotlight, he also greatly valued his privacy. Being able to disappear into unknown, unimportant Tom DuBelle was nice sometimes.

"You're not. When you didn't answer my calls, I went to the attorney's office on the other side of the business card Jake had. I had to beg them for information, but they took pity on me and gave me the last address of Mr. Harland's companion. They weren't sure it was you, but I guess it is."

"It was. For twenty-five years." Tom grimaced. Twenty-five long, irritating years. Thank God for performances. For long tours in remote lands. For an agent who understood he'd take anything, *anything* to escape. He could sell out in the music capitals of any country, but he'd gratefully play at a sleazy piano bar in Mozambique.

Jay was actually the reason Leo had come into the picture. Jay and the piano—the two things he cared about most had placed Tom with the person who'd driven him insane for a quarter of a century. Jay's father had died in a most opportune manner, resulting in his ability to file a large neglect lawsuit, which had brought them to Attorney Harland's Salt Lake office.

☆☆☆

Tom had accompanied Jay for emotional support. As usual, he'd come back to Utah without Jackie. He was always expected to handle the most difficult situations alone. Not that Jay seemed to resent being by himself. He told Tom that his presence wasn't necessary, and he'd be bored in the lobby for an hour.

I'd gladly be bored for you. In case you need me.

But when they walked into the ritzy building, Tom knew he'd be happy to wait as long as required. It was a huge office that echoed like a museum. The ends of his shoelaces clicked on the slick marble floor, and from the open lobby, he could tilt his head and see at least six levels. There was a wide, crescent-shaped bar at the end where three receptionists sat, and a trickling fountain near the entrance. But what drew Tom's eye was the mahogany grand piano near the left wall. It was corded off by a braided-rope barrier and five chrome posts, but the majestic creature looked sad at being neglected.

"I guess I didn't need to bring you a coloring book." Jay smirked and gave the name of the attorney he was meeting.

"Does anyone play your piano?" Tom asked the other free receptionist.

"No. The fourth floor doctors had someone come in and play, but it broke and they moved."

"So now it just sits there? Like a piece of furniture?"

"Isn't that what it is?" She gawked blankly.

"God, no." Tom couldn't believe people thought of grand pianos as just furniture. He didn't yet have one of his own, but he saw his upright as a living entity.

"He'll try to fix it, if you'll let him. And if you'll allow him to play it afterward," Jay said with a smile. In reply, the receptionist shrugged. "Go ahead. Apparently Mr. Harland is late anyway."

Tom had flown out the door and across the street to retrieve his tool bag from the car. He carried the kit everywhere since any instrument he played was likely in need of a little maintenance. When he returned, his hands quivered with excitement as he unhooked one end of the barrier and stepped inside the piano's cage. He struck each key separately and was delighted that no strings were broken. The hammers were only misaligned, a few were too high and hitting the stretch; and of course, it was out of tune.

Easy cheese.

Tom was pulling the action from the key frame the first time he heard that obnoxious voice.

"You got someone to fix this piece of shit?" A man said behind him.

Don't listen, sweetheart. He removed straws and wrappers that'd been squirreled underneath the action and dropped them to the floor, not bothering to look at the Neanderthal.

"What a waste of time. It's a nice ornament, sitting there and looking expensive. But what a fucking waste of time. Therese, I'm not paying a cent for this. Not a single, fucking red cent."

Tom had been glad when Leo Harland went to his office, even if he'd taken Jay. That douche bag didn't deserve to be in the presence of a grand piano.

"A nice ornament, sitting there and looking expensive?" Ridiculous. Tom worked his screwdriver between the hammer flanges to space them, tightening the screws in their proper position. *You might as well have a dead body lying at the side of your vestibule, asshole.*

It hadn't taken long before he slid the action into place and proceeded to tune it. It'd been tragic that the instrument had been condemned to sit idle over simple adjustments.

I'm so sorry you have to live with a man who doesn't understand you. Tom leaned over the rim with his hammer and rubber mute. He touched the keys he'd identified as being out of tune and brought them in line one by one. *A permit should be required to own a piano. There should be a vigorous background check and references provided.*

Jay had been away for half an hour when Tom screwed the key frame into the key bed and sat on the bench. As he always did, he laced his fingers together and turned his locked hands toward himself to crack his wrists. And the piano was so grateful to have the chance to breathe again, it answered his touch with a strong, beautiful tone. Tom sank wholly into the music.

He was playing *Liebestraum* when Jay returned. Or he thought that's what he'd been playing. As tended to happen, he'd vanished into himself until he was interrupted. But what better disruption than Jay's hand on his shoulder?

"He'd play for hours."

Tom glanced up. It'd been Jay's voice, but an unfamiliar hand patted his shoulder.

"You can stay. I wouldn't object."

The troll hadn't yet crawled under his bridge. He grinned at Tom. And touched him.

"No, thank you." Tom shrugged away the man's hand and pulled the fall over the keyboard. As he stood and pushed in the bench, he searched for Jay, who'd returned to the receptionists' desk.

"There's no need to rush."

"You were late for my friend's appointment, so you're probably late for the next," Tom said. "Time is money. You wouldn't want to *waste* any time."

"I get cranky in the morning," the attorney replied, though it was two in the afternoon. The man smiled, which irritated Tom as much as the excuse in lieu of an apology, and stuck out his hand. "Leo Harland. It's a pleasure to meet you."

"Tom DuBelle." He reluctantly took the hand. "It's a pleasure to have played your piano."

"I like that." Leo laughed and held his hand longer than necessary. "I've never been one for classical music, but maybe I haven't given it a chance."

"Hardly surprising." Tom nodded to Jay, who was now standing beside the attorney. "Can we go?"

"Sure, I—"

"Do you like concerts?" Leo interrupted Jay; another strike against him. "I'm sure there are some around here. This can't be the only fucking piano in Salt Lake."

"I prefer playing to listening." Tom didn't look at him and kept silently begging his friend to please, for the love of God, make a move to leave. But no such luck.

"Tom just got back from Boston. He played the full *Opus clavicembalisticum* at Symphony Hall. Not many people are capable of doing that." Jay nodded and his praise brought a flush to Tom's cheeks.

He'd played the *Opus clavicembalisticum* multiple times, but two days prior, Jay had been in the audience. Tom imagined he'd never performed as well. He played as if all the seats weren't full, and it was just Jay.

"What's that?" The attorney asked.

"What's what? Boston? It's the capital of Massachusetts. Surely they cover that in law school?" Tom said.

"No the *Opus clav*—whatever. The thing you played."

"It's a piano piece. It takes over four hours to play. You wouldn't enjoy it."

"Four fucking hours? Don't you have to get up and take a piss?"

"I'm quite capable of holding my bladder, thank you. Again, I'd think they'd discuss not pissing your pants in law school. Can we go, Jay?" Tom wanted to take his arm and pull him to the exit. If this torture went on much longer he'd have to.

"I don't know much about this stuff, but I could learn." Leo took a business card and pen from his suit coat. He turned the card over in the palm of his hand, wrote on it, and handed it to Tom. "Here's my personal cell. You could call me the next time you play someplace. Whether it's here or in Boston. If it's four hours, I can bring a diaper."

"Charming." Tom shoved the card in his tool bag.

"I'm not graceful about these things. But still, I hope you call." The attorney rubbed the back of his neck.

"I'm a busy man. I don't like *wasting* time." Tom took a step nearer to Jay and touched his sleeve. Thankfully, this got him to move.

"Don't I owe you anything for fixing it?"

"Not a 'single, fucking red cent,'" he said loudly without looking back.

"It was nice to meet you, Tommy!"

Tom grimaced. He hated being called "Tommy."

"I hope you had *nothing* whatsoever to do with that," he whispered to Jay as they exited the building.

Jay hadn't had anything to do with that particular event. He assured Tom that the most he'd done was confirm to Leo that no, he and Tom weren't a couple. And that might've been all, had Jay not answered honestly the questions Leo posed to him about Tom during their next appointment. Which is how the ultimate guilt trip arrived at his front door two weeks later.

"What the fuck is wrong with you?" Tom yelled into the phone. Four men had shown up and were asking where he wanted his grand piano unloaded.

"I knew that would get you to call me."

"Fuck you. I'm a concert pianist. Don't you think I have a fucking piano?"

"Your friend said you had an upright, but you prefer playing a grand. These are two different things. I found that out myself. And I researched the *Opus clavicembalisticum*. I downloaded a recording and listened to it." Leo slaughtered the pronunciation of the piece. "And I located a piano bar on State Street. They prefer contemporary to classical, but you could play whatever you wanted. I'd see to it."

Only Jay had ever shown this level of attentiveness to Tom, and that'd never been a romantic interest, as Leo's plainly was.

"You really wouldn't have a drink with a guy who gave you a piano?"

No, he really wouldn't. He had no intention of accepting the piano. What made him refrain from an outright rejection was a combination of Leo's effort and Jay.

Tom wasn't familiar with lawsuits, but it seemed the case would be clear cut. There'd be a substantial settlement, and he knew what Jay would do with it. It could be useful to be on close terms with an attorney. Based on Leo's crass behavior, he might be adept and amiable with shady dealings. Acquiring his help might play right into Tom's hand to get what he wanted.

"Come on, Tommy. Please?"

"Fine, but my name is Tom."

"*I* call you *Tommy*. That's my *special* name for you."

It'd been a grueling twenty-five years. Leo hadn't changed, but neither had Tom. Leo's devotion to him and his endeavors to understand and appreciate what Tom loved were occasionally endearing, but by and large insufferable. The well-intentioned, persistent undertakings had been in vain. Tom had never loved him back.

Ah, unrequited love, you fucking bitch.

☆☆☆

"I'm sorry for your loss," Luke said, bringing Tom from his memories.

I told you. No one should have to bury anyone until they're so fucking sick of them that they'd sooner kill them personally than have to spend another second sharing the same air. I was so ready to bury Leo. Thank God he was older than me.

"Thank you."

"I don't care that you're gay." Luke still looked out the window, but he'd let his bag drop to the floor.

"I wouldn't give a fuck if you did. It's none of your business," Tom snapped. "And I should sue that law firm for releasing my information."

"No one is hiding anything from me anymore." Luke turned to him with a smile. Tom didn't want to care, but he was glad the boy appeared to be feeling better, even as he felt himself deteriorating. He knew he wasn't hiding the pain effectively when Luke's expression became one of alarm. "Are you okay, Tom?"

"I'm fine." He covered his mouth. "I just need a glass of water."

"I can get it for you. Point me to your kitchen, and you can relax."

"No." Tom felt the hand over his mouth was the only thing keeping down his stomach contents, and he moved from the door. "Enjoy the view. You won't be staying long."

Tom walked to the kitchen, bracing his shoulder along the wall for stability.

I'll try to take the nausea meds. Maybe I can keep them down long enough to play twenty questions and get him out.

He made it to the sink without collapsing in a puddle of vomit. And when he brought up the granola bar and sour acid, it wasn't as bad as it usually was. He had to clutch the counter and shake, but he maintained the strength to stand.

Tom stared into the sink, and recognized the white OxyContin pills amid the tan oatmeal flakes and other crunchies. They were partially digested, which explained why the pain had eased.

"Are you okay?"

He jumped at Luke's question and turned to glare at the boy, keeping his grip on the counter.

"Is it customary in Pennsylvania to wander a person's house without their permission?"

"I'm sorry. I was worried."

The concern in the boy's eyes allayed Tom's annoyance. At least the actual throwing up hadn't been interrupted, and he felt more under control at present.

"I'm fine. Sit there." He motioned to a row of stools in front of the kitchen bar. When he returned to the sink, he heard the squeak of a stool. "Now tell me what you want."

"I want to know everything."

"Narrow down 'everything.' I'm not a fucking yogi on a Himalayan mountaintop."

"Tell me where I came from."

"I'm not a priest either. However, there's no shortage of religions that would *love* to answer that question for you." Tom flinched and eyed the pills nestled in the gruel. "The Mormons are on every corner. Go ask them."

"No, I want to know how *I personally, physically* got here."

Oh, what the fuck? When you die, you're just going to shit your pants.

Tom dug the two partially digested pills from the vomit with his fingertip. He placed them back in his mouth and swallowed.

It's not like you don't know where they've been.

"If you want to know how you physically got here, visit any elementary class." He straightened his shoulders and turned on the sink and garbage disposal. "They'll give you a nice pamphlet. Be aware there are a lot of 'icky' pictures."

"Are you my real father?"

For twenty-six years, Tom had never wavered in how he'd respond to this question, were it ever asked of him.

"Nope." He flipped off the disposal and faced Luke.

"Fine." Irritation flashed across the boy's eyes. "Are you my *biological* father? Did you sleep with my mother?"

The amusing way Luke phrased his question made Tom chuckle.

"Speaking of icky things."

"Did you?"

"I always pictured that having sex with your mom would be a praying mantis transaction. And I still have my head." Tom smiled. "So the answer is no. I didn't have sex with your mother. Now, did I have a contribution in your creation? *That* may be true. Trivial, but true."

He went back to the sink. He shouldn't talk so much. It was easier to keep the nausea at bay if he didn't waste his breath with words.

"It's not trivial. Not to me."

"Well, to me it is. I obviously haven't wanted anything to do with you, have I?"

Tom considered adding that neither of the children had needed him. They had the two parents Jay wanted them to have. What purpose was there for him or to be served by him?

"Maybe he wouldn't let you. He was jealous of you. He kept you away."

Tom had to laugh.

"Don't try to demonize your dad with me, Luke. I knew him better than anyone else, and you have no concept of how close we were. If I'd wanted to see you, it wouldn't have been an issue. I didn't want to."

"Why not?"

"Because I don't care!" Tom glanced over his shoulder and tried to appear appalled that anyone would assume otherwise. "Why would I? You're not *my* son. I jacked off in a tube. For all you know, I've jacked off in hundreds of tubes. All the thought I've put into you in the past twenty-six years was that initial five minutes with a porno mag. And it wasn't even a good porno."

Again he'd spoken too much, too fast, and he began to cough. His stomach contents smoldered and writhed to come up. *Keep it together, Tom. You're being too much of an asshole for him to want to stay much longer.*

When he felt Luke next to him, Tom was relieved he'd had the foresight to wash the vomit down the sink. The boy turned on the faucet and filled a glass. He offered it, waiting until Tom could remove a hand from his mouth and take it.

"Then why did he talk to you about us?"

"I couldn't get him to *shut up* about you." He took a sip of the water.

"Why did you ask me about New York?"

"I like New York. I lived there, remember?"

"Why did you want a sonogram picture?"

Tom knew he shouldn't, but he took two large mouthfuls of water to buy himself time to think.

"Morbid curiosity." He set the glass on the counter. "Are we finished here? You said that's all you wanted to know."

"I have the picture."

It was appealing. So tempting to—

"Show it to me then."

The words left Tom's mouth before he could finish mulling it over or construct a sly way to get what he wanted and maintain the indifference. He'd never see the child. Even if Jay had been alive and none of this drama had cropped up, Tom was still going to die ahead of its birth.

Tom supposed that wanting to see the sonogram had to do with his approaching death, whether by his own hand now, or in six months. Though he hadn't solicited them, Jay had sent shadowy pictures of the first child who hadn't survived. Fatherhood had been Jay's desire, not Tom's. But as his life started to curve away from him, the weekly updates had become important. He'd eagerly anticipated that first sonogram. It would resemble a wad of gum, but he wanted to see it. Beyond rationale and convention.

I know it's selfish and narcissistic. I don't feel I'm their father or that this would be my grandchild. But I had a part in it. There will be another life, a chain continuing. A part of me is going to live on. Somehow it makes dying before I'm fifty not as bad. My life isn't as insignificant.

"I want you to tell me everything first."

Do you really have the balls to dangle that in front of a sick, dying man, you little fuck? But his thought did provide an approach to obtain the picture and get rid of Luke. It'd be like succeeding at having breakfast on a closed patio. He'd play the ultimate trump card. The timing also couldn't have been better. It was becoming too strenuous to hide the pain and nausea. He needed Luke to go soon.

"Even if I thought your dad wanted you to know everything, which I'm not sure he would, I don't have the energy for trips along memory lane," Tom said. "I don't want to be your Virgil. I don't have fucking time for it."

"What do you mean you don't have time?" The boy followed the setup perfectly. "You're retired from whatever. You said you lived alone and did what you pleased. What else do you have to do?"

"I'm dying, you fucking asshole. If I'm lucky, I have six months left, and I don't want to spend my remaining time recalling what are, for me, painful memories. I want to be left alone."

It occurred to Tom that this was the first time he'd said it aloud, besides to the waitress at the restaurant. However, she'd been a stranger. Telling Luke was similar to how it would've been to tell Jay.

But it's not exactly the same. If Jay were in front of me, and I told him I had six months to live, he wouldn't have stood there. He'd have enveloped me in his arms. And I feel so unstable right now that we would've sunk to the kitchen floor. He'd let me cling to him and cry into his shoulder. It's not fair I have to go through so much pain and die when I'm still young. There are jackasses that'll live into their nineties and still run marathons. I won't make it to forty-nine. He would let me get it all out.

There were many reasons why Tom wished he'd told Jay the truth. But currently, the most selfish one reigned supreme. He'd missed the opportunity to tell someone who would miss him. Who'd be pained at the prospect of him no longer being there and would mourn for him. Tom had cheated himself from the satisfaction of having someone be as upset as he was.

It's awful, and you should want to spare your loved ones the pain. But it would've been nice to feel someone agree that it's fucked-up. Not because cancer itself is fucked-up. It is, but it's fucked-up that it's happening to me. That I'm the one who's dying. Whatever the method.

When someone was hurt in this way, their pain was like a refraction of light through a lens. When it came through the lens, and the beam was focused, the image changed and was no longer one of pain. It was truly one of love. To feel pain was to love. And Jay would've been devastated.

I'd have pressed my face to the collar of your shirt and felt you shaking. And your grief, your sadness, would've made me feel better. In seeing your tears, I'd know I was loved.

That's why it wasn't the same with Luke, no matter how tempted Tom was to pretend he was talking to Jay. There was sorrow in his eyes only because death was unfortunate and people were expected to feel bad about it. It wasn't that Tom meant anything to him. Not that Tom wanted to mean anything to him.

"You're dying?"

"Yes. So can we cut the shit? You know all you need to. Your father was a good man. He loved you. Let me see the picture."

"But I didn't know him."

So much for the trump card.

"Yes, you did. You knew the *real* him."

"I also want to know you."

"I'm no one to you. I don't know how much clearer I can make that."

"But—"

"No one!" Tom cut off his protest. He folded his arms across his chest, digging his fingers hard into his biceps to put his mind somewhere other than his stomach. "I don't want to be known by you! I don't want to know you!"

Was it the shouting that was too much? That cranked the nausea to the max? He was going to be sick again. Not vomiting a granola bar sick. Violent, leaning-over-the-toilet-for-hours sick, as he'd been when he'd received the call four days ago. He didn't have more time to waste on this mess. He had to escape.

But Luke didn't seem to be going anywhere. And despite the room starting to spin, Tom still wanted that Goddamn sonogram.

"Fine. You can stay the night, since you seem intent on disturbing me." He crossed the kitchen. "Take the spare room down the hall, but I want you gone tomorrow. Let a dying man rot in peace."

Tom turned abruptly and left. As he'd hoped, he made it into the bathroom connected to his bedroom. He closed the door and got his head over the toilet bowl just in time.

It took a few minutes before he could form a coherent thought.

I'd be dead by now. So fucking dead that flesh-eating flies would be boring through the walls to get to me. This is why you don't have kids. Why you don't help anyone have kids. They might find out and show up on your doorstep just as you're ready to axe yourself.

He leaned his cheek on the porcelain rim. It would be a long night.

☆☆☆

Tom remembered crawling into bed at around one in the morning. It'd been a bad round, particularly since he hadn't eaten much. But dry heaving never lasted forever, only for what seemed like forever.

He thought maybe he'd passed out. Only whenever he'd blacked out previously, he hadn't dreamed. And this time he'd had an odd dream that began as soon as he hit the pillow.

Tom dreamed that he was thirsty. Horribly thirsty. Gargling-sand thirsty. In the dream, he'd been sleeping, and the thirst woke him. A painter painting himself painting.

His dream-self hadn't felt the pain or weakness that followed a vomiting episode, and he walked to his kitchen like a normal, healthy person. He trailed his fingertips against the wall as if he were a child running a stick along a picket fence.

He hadn't needed to turn on the light. He just took a glass from the cupboard and turned on the water. He filled and drained the glass six times. It felt wonderful. It tasted wonderful. Nothing had that alkaline, metallic taste in dreams.

Cancer fucked everything up, even getting a drink in the middle of the night. Maybe that's why he was having a basic dream. Life should be this simple again. He longed for the mundane.

But nothing nice could last.

Halfway through his seventh glass of water, Tom could no longer hold the glass. It shattered on the floor, and his body shook with such ferocity that he couldn't stand. He collapsed on the tiles, shivering and vulnerable.

And he was frightened, so very frightened. Although he'd been intent on taking his own life, he didn't want to die on the kitchen floor, writhing like a dog that had gotten into antifreeze. He'd wanted to die hours ago, falling asleep on the couch in front of his piano. But no, if he could have any death...

He struck his arm against the kitchen floor, unable to stop the repetitive movement.

"I want you to be here with me! You were supposed to be *here with me!*" Tom cried. "You were supposed to drop everything and come to me! And comfort me! And talk to me about when we were young and were going to live forever! I want you to stay by me, and hold my hand when I go! I don't want to be alone! Why did you have to die and leave me? Why did you have to leave in the fucking first place? Why didn't you stay with me? I don't want to die like this! You motherfucker! I don't want to die like this!"

And God had heard. Miraculously the clouds parted. He opened his eyes and there he was, brightness surrounding him.

"Tom?" Jay knelt, taking his hands.

"I really am dead."

He was happy. The pain was over. The humiliation. The shit life that had been a waste anyway. And Jay was there. That above all. A heat radiated through him as if he were standing before a curtain of fire.

"No, you're alive. Here, let me help you."

He was disappointed to not be dead. He wanted to go wherever Jay would lead him. In this state, where all the constraints were severed, Jay couldn't leave. If there was a paradise, and his suffering was rewarded with attaining everything he wished for, he wanted this now. He contemplated arguing with the angel, demanding to die. But this wasn't a random harp-toting, robed figure. This was Jay. And Tom had never been able to do anything but follow him.

The shaking stopped as Jay held his arm and helped him up. Strength seemed to flow from the spirit directly into him, and he only needed to lean lightly on his friend as they walked down the hall. He noticed that the farther from the kitchen they went, the more the glow around Jay dimmed, until he looked like a normal human being, instead of an angel.

"You came back for me," Tom said.

"I heard you calling. I couldn't leave you."

They were at the doorway to Tom's bedroom, and Jay leaned away, sending him into a near panic. He was reassured when Jay returned, and Tom smiled since the radiance surrounding him was back too.

"You'll stay with me, Jay. Won't you? This time you'll stay?"

The angel led him to his bed, where he allowed himself to be tucked in. But the lack of response alarmed him, and he caught Jay's wrist.

"Please, stay with me. You have to. There's no reason why you can't."

Concern streaked across Jay's perfect, golden face. Who knew what responsibilities an angel had? He was asking too much again, keeping Jay from more important things. But he couldn't bear it. Tom reached up and smoothed a piece of Jay's hair from his forehead. He wanted to die so much.

"I won't be long. I'll try. Just don't leave me."

Jay pulled his wrist free, but he hadn't left. Instead, he knelt beside the bed and took Tom's hands.

"I'll stay."

And in the dream, the dream-Tom fell asleep, never having felt so complete.

He had other random dreams within dreams that night, but only bits and pieces stuck with him. They were mostly episodes of being sick again. Vomiting into the toilet until his throat was raw. Not making it to the bathroom and being sick on the floor. A horrible nightmare where the pain in his abdomen came back. It advanced like a serpent, winding itself around his spinal cord and inching higher and higher. It reared its triangular head, and he saw the red eyes as it opened its mouth to sink its fangs into his brain stem. He dreamed that he woke screaming.

But it wasn't all bad. In every snippet, Jay was there, keeping his promise to stay with Tom until he died. When he dreamed he was vomiting in the bathroom, his friend sat beside him, rubbing his back. When he was sick on the floor, Jay helped him into bed and told him not to worry, not to be sorry, that he'd take care of the mess. And he wasn't abandoned during the worst dream either. The angel didn't kill the snake, but he held Tom's hand when he went through the pain. Jay caressed his hair and assured him that he wasn't alone, that he was safe.

So in spite of the insanity and terror, when Tom left this patchwork of dreams behind, he felt disappointed as Jay's presence slipped away. He kept his eyes closed and lay still, attempting to recapture the sense of his friend being near, touching his arm, and holding his hands. He moved his thumb and first finger together, trying to feel again the individual strands of his hair. He reviewed his dreams until they were overplayed, and he couldn't hold on to Jay any longer.

☆☆☆

Tom propped himself up on his elbows. He surveyed the room—it was the same as always, and no apparitions lurked in its corners. His windows were open. He didn't remember opening them, but it was possible that he'd been proactive prior to falling into a bizarrely active sleep. The February air swept its freshness into the room and circulated out the sickness. He loved the cold.

And how are we feeling today, Tom? Moderately well, having spent the past several hours dreaming that you're dying, and you had Jay back?

He did feel surprisingly improved. Shaky, since he needed to shovel something down his throat, even if it'd taste like magnets, but the pain and nausea were absent.

And we mustn't be ungrateful for small blessings. Tom smirked and swung his legs over the bedside. *Whether it's two degrees or two symptoms. Every little bit—*

But he couldn't finish the idiom. He looked at the floor and realized he was about to step on Luke. The boy was asleep by his bed, his arm tucked under his head as an improvised pillow.

Chapter Fourteen

Salt Lake City, Utah
February 2038: Luke

"Old man? My God, you're cruel, *boy*."

"You're such a vulgar *boy*."

"Or you can be a good *boy* and stay sober."

"I'm leading. Leading. Can you stop acting like a little *boy*?"

"You're stupid. A fucking, stupid little *boy*. And that's all you'll ever be."

These statements played through Luke's head as he sagged against the living room doorframe and watched Tom DuBelle play his piano.

When he woke on the floor, he'd initially been so panicked that he hadn't noticed the music. He'd bolted up, terrified and panting as if from a nightmare. But he'd gone to sleep from a nightmare and actually awoken from nothing. The nothing of total physical, mental, and emotional exhaustion.

The bed had been empty. Tom's absence sent his adrenaline pumping until Luke registered that the bed had been made and a thin blanket had been tucked around him.

But where is he? What if Tom had spent all his energy stealthily making the bed and finding a blanket only to pass out in the hallway? The image of Tom lying dead somewhere brought Luke to his feet. But as he was getting ready to search the apartment for a body, he heard the piano music.

It leaked slowly into the bedroom through the door gap.

If you're near to death, you don't go to the trouble of shutting the door except for a crack. Luke pushed it open and followed the music.

From the full, swelling tones that flowed from the front of the condo, the sound couldn't be a recording. When he saw Tom at the grand, with all his picture frames back on the lid, all Luke could do for several minutes was breathe.

Tom leaned over his piano, and in the warmth of the notes, Luke heard how his fingers caressed the keys. It could hardly be called "playing," since it was more than just striking keys in a predetermined order. The action was living, and the piano was an extension of his voice. Tom moved with a gentle consistency, leaning in and out as if he was breathing air into a balloon. The emotional, hypnotic way he coaxed the instrument on made Luke feel as if he'd stumbled into Tom's sacrosanct paradise. Yet he felt as compelled to interject as he did to back away. So he resigned himself to stand in the doorway and listen. And wonder.

What Tom played was familiar—*Cavalleria Rusticana's* "Intermezzo". It was one of his father's favorite pieces of music, one that Jay played over and over again.

Are you thinking of him?

He expected Tom to turn as the last notes folded into each other, but instead, he played as if the music had never been meant to end. It transformed into another piece Luke knew.

The "Flower Song" was something else Jay had listened to so constantly that Luke knew the gibberish by heart. He could hear the voice of his father's favorite tenor overlaying the piano. *You are thinking of him. Are you thinking about him in general? Or how you thought I was him? Do you remember that? Maybe you don't know what I was doing on your bedroom floor this morning.*

His knees felt weak as he reflected on last night. Luke was exhausted. More so than he ever remembered feeling.

He'd pulled all-nighters. It was fun to sleep over at a friend's house and chug bottles of soda during Scrabble. Or when he was working, and he'd be awake with the rest of the cast, running lines until the words made no sense, and the sun broke over the horizon.

Or staying up all night with Dad, watching Robert Cuccioli.

And he'd taken care of sick people. It was undesirable, but when Beau had had the flu, he'd brought her soup and offered her tissues. He'd certainly cleaned up vomit. Granted, it was more often than not a dead person's vomit, but vomit was vomit.

There was that teenager who committed suicide on Madison Street. He let his grandpa's old car run with the garage door down. I helped Dad get what was left of him in the bag. He was melting in my hands. Globs sliding from the bones like fucking scrambled eggs.

That liquefying body had been the most disgusting thing he'd seen...he'd touched. He could handle vomit. Helping Jay had numbed Luke to many things.

But none of the late nights, none of his time with the sick or grossly dead had prepped him for what'd happened twelve hours ago. Not even when his father had died in his arms. Potentially, that experience could've been the crossroads. But watching Jay die had been over too quickly for them both.

Last night, Tom had suffered for hours. There'd been nothing Luke could do to stop or ease it. He'd just been a powerless witness to misery. And the ordeal wasn't over. Tom appeared to be feeling better at present, yet he'd continue to suffer until he died. And Luke would remain helpless to do anything. It was only pain—without complications. There was no question of fairness or equality. No one to blame or misinterpretations to make. No pride. No conspiracies. Nothing and no one to fall back on. Nowhere to run away.

And Luke had never been in a situation like that.

He swallowed and tried to focus on the music pouring from the piano rather than what had happened. But music was the only thing that had prevented him from turning away from the condo door in the first place.

If you hadn't been playing the piano, I'd be in Pennsylvania. Or New York. Luke watched Tom, who hadn't yet ceased playing and didn't appear likely to stop any time soon. *And if I were in Pennsylvania or New York—if I'd been anywhere else last night—what would've happened to you?*

☆☆☆

Luke knew something was wrong with Tom before the incident. From him even initially opening the door, it was obvious. The hostility contradicted their other interactions, even when Tom had been angry at the end of their breakfast engagement. The shaking, the twisted look that kept coming into his eyes, the way he grasped the sink as if it were a crutch? Tom was sick. He was in pain. And he was trying to hide it.

Everyone is always trying to hide things from me, Luke had bitterly thought when Tom staggered down the hallway to his kitchen.

The bitter conclusion that once again he was being deceived made him decide that, while Tom was pushing sensitive buttons to frustrate him enough to leave, Luke wasn't going anywhere. Not until his questions were answered. If Tom threw him out, he'd pitch a tent in the hallway.

His resolution only faltered slightly when Tom said he was dying.

For being raised around so much death, you'd think I'd know what to say. Should I ask what's killing him? Volunteer to help? Say I'm sorry? Am I sorry? He didn't know the man. Would he be sorry if Tom dropped dead before he got the answers he wanted? Yes. But after he ceased to be of any use?

I'm a dick, Luke thought. *You're not just a tool that can be disposed of once its purpose is fulfilled—a wet wipe or a fucking plastic spoon.*

Still, dick or not it wouldn't be fair if Tom died prior to answering what he needed. And even if no one else believed in the concept of fairness, Luke did. He was owed the information he came for, and he was determined that Tom would deliver it, no matter how sick he was.

Luke stood in the kitchen for several minutes after Tom gave his reluctant invitation to stay before stumbling out. He'd heard a door at the end of the hall close but no other noise.

A wide range of emotions competed for dominance, including the doubt. Should he have come? Tom didn't want him there. He wasn't willing to answer his questions.

And what good does faith in fairness do if no one honors it? You'd like to think you'll be able to force answers out of him, but what are you going to do? Hold a gun to a terminally ill man's head? You can't make him do a thing for you.

Tom's unexpected enmity and cruel remarks also stung.

"I obviously haven't wanted anything to do with you, have I? If I'd wanted to see you, it wouldn't have been an issue. I didn't want to... I jacked off in a tube. All the thought I've put into you in the past twenty-six years was that initial five minutes with a porno mag... I don't want to be known by you! I don't want to know you!"

Wouldn't you be at all curious? Wouldn't you care about us?

And it struck him. None of these spiteful statements had been directed to an "us." At no time had Tom included Beau. He hadn't insinuated that the "you" he kept saying referred to Luke and his sister. It would've been simple to slip in an "either of" or "both of," but Tom hadn't. And his actions, the real ones he couldn't veil, revealed the truth. He wanted that sonogram picture. He wanted only Beau.

Like with everyone else, I'm second best. If not third. His heart shrunk. *And you don't know me to know that she's better. At least my parents had years of comparison to make their decision. How many times have you thought about her? Wanted to see her? Know her? Or what if you already do know her?*

If Beau had known for years about their father's secret past, maybe she'd met Tom. And how did he know Tom also hadn't met Jake? Again, Jake had been identified as the preferable son.

He walked into Tom's living room. The strategy of trying to feel hatred toward everyone in the universe, instead of sorry for himself worked as well as it usually didn't. The struggle just wasn't worth fighting.

Luke put his hand over the piano's cheek block and surveyed the illuminated buildings.

I just want to be as good as everyone else. If you don't care about us both, fine. But why am I always inferior? What's wrong with me?

He wasn't sure if there was anything Tom could tell him that would resolve this question or where he could find the answer for himself. At his core, Luke knew why Beau or Jake were favored. They *were* better than him. He couldn't fool anyone into believing otherwise. A stranger who lived two thousand miles away and had never seen him knew immediately. Luke wasn't worth caring about. He wasn't worth anything.

I'll stay tonight, but tomorrow I'm leaving. Answers or no answers. I don't know where I'll go, but it won't be to anyone else. I'll always find the same.

The piano bench was halfway out, and he sat on its corner so he could still survey the city. On a whim, he placed his fingers to the far right keys and gave B a tap.

But the resonance inside the piano wasn't right. And when he pressed the key a second time, again it returned an abnormal sound. Luke leaned back to peer down the hallway. No one had been there, and no light filtered from any open doors.

He put his fingers on the high keys and hit all five separately, ending in the B. They were each horribly off, and not only with the pitch. A grand should sing every note with a rich quality, but the chords sounded weighed down. He'd heard Tom playing his piano just over an hour ago, and the quality hadn't been stifled.

Luke stood and lifted the top. The cause became apparent right away. There were half a dozen upside-down picture frames spread across the treble strings. He leaned aside once again to ensure the hallway was empty before turning the first one over.

He almost dropped the lid, but fortunately remembered himself in time to lower it quietly. He settled on the piano bench with the frame in his hands.

It's me.

Not a family portrait. And it wasn't of him as an infant or small child. It also wasn't his graduation photo. It was a picture of him a year ago. From the last performance he'd played before leaving to New York. The role he'd been so proud of, that his father had helped him practice. But he'd never seen a copy of this picture.

Luke closed his eyes and remembered the instant when someone must've taken the shot.

It'd been the big number. The show's pinnacle. And the moment had been all his. He shared the stage with no one. The new scenery had already been pushed forward as he stood singing, looking over the audience. And the backdrop that finished the setting change had been halfway down. Luke had started the final verse. He'd removed his jacket and tossed it stage left. He'd raised his right hand. And that's when the picture had been snapped.

God. To feel that rush. To be there again.

Be there.

Luke wondered...

He reopened the lid of Tom's piano and turned the other frames over one by one. Baby pictures of him and Beau were there, as well as the graduation pictures. A family portrait from a few years ago. A frame of his sister and Jake kissing in front of their wedding cake. But these photographs were professionally taken.

Dad could've sent them. And I guess he could've taken this picture of me too, but wouldn't I have seen it? The rest are copies.

He pictured the theater layout in his head.

Dad was there every night. He sat in the same reserved spot on the far left side. I felt him watching me there.

But Luke could tell from his body position in the picture, and from the angle of the stage, that the photographer had been on the right.

"Did you really come to see me perform?" Luke whispered, setting the frame in his lap. "You traveled two thousand miles to see me sing on stage and take a photo?"

He searched his memory for Tom. Tried to recall noticing him, speaking to him, shaking his hand. But there was nothing, and he could've been at any of the dozen shows. He'd entered and departed like a ghost, taking only the picture to place with the others.

That's what you were doing when you told me to wait by the door. Luke imagined Tom gathering the frames and hiding them inside his piano. *You do care. You just don't want me to know—*

A door opened and fear branched through him. He was already on unstable ground with Tom. He'd be rightfully angry to find Luke poking around.

Luke hit the light switch, bathing the room in blackness. He shrank into the couch and waited for the light to reveal him. But it didn't. There was no light from the hallway, and he only faintly heard running water in the kitchen. His nerves started to unwind.

He's only getting a drink.

Since Tom hadn't rotated the vertical blinds closed, the illuminated cityscape gave vague shadows to the room's objects. Luke made out the framed photograph he'd left on the piano bench in the hurry to mask himself. He deliberated trying to retrieve it and push it under the couch, but the running water stopped, making it impossible for him to judge Tom's location.

The water started again. But also, right as he moved to hide the picture, it stopped. This pattern repeated three more times, until he wondered if Tom was playing a game. Did he have a hidden camera in the living room? Was he watching Luke begin to get up and then cower into hiding as he turned the water on and off? Manipulating the terror in someone who had their hand in the cookie jar? The water stopped a seventh time, and Luke sighed in frustration.

Just catch me having snooped in your things. Stop toying with me. He waited for the water to come back on.

But it didn't. Instead he heard a glass breaking. And Tom calling, crying. Luke cautiously peeked at the dim outline of the hallway.

"I want you to be here with me! You were supposed to be *here with me!* You were supposed to drop everything and come to me! And comfort me! And talk to me about when we were young and were going to live forever! I want you to stay by me, and hold my hand when I go!"

Luke decided it was worth risking Tom's wrath to ensure everything was all right. He expected the kitchen light to be on and lead him down the hallway, but it wasn't. He followed the wall with the flat of his hand.

"I don't want to be alone! Why did you have to die and leave me? Why did you have to leave in the fucking first place? Why didn't you stay with me?"

You're drunk. Drunk and talking to ghosts.

Luke winced as he hit his knee on one of the kitchen barstools.

"I don't want to die like this! You motherfucker! I don't want to die like this!"

He felt for the switch and turned on the lights. He stepped around the bar, squinting as his eyes adjusted to the brightness. And he froze.

Tom lay on the kitchen floor.

Luke returned to seeing his father being hit by the Honda Civic. Of holding Jay's head in his lap with blood gushing from the back of his skull. It was happening again. Tom was going to die.

His chest repeatedly seized in panic as he knelt by Tom and took his hands.

It's happening again. All over again.

But Tom did what Jay hadn't. He opened his eyes. Although he didn't seem able to concentrate on Luke, they were still open. He was alive.

Luke helped him up and led him through the dark hall to his bedroom. Tom's skin felt like he'd been sitting in the sun for hours. He kept looking at Luke in a strange way of seeing past him. And while Luke tried to remain levelheaded, inside he neared hysteria.

Just get him in bed. Then find a thermometer. Should I call 9-1-1? Oh, my God. Oh, my God.

He didn't know what to do. Tom hadn't said what he was dying from. Was this the end? Luke had been around dead bodies for twenty-six years, but he'd never seen someone die until Jay. Was this what happened when you didn't die in a car accident? Did you become pliant and obedient? Lose your awareness?

"You'll stay with me, Jay. Won't you? This time you'll stay?"

Did you hallucinate? He decided against correcting Tom. If he wasn't thinking lucidly, he might argue, and there wasn't time. Luke needed to take action. Fuck the thermometer. He needed ice. Bags of ice. He needed to build a fucking igloo.

"Please, stay with me. You have to. There's no reason why you can't."

Tom grabbed his wrist. With his other hand, he touched a piece of Luke's hair that'd fallen across his forehead. The tender way with which Tom pushed back the lock of hair suspended the anxiety.

"I won't be long. I'll try not to be. Just don't leave me."

And Luke knew he couldn't. If Tom was about to die, and he wanted Jay to stay with him until the end, how could he refuse?

"I'll stay."

Tom smiled. Luke knelt by the bed and tried to return the smile, though it felt cracked.

But please don't die right now. I can't handle this. You said yourself, "A boy shouldn't have to bury his father." You're not my father, but you're something. Even if you refuse to tell me anything. I know you care. Tom had closed his eyes. *I don't want to lose anyone else. I can't bear to lose anyone else, Tom. Please don't die.*

As minutes went by, Tom's breaths grew relaxed, and the pulse Luke felt from holding his hands kept steady. He at last separated from Tom to take further action.

Luke went to the windows on the right side of the bedroom. He threw them open to let the winter air in, still so overwhelmed he barely sensed the cold. He saturated a washcloth in the adjacent bathroom's sink. After wringing the excess water, he returned to Tom's side and sponged the cloth across his tacky forehead.

Luke only wondered if he should leave when Tom's temperature seemed to be reducing. But as he was about to, Tom sat up with a start. He was a zombie, not acknowledging Luke's existence and intent on a singular purpose—to be sick in the bathroom.

It felt like Tom spent hours vomiting into the toilet while Luke watched, unsure what to do. He felt relieved when the sleep walker initially returned to bed; however, Tom was up again to the bathroom dry heaving only moments after being down. Then back to bed. To the toilet. To the bed. All without a word.

What do I do? There's nothing to do! Nothing!

On one of these trips, Tom stumbled to the floor and expelled a trace amount of stomach acid. He spoke for the first time in hours, apologizing to Jay for the mess.

Luke knelt beside him on the floor. He said not to worry; he'd take care of it. And when he patted Tom's shoulder, the touch appeared to relieve him. So over the toilet a couple of minutes later, Luke sat next to him with his hand on his back. To some degree, it put him at ease to provide a small measure of comfort.

But the pain. When Tom woke, thrashing from the pain, it was like lighting a firecracker under a coffee can. Luke couldn't think of anything he'd experienced that compared with what he saw. The unpleasantness in his life had been only that—discomfort. Pain had been simple to remedy. It was temporary and able to be walked off. This wasn't crushing a hand in a car door though. It was a struggle with internal torment that couldn't be escaped. It was being backed into a corner by a bull and gored again and again.

"Do you have pills, Tom? Anything?"

There was no answer except for the screaming. Something about it wrapping around his spine, biting into his brain. God knew what "it" referred to.

Think! Goddamn it! They're probably in the kitchen. But I can't leave him!

Then he noticed the luggage by the door—the carry-on bag slung over a chair. The bulb in his mind flickered. Tom would've taken any medication with him to Pennsylvania.

Please be here, please be here! Luke tore through the bag and could've wept for the relief of finding pill bottles in the bottom.

He skimmed the instructions before dumping out the doses the labels advised and forcing them down Tom's throat. After that, there'd been nothing to do but crouch beside the bed and let Tom crush his hand as he prayed for the medication to take away the pain.

"It's okay. You're not alone. You're safe. It'll be okay." Luke stroked the hair from his face with his free hand, speaking for both of them. He didn't know if Tom could hear him anymore.

Several minutes passed until the pills worked. The violent tremors stopped, and Tom loosened the grip on Luke's hand, his breaths evening out as if he was asleep.

Thank you, God. Luke pressed his forehead into the bedspread and began to cry. *Thank you for sparing him. Not so he can indulge me. Not so—*

He jumped to feel a touch on his head.

"Shh, shh." Tom didn't open his eyes. "It's okay."

Luke pushed his face into the comforter and howled. Tom trying to console him made it worse. Clips of the last few days spiraled through his mind:

Jay dying in his lap without waking up. Jake pulling the rings from his father's dead hands. Beau and Jackie clinging to him like they never had. And all of them turning against him. Yelling at him. Hating him. Driving him from their lives. The things Tom had said too. Adamant that he didn't care. Trying to lie with the cruel statements and excuses. Everyone lying to him. Hiding from him. But the strongest image which kept overshadowing everything else...

"I was thinking how we watched that recording of Robert Cuccioli a hundred times. We stayed up all night the day you got the call, watching his every move because you wanted to nail that part." Jay was driving past the onramp to the freeway. He was going to take the long way.

Why didn't you take the long way? Why?

"And you absolutely did. Absolutely! You were meant for that role. It was like a second skin on you."

You were there every night. You reserved that seat in the front row for each performance. Beau came once. Mom came once. But you were there every night!

"I was so proud of you." His father had reached over and patted his arm. "I *am* proud of you."

But Luke had shrugged off the touch and said nothing.

I'd give anything *to feel you touch me again. I promise I wouldn't turn you away.* He clutched the blanket to his face and tried to pretend it was Jay petting his hair, not Tom. *Why didn't you take the long way? Why didn't you get gas on the way down? Or at any other place. Any other fucking one!*

He remembered the van pulling into the gas station.

"I'll be right back. Do you want anything?"

"Not from you."

Luke felt lightheaded, and his throat ached from gasps of air erratically taken between sobs.

"I'm sorry, I'm sorry, I'm sorry."

"Don't cry. I understand," Tom said and found Luke's hand. "I understand why."

He couldn't know what was going through Luke's thoughts, and no one could understand why. Even he didn't.

"What?" Luke rasped.

"I understand why. It's not your fault."

But it is my fault. It's all my fault.

"I have to go sometime."

But not at fifty. I wasn't ready. I wasn't ready for you to die.

"I know why you're sad that you can't do anything about it. But it's okay."

"It's not okay! It's not!" Luke said aloud.

"No, it's not okay. But *I'm* okay. I. Am. Okay." Tom spoke the last three words slowly. Deliberately. As if each was its own sentence. "I understand why you couldn't kill it, Jay."

Tom's last statement was overpowered by what he'd said before it.

"I am okay." Luke replayed the phrase as he lifted his face. His cheeks and temples tingled like the skin had fallen asleep. He looked at Tom, who'd been tranquil and unaware of his hallucination's impact.

"I am okay." "I" as in "you." You are okay.

The situation wasn't okay. Luke may not be okay. But *Tom* was okay. And that mattered to him...deeply. Waves of emotional pain crested and fell within him, but hearing that Tom was no longer suffering comforted Luke.

The same could be said of his father's death. It was a horrible circumstance. Fucked-up, in no small part thanks to Luke, and he was devastated. Perhaps he hadn't understood how upset he was until right then. He'd been deflecting and redirecting his attention since the accident happened. Returning to the fight with Jay, his rivalry with Jake, the Tom DuBelle mystery. He'd been so eager to feed into these things and avoid his grief.

Dad is dead.

Luke was far from okay. But wherever Jay was, nothing could hurt him any longer. His father was okay. It didn't erase the shame, but somehow, the burden lifted an inch or two from his shoulders.

But what did you even think when this delirium and sickness started? You thanked God for sparing Tom, but why?

For what reason did he want Tom to live? He didn't want him to die, but why did he want him to *live* when he was in such pain? He'd told God it wasn't to indulge himself, but had he thrown that out because it was actually the *primary* motive? He wanted answers. It was fairness again—it wouldn't be fair to make this journey and have his well of knowledge die on him.

I wanted him kept alive for me. To give me what I want. I thank God for bringing him through only for myself. It had nothing to do with his welfare.

Of all the many terrible things Luke had ever thought, he knew the gratitude for keeping Tom alive to serve his selfishness was the worst. Tom was a human being with a greater purpose than being Luke's encyclopedia.

Being okay with living *or* dying transcended his personal goals and agenda. Acceptance of whatever happened. And it wasn't *him* being okay.

There are more important things than me and doing what I want. I can be okay—eventually, I can get there. If others are okay, everything will be all right.

☆☆☆

As he stood inside the doorframe the next morning watching Tom at the piano, it occurred to him he'd finally been pushed toward growing up. The point where he'd decided that he could only focus on the present moment and calmly, selflessly accept a situation had been when Luke stopped being "boy."

He wasn't sure if he should be happy about this. Grief sounded overdramatic, but it didn't feel like a misplaced emotion. Being "boy" had been easy. It was a volatile rollercoaster, but he got his way. Everyone cut him slack, and he rarely had to make excuses for his behavior—they were made for him. He did whatever he wanted, he was free to always back out or pass the buck. But now he felt the concrete, which had been poured around him in the night, starting to set. "Boy" was gone. Another thing he couldn't reclaim.

Further indication of the changeover was how Luke didn't dwell long on his loss. His concentration turned to Tom, who still didn't seem aware of his presence, although his playing had become different. He'd transitioned from mellow, familiar pieces that Luke assumed reminded him of Jay and instead struck the keys with a frenzied speed that made him think of fast-falling sleet in a blizzard. An anxious feeling hung in the air until Tom ran the side of his right hand across the keyboard.

After Tom performed this move twice, he returned to the delicate notes that weren't as distracting to think over. But even though he'd stood there for several minutes rehashing the confused and painful events of last night, Luke still had much to sort out. Chief among his problems being that Tom's grudging invitation had been for one night only.

How will I convince him to let me stay? It wasn't just for himself that Luke wanted to stay, though he was terrified to call his mother and sister. Tom needed someone to be with him. *That might as well be me. It should be me.*

He remembered parts of Tom's initial cries to Jay—he was supposed to "drop everything and come." Had Jay known Tom was dying? Was he planning on "dropping everything" and going to his friend's side? Would he have done this?

Yes. Luke decided he must not have known about Tom's condition.

If you had, you'd have been here. You would've classified it as a "good deed of truth." Luke shifted from one foot to the other.

"Someday, this will be you...doing what I'm doing... Eventually, you'll be where I am." It was like his father stood in front of him. *Here I am. Where you should've been. This is me. And I have to do this. But how?*

Tom didn't seem the type who'd welcome the insinuation that he needed taking care of by anyone. He had too much pride and independence to own up to caring about Luke at all. He'd be adamant that he didn't need help. Maybe Jay could've swayed him, but aside from Tom's picture stash, there was no indication that Luke held any influence.

Unfortunately, he wasn't able to invest more in strategizing the right approach. There was a pause in the piano music, and before Tom spoke, the first five notes of the next piece arrested him. Luke would have to wing his request to stay and hope he could be more persuasive than he felt he was.

Chapter Fifteen

In the middle of the "Revolutionary Etude," Tom became conscious of Luke's presence. How long he'd been there was impossible to know. There was nothing Tom loved more than losing himself and letting his mind wander, fusing piece into piece, guided by what he was thinking or feeling. All his surroundings washed out, and when he emerged from this trance, he'd have no idea what he'd played or how much time had passed. Luke could've been standing in the doorway for hours or minutes.

He continued playing and peered between the grand's open lid at the window. Through the glass, he saw the reflection of the room behind him.

Another great thing about these windows.

Luke's eyes were lowered to the floor, and Tom didn't feel any waves of anxiety, which was fine, as Tom was pleased to continue playing. However, now that he was cognizant of an audience, the reverie of playing for only himself slipped away, and nagging showmanship asserted itself.

Tom let Chopin fade into his favorite piece to perform, Carl Vine's "Sonata No. 1." He loved how the first slow, dissonant measures skyrocketed to a lightning fast, invigorating tempo. It was as enjoyable to watch as to hear. There were electrifying spots where he had to hit treble keys, or play a quick, high octave, and instead of moving his right hand up, he'd dart his left over to strike what he needed. He had to be quick to not create a gap and accurate enough to hit the keys he was going for.

But it's right on the money. He grinned. *And next I do this.*

Tom placed the side of his right pinky and ring finger on the low A next to the keyblock and swiped his hand across the length of the keyboard in a dazzling glissando. He'd done it hundreds of times, but it was still thrilling.

As freeing as it was to play his personal repertoire, a close second was the pleasure of being an entertainer.

I know the draw it has on you. I understand wanting to do nothing else, and being swept away by what you love.

Tom followed the notes in his head as they decelerated. There could be several minutes of glittering melodies, but it was a good time to pull back.

For the first time in what may've been hours, Tom stopped and removed his hands from the keys. He then replaced his right and played five slow notes.

"You'll know this one," Tom said. He needlessly adjusted one of the photographs he'd replaced on the piano, before putting his left hand on the keyboard and resuming his performance.

He glanced at Luke's reflection and was satisfied to see the boy's discomfort as he struggled with a response.

It's embarrassing to have been caught invading someone's privacy, isn't it? Though no less humiliating than being sick in front of a stranger. Wailing, or psychotic, or whatever happened last night. Still, you shouldn't have been prodding into anything. Tom sighed. Since there'd been only one picture left on the piano bench, he knew what was going through Luke's mind.

"The answer to your question is yes."

"What question?"

"The one you're thinking. Yes, I was there. And I've been to other things. That wasn't the first time I'd seen you in person. For the first several months of your life, I saw you every day, actually."

"I was wondering that last night, but it wasn't what I was going to ask you now."

"Ask away. We'll see how inclined I am to answer."

"I wanted to ask how you were feeling this morning."

"Afternoon."

"Afternoon. You seem better."

It surprised Tom that Luke's attention hadn't been diverted. He'd wagered on easily manipulating the conversation to avoid an awkward discussion of last night. Admitting he cared for Luke was the lesser of the two evils.

"I am. But don't even try thinking it's because of you. That you've given me a 'reason to live' or some bullshit. It has nothing to do with you."

"What is it then?"

"It's because of the fucking pills I assume you shoved down my throat."

"If they make you feel better, why don't you take them?"

"Whether, or how often, I take my medication is no concern of yours. You don't know I didn't take them, and those are strong meds. You might've killed me with an overdose. Is that what you were trying to do?"

"I... I didn't know what else to do, Tom."

Tom shifted on the bench to face Luke. The reflection in the window had hidden the exhaustion in Luke's face, the worry in his eyes. But while Tom felt kindhearted in a way, and sorry for giving him a hard time, he didn't feel grateful. Luke had been kind and hadn't left him last night. But Tom wouldn't have even been in that situation had Luke not interrupted his suicide.

"You look worse than I do, but I don't think the pills would help you much. Sit down."

"I'm sorry if that's not what I should've done. I didn't know what else to do." Luke repeated. He flopped onto the couch, and leaned his elbow on the arm, cradling his forehead in his hand. "You were in so much pain."

"Having one's insides eaten away isn't something I'd highly recommend."

Luke opened one eye. "My two grandmas had cancer. It was horrible."

"There are more centenarians today than there have ever been. I could've lived another fifty years. It's stealing half my life from me." Tom leaned back against the keyslip and folded his arms. "At my age, your grandmothers were still happy, healthy, independent people. Did the cancer kill them when they were forty-eight? No. *That* is horrible."

"Dad was only fifty."

"Also horrible."

"Barely fifty," Luke said as if Tom hadn't spoken. "I didn't come home for his fiftieth birthday. I was in New York. I knew it was his birthday, but I didn't care. I assumed he'd have more. I didn't send a card. I didn't call. Beau called me and tried to put Dad on the line. I hung up as soon as I heard his voice."

"He told me about that. It really upset him. You were a fucking asshole." Tom was glad this topic had surfaced. If there was one subject that'd provoke Luke to the rage that would culminate in him leaving, this was it.

"You don't know the things he said to me." Luke said the words in an attitude of weary defeat.

"I know exactly what he said."

"You know what he *said* he said to me."

"Wrong. I was there." Tom smiled slowly when Luke lifted his head. "I was at your last performance, and Jay wanted to have a drink with me after he talked to you. Coincidentally, I happened to be in the same restaurant." He shrugged. There wasn't much point in petty lies. "Well, not coincidentally, but I was there at the bar. I heard everything."

"So how can you possibly defend him?"

There's the flame. There it is.

"I feel guilty about how I treated him, I admit that," Luke said. "I didn't expect him to die before I could prove him wrong, or apologize for my piece. But he shouldn't have bashed my dream. He should've believed in me and been proud of me for *my* accomplishments." He gestured toward Tom. "I mean, you're a performer, aren't you?"

"I've played the piano for thousands of people in concert halls all over the world."

"And I'm sure there are those who'd dare to call that a waste of time. To call that 'shit' because it's different from *their* opinion of success."

Tom chuckled, Leo's voice echoing in his mind.

"That isn't what your dad said, but I'll play along since your argument is flawed anyway. No one would call what I do a waste of time, or 'shit' even if they didn't understand it. Do you know why?"

"That is what—"

"You're a revisionist. I get that. Or have selective hearing, whatever. But shut up and listen for a change. No one would say those things about me. As I told you, I've played the piano for *thousands* of people in concert halls *all over the world.*"

"So I just hadn't done more yet, and—"

"Not 'yet'. Never. You had no intention of leaving to try for anything larger, Luke. And though, again, it isn't what Jay said, it's true that you were 'wasting your time' on 'shit' by not pursuing your goals. I don't need to defend him. He was right."

He could tell Luke was fuming as he stared at his knees. But he still didn't leave. If Tom pushed harder he could succeed; however, he paused from grinding his heel in that sore spot.

"You don't understand how hard it was for him to talk to you," Tom said.

"Everyone always says that. *You* don't understand how hard it was for *him*. Why don't people understand how hard it was for *me* to hear that?"

"Oh, I understand how hard it was for you to hear. Could he have said it differently and added things you *wanted* to hear, so you wouldn't throw a tantrum? I believe so. But I try not to judge. I don't know what it's like to be a father and have to tell a son I'm proud of that he's stagnant and could do better. Yes, it was hard for *you* to hear. You're such a narcissist."

"He wasn't proud of me."

"Then you're a stupid narcissist."

Tom turned to watch Luke through the window reflection as he started to play again. The "Intermezzo" from *Cavalleria Rusticana* rushed from his fingertips. It reminded him of Jay, and he didn't have to think through any portion. He could have a conversation, made easier with his back to Luke.

"I know you have this competitiveness, this jealousy between you, Ginger, and Beau. Your father had a problem with his brother too. He—"

"Jake is not my brother," the boy snapped.

"Did you fly two thousand miles to be a jackass? You should refrain from interrupting me. You never know when I might tire of you and throw you out of my house." In the shadowed reflection in the window, Tom saw Luke freeze, and concealed a smile. "As I was saying, Jay had a problem with his brother. Gordy was a pile of trash. Did you have the misfortune to meet him?"

"No, we were only seven when he died. Meecie had moved in a couple years prior, and she was really upset."

"I imagine she was, but Jay was on the opposite end of the spectrum."

"He was professional," Luke said. "He was as collected about Gordy as he was about Meecie. Even when Beau lost her baby. Nothing could shake him. He went to Chicago, took care of things, and brought Gordy's ashes back. Like he would for anyone else."

"You should take a lesson from your dad. He was a great actor. When he called to tell me Gordy had died he said, 'That asshole rotted in his apartment for a week. Ruined a perfectly decent couch.' Jay was a good man to most people, but he had zero tolerance for Gordy. He *hated* his brother."

"I don't hate Jake. I hate that Dad loved him more than me."

"That is far from accurate. Jay loved Ginger as a son, but it wasn't the same. It wasn't like you. You were always..." Tom searched for the right words. Once found, he was silent, wondering if he should say them. Would Jay want him to say it? But he might as well. "He favored you, to be honest. Not just above Ginger, but your sister too. He said that to me on more than one occasion. The only reason you wouldn't recognize the partiality was that he also worried the most about you."

"Why would he worry about me more? I'm weaker? I'm not as good?"

"No. On top of the other reasons I'd think would cause a father to be concerned for his son, he wanted so much for you—"

"He wanted me to be him. To forget what I wanted to do and carry on beside him like an obedient son."

"One more." Tom kept his voice steady and didn't turn around. "If you cut me off one more time, I'll throw you out. And no amount of sniveling will persuade me to let you back in. I'll call the police."

The only response was his adagio playing of the "Moonlight Sonata."

Why do you want to stay? Answers to your questions? Perhaps you have nowhere else to go? But if Jackie kicked you out, there's New York. So what do you really want? He viewed the boy's reflection in the window. *Why are you trying to keep yourself in check?*

"Anyway," he continued at last, "Jay is the last person who'd demand conformity of anyone. The only expectation he had was for you to do something with your life. The only pressure was for you to get off your ass. He would've done anything to support you. He wanted the world for you, Luke. Yet you had no ambition, no desire to take it. You were complacent with mediocrity."

"But when mediocre is all you are." Luke slouched farther on the couch and trailed into incoherent mumbles.

"Then you fix it. You don't settle for *second best*. Your dad understood that because of what he went through. When you know who you are and what you want, you have to try and take it. And you were never going to try if he didn't say anything."

"He didn't know that. I could've been waiting for the right time."

"Another edited history. You *told* him. I was there. I heard you."

☆☆☆

Over a year ago, Tom had been two vodka tonics in and spinning a peanut shell on the lacquered bar, when he noticed Jay's voice behind him.

"Here is fine," Jay said.

It was good that the conversation hadn't taken as long as Tom expected. Being halfway through his third vodka, he'd begun to feel drowsy. Jay would keep him awake by spending the first fifteen minutes admonishing him for drinking too much.

Liver cirrhosis could cause pain in that particular vicinity, Tom had thought. *You'll love that, won't you? I'll never hear the end of it.*

But as he'd been about to turn and greet his friend, he heard not only two chairs pull out, but two voices as well.

"Always this place. Why? The food is *not* that great, Dad. It's not."

Tom choked, so he hadn't heard Jay's reply. He covered his mouth in the crook of his elbow and coughed until his eyes watered.

You're a fucking dick, Jay. I should leave.

A hand patted his shoulder.

"Are you okay, buddy? Just breathe," Jay said. "It'll be okay."

"I'm. Fine," he wheezed, in two separate breaths between his teeth.

"Take it easy on the drinks." Jay's gaze darted to the two empty glasses and half-filled third.

Tom picked up the glass and drained it in two swallows. He raised his hand for the bartender to bring another.

☆

"Wait, you were the coughing drunk?" Luke's question made Tom laugh, and he forgave the disruption.

"Yes." He quirked an eyebrow and smiled. "I was the coughing drunk. I'm the king of bad first impressions. You can ask your mom. When Jay introduced us, one of the first things I told her was how I'd fucked a random guy behind a dumpster the night before."

"That's why she doesn't like you?"

"There are *plenty* of reasons she doesn't like me. I doubt my sexual escapades make the top five. I wasn't her preference when it came to you two, and I understand that she was vehemently opposed to my involvement. However, it wasn't her decision. That's a different story though."

☆

The amount of alcohol Tom had quickly consumed dulled him for some time. He listened to the first of Jay and Luke's conversation, but he'd been so lightheaded that their words floated out of his mind as soon as they entered. His brain was like a truck stop on the highway as he sat at the bar spinning his peanut shell.

But there'd just been small talk between father and son in the beginning, so it was of no consequence if he retained it. By the time Jay raised the sensitive topic, Tom had been sipping club soda and feeling more lucid.

"What are you planning to do now that the show's over?" Jay had asked.

"I'll audition for the next. After how well I did with this, it's in the bag. Don't you think? All smooth sailing."

Cocky little bastard. There was a time when people would've called Tom a cocky little bastard too. Both him and Jay. It didn't take much for them to become full of themselves. It'd always been a personal challenge to stay grounded.

"It's only summer stock theater, though," Jay said.

"I know. I'm going to keep with them. Land every lead."

"So your plan is to stay here indefinitely? You'll keep on performing with this theater?"

"Yes. Why ruin a good thing?"

"And you'll help with the funeral home in your spare time? When Ginger and I need you? Just pickups and odd jobs?"

Tom winced. *I told you not to mention the funeral home. It will feed these notions he has.*

He knew why Jay had brought it up though. Luke received no compensation for his performances at the theater, and the funeral home was his only source of income. Jay had commented to Tom that "juggling fucking bowling pins" at a renaissance fair was more lucrative. People were paid minimum wage for that. The boy loved what he was doing, but it was a dead end. Jay had actually wanted to talk with Luke sooner, but Tom had advised him to wait. One good thing could come from summer stock theater—experience.

"Do you know how cutthroat it is, whether he plans to go to school or directly into the industry?" Tom had said. "Thousands of students apply for the musical theater program at Carnegie Mellon. Do you know how many they accept? It's in the single digits, Jay. And they won't waste their time letting him audition if he doesn't have more to say than 'I was in a high school play and liked it.' He needs experience to build a portfolio. It's the same if he goes to New York. Sit back and let him improve his chances."

But Luke now had several performances under his belt that might sway a conservatory to review him, or secure auditions on a larger platform. Investing further at a free stock theater was no longer conducive to making a career in Broadway. It was time to have the discussion.

"'Just pickups and odd jobs?' Dad, I'm not going over this again," Luke had seized on it, as Tom anticipated he would. "I told you, I don't want to do more than I'm already doing. I can barely tolerate that. And you don't need me. You have Jake."

"Of course, I need you. You're part of the team. We couldn't do it without you," Jay said.

I see what you're doing, but you're making it worse.

"You'll have to. I'm not giving this up."

"I didn't tell you to give it up. I can't make you do what you don't want to do. "

"That's right, you can't. But you'd *love* it if I would. You'd *love* me to give it all up."

Tom sensed Jay's hesitation. He imagined his nervous tick of flexing the fingers of his right hand.

Lie to the kid. Don't pick at semantics. Concede, say what he wants you to say, and circle back.

"Yes, I'd love you to give it up. Not 'all,' just 'it.' Give 'it' up *here*," Jay had said, and Tom put his head in his hands. "You're wasting your time *here*."

"Wasting my time? How could you say that?"

"Luke, if you want this to be more than a hobby, you *are* wasting your time. Central Pennsylvania is not where you start a Broadway career. You have enough experience that you can try to get into a conservatory or go to New York. And I'm not only speaking on behalf of myself. Mom agrees."

"Are you saying you want me to leave? Are you kicking me out?" Luke raised his voice.

"I'm not saying I *want* you to leave. I'm saying you *should*."

No one gets word play when they're angry, Jay. It's condescending.

"That's the same fucking thing!"

"No, it's not. I want a lot of things. But—"

"I know what you want. You want your *perfect* world with your *perfect* son who takes over the *perfect* business that you built. Who worships the ground you walk on and does every single thing you command! That's what you want! And how great for you. You already have it! Jake is a good bitch for you. How 'coincidental' that he falls for Beau so you can officially bring him in and play happy family."

Tom had casually turned to the left and pretended to watch the sports game on television, keeping them in the corner of his eye. He'd seen Luke make air quotations around the word "coincidental" and the anger on Jay's face as the tirade ended.

"You're out of line. Ginger isn't a replacement—"

"No, he couldn't be a replacement," Luke interrupted Jay again. "To 'replace' there has to be an original. And I've always been a huge disappointment. Don't lie. I know I have."

"That is not—"

You should've had Jackie here. She'd have shut down this bullshit.

"The closest I've felt to you has been the past couple months. I let myself believe you'd gotten over the fact that I'm not how you want me to be. That maybe you'd accepted me." Luke uncrossed his arms and made a dramatic gesture. "So what has all this been, Dad? Was it difficult for you to spend time with me the last few weeks? Were you gritting your teeth when you helped me practice? Has it been torture for you to sit through every performance?"

Tom had rolled his eyes and taken a drink.

"If it was torture for me to be at every performance, why was I there?"

"Maybe you were waiting for me to fall on my ass. Hoping I would."

"I've never wanted you to be anything but happy and successful."

"Then fucking leave me alone! Let me be who I am and accept it!"

Tom tried to catch Jay's attention. *Here's your opportunity to tell him. You don't have to bring me into it. But tell him you know what being rejected for who you are is. Tell him you understand and why.*

Tom had been unable to make eye contact to communicate anything.

"You can be whoever you want, Luke! Go whore yourself for all I care! But you have to be responsible! You're twenty-five!" Jay dropped his voice. "You're a man, not a little boy. You've never worked for anyone but me. You've never had a real job. You have no degree, and you're not qualified to do anything. Singing on a stage won't get you anywhere here. I worry about you. How will you support yourself when I'm gone?"

You've called him a stupid, insignificant leech. He's gone, my friend. He won't hear anything more.

"It's always all about you isn't it? You care so much, yet every conversation is brought back to you!"

"This isn't about me. It's—"

If he interrupted me that much I'd reach across the table at him. Tom set down the empty glass and shook his head to decline another. *But that's why you're not a father, Tom. People don't take kindly to punching anyone in the face. Whether it's your child or not. Even if he's being an asswipe and deserves it.*

"You're right. It's not. I'm a big disappointment to you, but I like who I am. And I'm going to do what I want to do."

"You're not a disappointment, and should do what makes you happy. But if this is something you want, you're wasting your time on this shit here," Jay said. The concern had returned, but Tom knew it was futile. Jay had misspoken and once again made a comment the boy would latch onto like a rabid pit bull. "You need a bigger venue. Go to New York or California, somewhere bigger than here. Or go to school."

"*Shit?* How could I have been so stupid to think you cared!"

If Jay hadn't been upset, Tom would've found his accuracy at predicting Luke's reactions quite amusing.

I'm sorry, this is all me coming at you. I remember having these fights with my parents. Where I only heard what I wanted and skewed their words to match my views. I should've fought with you more, Jay. You'd be more prepared.

Tom glanced at Jay again and sighed.

I'd get into fantastic fights with Leo—it was fun to rub him against the grain. But you? It doesn't matter how angry I am. I look at you and just crumble. Maybe if I can pretend you're someone else I'll give you a good fight, you son of a bitch.

"You'd like it if I left. You wouldn't have to see me every day to be reminded of your son, the failure. Who 'wastes his time on shit.' You could pretend there's only ever been Jake." Luke had tossed his head, and Tom masked a laugh by coughing again.

God, you belong in a soap opera.

"I don't want you to leave. I'd miss—"

Tom was glad he hadn't been able to see the pained look in Jay's eyes. If he could've, he'd have violated the principal rule and interrupted.

"Save it. I'm happy to make myself disappear. I'll go and prove you wrong. But it'll be too late." Luke stood and shoved his chair under the table. "You've chosen your son, so go fuck yourself, Jay."

Tom didn't tell Luke what'd happened after he marched out to act upon his threat. He didn't disclose how his father had been brokenhearted, and it'd only been due to Tom's insistence that Jay hadn't followed the boy and begged him to stay.

He'd known that Jay pursuing Luke would've prevented him from leaving. The boy didn't even necessarily need an apology. He wanted to feel valued. Things and people weren't chased if they weren't loved. But Tom had kept him back.

There's just something wonderful, gorgeous about Jay being upset. And this is it...

Jay had allowed Tom to be near him. To take him in his arms and hold him for a few moments. So fuck the situation. Fuck the consequences. Fuck the boy. Let Jay be upset always. Had he ever been this aware of his own heartbeat? Jay was so close Tom caught the scent of his cologne and felt his hair grazing his cheek. It was more intoxicating than the vodka tonics—than the piano. Even a year later, Tom had to literally shake his head to eject the memory and return to the reason he was relaying the event to begin with.

☆☆☆

"Jay was trying to be a good father to you," Tom said to Luke's reflection in the window. "A good father pushes his child when he needs to be pushed. He knew you were misunderstanding what he was trying to say, and that your interpretations were hurting you. But he was right to encourage you."

Luke lay on the couch now, his arm over his eyes. "I just don't understand why he couldn't have been happy for me. Why he couldn't have been proud and left it at that."

"Your dad was proud of you. But he was so proud of you that even if *you* were okay being average and not trying for anything greater, *he* wasn't."

"He wanted me to be him."

"He wanted you to have the same success he had. To be as happy as he was. To take the risk and have your *moment* at the phenomenal. Listen to me." Tom faced him and spoke again when Luke met his eyes. "There's no need for you to maintain charades in front of a dying man. Who would I tell your secrets to? Let your guard down. You can be wrong. Because you know you *are* wrong. What Jay said came from genuine love for you." He swallowed.

"You and Beau weren't like other children. You weren't accidents. You weren't whims. You weren't patiently counted on to appear. You were passionately, manically desired and sought after at great mental, emotional, financial, and physical cost. Trust me, Luke; he went through hell to get you. You don't know how badly he wanted you. For his entire life."

Tom turned, unable to bear looking at Luke any longer.

And no one knows how I took advantage of that desire when Jay came to me and asked, he thought as he cleared his throat. *How I did it, not in the service of my friend, but only for myself. I assumed that if I could give him what he'd always wanted, he'd stay with me.*

Tom wasn't aware of what he played as he slipped into thinking about the most painful and humiliating juncture of his life.

Worse than when you bailed me out of jail. Worse than the car accident. Worse than my mom dying. Having you turn me away was more horrible than your own death, Jay. And how awful is it to know that's true?

☆☆☆

They'd been alone a lot. With a big trial in Saint George, it was easier for Leo to only come home on weekends. And Jackie was away often too. Her literary agency had still been new.

"Marketing necessitates travel," Jackie said, though she didn't travel well. "That's how you *know* I hate it here, Jay. I'd rather be drugged off my ass on Dramamine than stay in this shit hole."

Where they were staying was hardly a shit hole. Tom had recently moved into Leo's seven thousand square foot house, where his friend and his friend's wife were invited to stay as long as they needed. It was much larger than Jay's house in Pennsylvania, and worth more than his funeral home. The shit hole she referred to was the state of Utah itself.

But their absence suited Tom perfectly. When Leo had decided he shouldn't commute daily, Tom canceled an upcoming performance at the Opernhaus Dortmund that'd been planned for months. He told the Germans he was ill—nigh unto death. To Leo, Jay, and Jackie, he said the Germans had canceled on him, the bastards. But in actuality, Tom needed to take the window of opportunity.

Stupid. Just fucking stupid.

He waited, like a spider. Building his courage and confidence on the belief that after all he was doing for him, Jay couldn't refuse. Not only had Tom provided the means for giving Jay what he wanted, but he'd also opened his home to him. Or rather, Leo's home, not that the detail mattered. Jay had a place to crash for the next year or so, quarantined and isolated. Jackie would be with him, but her presence was also a technicality. And, thanks to Leo, they'd conceal everything. The birth certificates were going to say whatever Jay wanted, and the hospital and medical records would disappear.

"You don't become this successful without making unsavory connections who remember when you've done them a favor," Leo had said, gesturing to the lavish furnishing of his home. "And you also make connections of the savory variety too. Right, Tommy?"

He wrapped his arm halfway around Tom's waist and hooked a hand into the back pocket of his jeans, a move Tom loathed. The man had his own fucking pockets to stick his meaty hands in. But it was the same as that infuriating nickname.

He'd told Leo several times not to call him Tommy. But Leo was the type who, when told to stop something, only increased doing it. So Tom's name was butchered, and his pockets were always stretched out. But Tom tried to remember that these were temporary annoyances.

Leo was a mosquito. He had to be endured in exchange for amazing summer evenings. And when those evenings opened into an infinite night of perfection, he'd citronella the shit out of that exasperating pest. The payoff outweighed his annoyance. His early guess that the attorney could be of use to him had been correct. How else would Jay have accomplished a cover-up if not for Leo's network?

In addition to Jay owing him one—

I mean really *owing me. And I'm only asking for one,* Tom rationalized. *I gave you two lives for the price of one. That's more than fair. Numerically, I'm getting the short end of the stick.*

It was the most logical choice, and Tom was sure Jay could be convinced. So after weeks of waiting for the right time, he took his chance.

They were walking in the cemetery. Tom didn't care for cemeteries, and he'd never been fascinated with death or dead bodies. But it wasn't important. Jay had wanted to be a funeral director as long as Tom had known him, and Tom had long ago moved beyond any trepidation. He could live in a funeral home. He would get used to calls for removals in the middle of the night and on holidays. He'd gladly handle Jay coming home with his clothes and hair smelling like formaldehyde and rotting flesh. If it was Jay who was coming home, it was worth getting over.

Jay had been in a good mood, though Jackie was away. It'd been the first week of June, before the weather was too hot to be outside, let alone in a hooded sweatshirt. And the graves were still freshly decorated with orange, yellow, and red mums from Memorial Day, which made Jay happy.

"They don't do this in Pennsylvania."

"That's too bad. They should." Tom's hands were in his pockets. It was seventy degrees, but he decided he had no right to be comfortable around Jay, so he wore jeans and a long-sleeved button-up.

"But they won't."

"They should get better food too. Nasty shit." It would benefit Tom's case for these comparisons to be fresh.

"If there was better food, I'd have no reason to come back."

"I'd still be here."

"Oh, you're never here. You're playing your piano in exciting places I've never heard of." Jay laughed.

"But I could stay here. I could be wherever you'd want me to be. Do whatever you want me to do." A tingling sensation swept up the back of his neck and across his face.

Corny. Cheesy. Awful.

"If I told you to jump off a bridge?"

"Don't ask if you don't want me to." Tom's laugh seemed to come out sideways, and it didn't make sense.

Around you, simple things don't make sense.

Jay had been kicking a soda bottle across the grass, and he passed it to Tom. But Tom wasn't in the mood to play. He'd lose his nerve if he didn't do it now.

"Jay, you know I feel the same about you, right?" Tom picked up the bottle. There'd been a garbage can several yards away, and he started in its direction.

"I have no patience to convince anyone of who I am anymore. Whatever state I'm in, I'm the same guy. If your perception of me was any different, I'd be out the door. Figuratively speaking. Since we're outside, I'd be down the street." Jay smiled as he caught up with Tom.

"I don't mean about that." Tom tossed the bottle in the trash and pushed his hands back into his pockets. He avoided looking at Jay as they walked across the trimmed grass.

"What do you mean then?"

Tom had composed a list of reasons that would appeal to Jay's logic and feelings. Irrefutable reasoning that couldn't be dismissed. He'd been practicing the list to make sure he didn't forget a single line. Since he didn't know which factor would sway Jay, none could be disregarded. Tom rehearsed as diligently as for a performance. Every piece of music. Up and down. Like scales.

You never forget the basics once you learn to play the piano. That's what you are to me. You're playing the piano. And I can no sooner forget those beginning scales as I can all the reasons I love you and why you should love me back.

He turned to Jay and caught his gaze. Jay had remarkably expressive light eyes. They were listed as blue on his driver's license, but they could look green or gray. Or a combination of the three. And Tom loved to look into his eyes. He'd completely forgotten his list.

Tom jerked his head away and frantically tried to remember anything. Any clauses of his grand argument. But his mind was empty except for the main construct—what he'd been envisioning and fantasizing for years.

After too many embarrassing seconds of failed recall, he gave up. He might as well blurt it out, and maybe the rest would follow. Or perhaps that's all he'd need. He didn't *know* that anything more would be necessary. It was possible Jay was just waiting for him to say it first.

He stopped walking and faced Jay.

"I want you to stay with me." The words sounded like they left his lips shaking. As if he was unsure. But he'd been absolutely positive. He repeated himself to seem stronger. "I want you to stay with me."

"Leo is generous to put us up for a few months, but I don't think he wants permanent house guests," Jay replied, though his face said that he knew Tom's true meaning.

It's kind to offer a way to retreat gracefully, but I don't want to take it back.

Jay's arms had been at his sides. Tom decided he was being reckless enough, so what harm was there in seizing every chance? Who knew if *that* could be the tipping point? Jackie wasn't affectionate, but Tom could be. He didn't understand how Jackie was okay in leaving Jay, with not sitting close to him, holding his hand, or lightly touching his cheek.

"No." Tom stepped near to him and took Jay's hand. He held it in both of his and pressed it gently. "Not with anyone else. Just with me. Stay with me."

"I can't do that, Tom." Jay tried to pull his hand back.

"Please just listen before you say no."

"I don't need to listen. I'm immensely grateful for all you've done, but I can't stay with you. Nothing you say can convince me otherwise." He freed his hand and plunged it into the pocket of his sweatshirt with the other, giving a weak smile. "And you don't want to leave Leo. You're just nostalgic. He's good to you. He's the best one you've had."

"You're the best."

"You never *had* me to know that. I've never insinuated or alluded to feeling anything but friendship for you. Never."

"But I'd leave him." Tom ignored the last half of what Jay had said. "The only reason I'm staying with him is for you. I tolerate him because of what he can do for *you*. When it's over and he no longer serves a purpose, I'm done. I can barely stand him."

"That's an awful thing to say."

"I'm an awful person sometimes." He tried to remain poised. Jay couldn't be expected to acquiesce immediately. He'd anticipated having to coax him. Hence the list. The fucked-up and forgotten list. "But so are you. We know that about each other." Yes! That was a reason. "I know you better than anyone else, Jay. You could leave Jackie. Nothing is stopping you. However many years you've been together, no one will ever know you or understand you like I do. I was there. I grew up with you. I saw what you went through."

"Oh, yes? And you're going to say how you loved me before and after, right?"

This was true, but Tom knew confessing it would taint anything else he could say. Jay had always been appealing, and Tom had been fascinated with him even before he'd changed his name and started hormones.

It was a cliché, stereotypical scenario. Tom had moved into the neighborhood, and in the house next door lived the slender, beautiful girl with long dark hair and light-colored eyes. His parents had been thrilled—maybe this girl could knock the "gay thing" out of their otherwise exceptional son. Tom had fallen. And he'd never been able to pick himself back up. Not because of a girl, but because of Jay. Jay had always been Jay.

But he didn't want to explain what he meant and risk losing everything. There'd be plenty of time to tell him once he accepted.

"You don't love when you're a kid. You do stupid shit with your best friend. Like building a tree house, or riding bikes, or doorbell ditching your own house to get your fat fucking brother off the couch. Remember that?" Tom returned Jay's grin. "See? You can't have that with anyone else but me. And you wouldn't want to."

"I wouldn't?" Jay's smile waned.

"No, you wouldn't." Tom kept speaking eagerly. "I know you care for Jackie. How couldn't you? But she'll find someone else. So will Leo. They'll be okay. You don't want to go back to Pennsylvania. You want to stay here with me."

"You're *very* wrong about that. I'll never move back here. There are things I miss, but—"

"We'll go wherever you want. I'll go with you anywhere. Or, you said I travel to 'exciting places.' I'll take you with me." He envisioned being where he'd already been, but with Jay. Places Tom knew Jay would love. He'd take Jay to see an Italian opera in a real Italian opera house. He hadn't performed in Italy yet, so it'd be a new adventure they could share.

"I'm not moving again or traveling. You can't uproot kids to hop all over the globe. I'm staying put."

That's right, I can't forget them. They're important—the crux of the entire thing.

"You're right. We'll stay. Wherever you like. I don't need to travel." He nodded.

"Yes, you do."

"I can get a stable, stationary job. I can become part of an orchestra again, or teach piano. I'll give up everything willingly, happily to be with you, Jay. To have a family with you." Tom gathered his courage and brushed Jay's face with the back of his two fingertips. "There's no reason why they can't have two fathers."

"No." Jay shook his head.

"This isn't the dark ages anymore. You can be a normal man. Tell them we used a surrogate mother. Tell them it had nothing to do with me. I don't care. We can say whatever you want."

"I said no."

"I've done immature stuff in the past." Tom began to grasp at straws. "But I'm ready to settle down. I could be a good father. A really good father. I'd be a better second father to them than Jackie would be a mother, and you know that."

"You're going too far, Tom." Jay's face darkened, but Tom took this to mean he'd hit the mark. Thank God.

"It's not too far when it's the truth. She's hardly capable of being a mother. Always making snide comments and cutting remarks at other people's expense. *I* don't do that. And she hates it here. She hates opera and piano. She hates your mother. She hates your brother. She hates me. And she'll hate those kids, Jay."

Tom could see him becoming upset; but the angrier Jay was at Jackie, the easier it'd be for him to leave her. And the sooner he'd do it. He should do it tomorrow. That's when she was scheduled to return and haunt them. Tom would have to hang on to Leo for a while longer, but he could tolerate being called "Tommy" for a few more weeks if he left with Jay afterward. So he prolonged the rant.

"Jackie won't hold them and kiss them and cuddle them like you will. Like I will. They're *my* children, Jay. *Our* children. Why would you want her to have any part of them? She'll scar them like your parents scarred you. She doesn't want them. She—"

"Neither do you!" Jay shouted. "You only say you want them because you think that'll make me change my mind!"

Tom felt daunted. Perhaps he'd pushed a bit much. "I won't deny that *you* are the most important to me, but that's how it's supposed to be. Kids leave, Jay. They grow up and start their own lives. You can't invest every piece of your soul in them." He touched Jay's arm. "That's what I'm here for. Someday, our children will leave us, and we'll only have each other."

When Jay had previously retracted his hand or moved his head to knock Tom away, it felt like he did it from discomfort. But yanking his arm back and retreating a couple of steps, he exuded more than uneasiness. He'd been furious.

"No, they'll leave *me*. They're not *ours*. They're mine. *Mine*," Jay said it savagely. "You agreed to that. And I don't care if no one wants them like I do. I'd give them enough of everything on my own if I had to! Fortunately, I'm not alone. I have my wife. And she's not a fucking Molly Mormon. She won't fall apart over every scratch or spoon-feed their egos. She's going to tell them they're being jackasses when they're being jackasses, and to shut up when they need to shut the fuck up! That's what children need!" He dropped his voice. "They need sincerity. That's love."

Tom didn't know how to respond. All his carefully constructed plans had broken apart as Jay yelled at him and defended Jackie's insensitivity. But he had stopped shouting. He'd lowered his voice. And were his last sentiments a hint of what Jay wanted to hear? What he *needed* to hear?

I'm not a romantic. I didn't want to tell you in a fucking hot air balloon at sunset or some shit. But I didn't picture it in a cemetery with you standing three feet away from me. Yet he proceeded. Nothing else had turned out as he planned it; however, that didn't mean things couldn't right themselves.

"Jay, I do love you. Sincerely. Genuinely. I love you." Tom took a deep breath. "Again, please stay with me."

And he waited for a response while Jay studied him.

I don't expect you to run into my arms or let me hold you. You don't have to say it back. Think about it. I'll give you all the time you need. I'll wait. I'll be patient, Tom pleaded in his head. He wondered if he should say these things aloud, but he had no voice. *Just please don't say 'no' right now. Please, Jay.*

When Jay's hands emerged from his pocket, he could've cried for joy.

"I'm sorry, Tom. I am..." Jay seemed to be struggling for words. "I am thankful for your help, but I can't be more than your friend. I love my wife. And I won't leave her."

Tom debated protesting. Demanding the simple, reasonable, and polite courtesy of him *considering*. At least *thinking* it over. For a few days. One day. A fucking hour. He knew the logic was there. If Jay would remove his loyalty to Jackie and decide based on common sense and reason, he'd come to the obvious conclusion that they were meant to be together.

But Tom felt his lungs were constricting, and he couldn't get enough oxygen. The landscape was spinning. The headstones bubbled like buoys on the ocean. He had no control over his speech. And to make matters worse—

A car horn honked repeatedly, startling them.

"I knew I'd find you morbid motherfuckers here!" Leo cranked down the window, and the horn blared three more times as the car pulled alongside the curb. "Surprised? I finished early today, so I decided, 'What the hell? I'm coming home to see my baby.'"

Tom said absolutely nothing.

"Get." Leo beeped the horn. "Your." He beeped it again. "Fine." Beep. "Ass." Beep. "In." Beep. "The." Beep. "Carrrrrr!" As he prolonged the last word, he placed the palm of his hand on the car horn and let it drone. "Get in the car, Tommy."

Goddamn it, he hated being called that. Leo honked the car horn yet again.

"Will you shut the fuck up?" Tom recovered his voice and pulled open the backseat door.

"Who am I going to wake?" Leo's hand hung out the window, and he struck the side of the car as he hooted. "I'm hilarious. Hilarious! How do you boys get along without me?"

"You'd be amazed how well I manage," Tom mumbled as he slumped into the back. Jay had already gotten into the backseat and was buckled on the other side, but Tom couldn't look at him. He still felt the dizziness in his head and tightness of his chest as two dark brown eyes leered at him from the rearview mirror.

"What're you doing back there?" Leo tilted the mirror to the left. "This isn't a *Driving Miss Daisy* episode. Get in the front."

"*Driving Miss Daisy* was a movie. Not a television show."

"I don't give a shit what it was. Get your ass in the front."

To pacify him, Tom climbed into the front seat, where Leo pulled him close. He closed his eyes and tried to pretend that the arm was Jay's. That the lips on his temple were Jay's. That the voice was Jay's.

"I missed you, Tommy."

Even if Jay decided to call him that, he would've forgiven it. He'd tolerate it. He would learn to love it, if it were Jay saying it to him.

But it hadn't been Jay. It was never going to be him. Calling him anything but "Tom" and thinking of him as nothing but a friend. A friend to whom he was indebted, but just a friend.

For the next few days, there'd been strangeness between the two of them that took Jay farther away. He assumed from Jackie's increased hostility that the incident had been divulged to her, and he contemplated inventing a version to tell Leo. A story that would really get him bent out of shape. That would make him insist that childhood friend, or no, Jay and Jackie weren't walking away with those kids.

"Now don't get all upset, Tommy, and don't tell your fucking friends. I'm only guarding your interests," Leo had said several weeks previously. "I drafted that contract myself, and it mentions one child. So if they try any funny business, or if you have second thoughts, babe, we'll play that loophole for all it's worth. Until you give up your rights for *two* children, they only get one. And by God, if you want them both, give me the go-ahead to play all the below-the-belt tricks I know, and you'll have them."

Tom was so upset that the option took on a definite appeal. Jay had always wanted to be a father. It would destroy him to have those long-sought-after children taken, not to mention the damage from the tactics Leo would use to get them. Tom assumed his methods would involve dragging Jay's name and situation through the mud—getting him declared an unfit parent based on being transgendered.

Jay wouldn't let the children go without a fight, but Tom knew he and Leo would eventually win.

It'll just be a waiting game. Time and money are nothing when one's attorney is being retained by ardent affection alone. Leo will draw legal proceedings on and on. He'll bleed them dry until they concede. They'd lose everything and Jay will be forced to give up his precious children because of something as dirty as money.

It also would kill Jay to relinquish one. And keeping one child sounded like it would be legally simple. Above-the-belt but equally cruel.

Not that I'm sure what I'd do with a child. I'd stop traveling for Jay, but only for him. If he's not part of the agreement, staying in one place for only a child isn't worth it.

At the time though, hurting Jay had been justification enough. He'd plan what to do with a child after he exacted his revenge.

And he could choose either one. Leo hadn't stipulated a specific child in the contract since they hadn't known there were two at the time. Oh,

Jay had been *so* excited about that. Yes, keeping only one child was the best plan.

When Tom hurt the worst, he spent time trying to decide which he'd pick—the boy or the girl. He should ask Jay. Simply inquire who he anticipated more.

A sweet baby girl, who you'll put in cute dresses and give your entire world to—Daddy's little girl? Or that charming boy, who would admire you and be your helper, your shadow?

Who did Jay want more? *That's* who he'd insist on keeping for himself.

It's probably the boy. You'll see yourself in him. You'll love him so much you'll ruin him. He'd be better with me. That's it. That's what I want. If I can't have you, I want the boy.

Tom continued to debate telling Leo, but as he'd resolved to unleash the firestorm, Jay had disturbed him at the piano four days after he'd placed his heart out to be crushed.

Tom had been bashing Prokofiev's "Sonata No. 7" with such fury that he'd stood, knocking the bench backward. He kept playing, and had it not been a quality piano, he might've smashed it to bits. When he heard the door open, he tensed with his back to the door and stopped the chaotic music.

Call me "Tommy." Do it. I'll whip the fucking bench into your head. I can't take anymore when there's no purpose for enduring you.

"Tom."

Thank God. Not that I want to see you, but I didn't want to kill Leo today. I need to call the Germans. See if they're willing to reschedule as soon as possible.

"Yes?" He faced Jay. It was difficult to not collapse. To not beg. To not threaten as he knew he could.

And threats could be effective. You want to be a father more than anything? That's your dream? The culmination of everything you've ever wanted? Then you stay with me. Or they stay with me. I get all of you, or just the children. I'll rip them from your arms if you won't stay with me, Jay. That would do it. You'll hate me at first, but you'll stay. And if you don't love me now, you'll learn to.

But when he met Jay's eyes, his temper dissolved. For the time being.

"What is it?" Tom withheld the tears. Those eyes drove back the strong desire for retribution, but they magnified the pain.

"I wanted you to be the first to know."

"To know what?"

That you're leaving now instead of waiting? That Jackie has convinced you I can't be trusted, so you'll never speak to me again? I can be trusted. I didn't attack you, did I? I told you my feelings, and you brutally shot me down, but how is that my fault?

"I don't know what I'll call the girl yet. But I want to name the boy after you," Jay said. "Not because of what happened a few days ago, and not despite it either. But you're my best friend. You've given me a wonderful gift, and I hope he'll be as good a man as his namesake." He paused. "I'm going to call him Luke."

And Tom knew he couldn't tell Leo. He could never do anything that would hurt Jay, or jeopardize his family, no matter how agonizing it was to be excluded from it. Though he'd agreed to their arrangement under the assumption that he could persuade Jay to stay with him, that supposition had been his own doing. There was no one to blame for the heartache but himself. As attempts to win him over would risk Jay's happiness, he had to forget how deeply he cared for him. And even if it was tolerated by Jay and Jackie, he couldn't get close to those children. They weren't his. Even if the boy carried his middle name.

☆☆☆

"Tom."

He jumped when he felt a hand on his shoulder, and his fingers left the piano keys as he turned to the right. Luke sat on the bench beside him. And the eyes he shared with Jay were clouded in concern.

"People are always disrupting me when I'm playing." Tom tried to smile.

"You've been playing for a long time. I've been trying to talk to you, but you weren't responding. I've been sitting here for ten minutes, and you didn't notice." Luke patted his shoulder. "Do you know who I am?"

"Yes, I know who you are. You're the fucking kid who keeps pestering me." Tom shrugged him away. "I'm sorry about last night, okay? When I don't take the meds, I get sick. I'm dying. It's not fun."

"Why didn't you take the meds?"

"I'm a grown man, and I decide for myself what I do or do not want to take."

Luke looked into his lap before turning his gaze back to Tom. "I think I should stay for a few days. To make sure you're okay."

"You think so, huh?" Tom laughed.

"What would've happened last night if I hadn't been there?"

"I can say with absolute certainty I would be dead right now." He made the statement with such a straight face that the boy seemed flabbergasted, which amused him.

"And?"

"And I wouldn't be in any more pain." Tom was starting to feel it again. At the same place, right in his lower back. It throbbed. The signal to take the meds. "Are you waiting for me to thank you for keeping me in pain?"

"I didn't think you wanted to die. No one *wants* to die."

"Believe me, when your entire torso feels like it's going through a food processor, you do."

But Tom had been feeling congenial toward Luke since discovering him asleep on the bedroom floor. And as painful and dark as the memories were, coming off them left a residue of compassion. Luke looked so much like Jay. Hadn't Jay been around this age when that unpleasantness happened? Yes.

Tom pressed Luke's arm. "Thank you. Not for saving my life. But for your kindness. *That* I can thank you for. Your dad would be proud of you. You're a good boy."

He was taken aback when Luke pulled away. And also perhaps a little hurt, but that may've been because Jay had done the same twenty-seven years earlier.

"I'm not a boy. I'm a man." Luke stood. "And I'm staying until I'm sure you'll be all right."

Tom scratched his chin and considered this resolution. Putting aside the pain and emotional distress Luke had already caused, and the potential for more, his motives remained questionable. And most important, Tom still didn't want to continue the farce of living any longer. He was ready to die. Well, not ready. He would've loved to have the next half of his life, but circumstances being what they were, he felt ready to die.

I was ready last night, Goddamn it. Until you showed up.

Of course, Luke could be of use to him in this area. If he was to commit suicide while he was there, his body wouldn't go a week before being found. That'd be nice. Considerate to the funeral director, the landlord, his neighbors, and his hardwood floors. Sure, that could work.

"Fine. But three things—" Tom raised each of his fingers in turn. "—first, this is *not* your home. However sick I may be, you will not try to boss me around or take control of anything. You will respect what I ask of you. Second, while I may be willing to answer questions about your dad, I, personally, am off limits. Don't ask about me. And the last is most important, so fucking pay attention."

He lowered all three fingers and took Luke's wrist.

"You will not, I repeat, *will not* call me or refer to me as anything, *anything* but 'Tom.' I won't give you more chances on that one. I have no son. If you imply otherwise, even in jest, even once, I will murder you in your sleep." Tom let go of him. "And I encourage you to take that threat literally. I only have six months to live, and whether I spend it here or in prison is irrelevant to me. Agreed?"

Luke nodded although he seemed nervous around the edges.

"Good." Tom turned to his piano and waved Luke away. "Then make yourself useful, and get me my pills that you spilled all over the floor. And bring me the sonogram."

"Can I get you anything else?"

"Go Betty Crocker some shit. I don't care what you do." He closed his eyes and put his fingers on the keyboard. He heard the boy leaving and was about to sweep into his other world again when he was once more interrupted.

"Tom."

"What?"

"You won't call me 'boy' either." Luke took a breath. "And I encourage *you* to take a death threat from *me* seriously. You have only six months to live, and if I murdered you in your sleep, I could probably get away with it."

He opened his eyes and saw Luke's reflection in the window. He stood in the doorframe and smiled. So Tom smiled back as he started to play his piano again.

"It's nice to have our homicidal tendencies in the open. Now go make me a fucking sandwich. And don't forget my picture."

Chapter Sixteen

Williamsport, Pennsylvania
March 2038

Ginger lay on the roof of the white van, looking at the stars. He'd parked in the cemetery, next to the turned earth that covered Jay's grave. The dead flowers had been removed weeks ago, so now it was only a bare, ugly spot with a rust-colored temporary name stake.

I haven't fucking ordered the headstone yet. Damn it.

He hoped the grass would grow over soon, not that it'd help anything other than making the place more aesthetically pleasing. More uniform, like every other grave.

Faster and faster every day, Jay was becoming like all the others. Not only the decomp, but eventually, the grave wouldn't be new. It wouldn't be fresh in anyone's mind, and a person would stroll through the cemetery without paying it a second glimpse. Jay would be reduced to a name engraved on a stone, and everything about him would be forgotten. Including how important he'd been to a young man who'd had nothing before meeting him. And the small, white container buried with him? That had already been forgotten. Less than a name on a stone, the box was nothing but Ginger's private secret.

His mind cycled through these and more morbid things. He could get himself really worked up if he gave in. But he wasn't currently dwelling on his dead father-in-law, his dead child, or death.

Ginger considered how he could lie undisturbed on top of the van for the rest of his life. He could bake in the sun until hawks picked the skin from his cheeks. No one cared if he fell and broke his neck. If he was upset, there was no one to whom it mattered. There wouldn't be anyone prodding him with a broom. Beau was gone.

The last time Ginger had seen her had been over a month ago. She had turned her back to him after throwing a suitcase of his clothes on the sidewalk outside the funeral home. He'd tried to talk to her, but she'd refused to grant him a single word. She just drove away. He'd been waiting since then to be served with divorce papers.

"Did she say she was going to divorce you?" Jackie had asked him that morning.

Beau had forbidden Ginger to "go crawling" to her mother, but that ban had been abolished. By his mother-in-law.

For the first couple of days, he'd stayed at the funeral home until Jackie had shown up and told him he was to move in to her house. He could have the spare room. No, Beau hadn't forgiven him, but it was *her* house, not Beau's. And yes, Jackie herself still wasn't happy with him, but life was too short for this shit. Jay wouldn't want him sleeping on the couch in the funeral home. Moreover, if Luke should call, Jackie was sure, based on the events, he'd call Ginger. She wanted to keep him close, so if and when that call came, she could speak to her son. Also, his slacks were wrinkled and needed ironing badly. This was a business, not a homeless shelter.

"Well? Did she say she was going to divorce you?" His mother-in-law repeated, which had become a regular occurrence.

Sometimes a tunnel vision overtook Ginger; everything around grew dark, and all he could see was a pinpoint of light in the distance. It could've been the depression. Or maybe he was sick. He hadn't been sleeping well or eating much—his clothes hung on him, and he shivered a lot.

"No. She didn't specifically say that."

"I wouldn't worry about what hasn't happened."

"Did she tell you she'd divorce me?" Ginger had glanced up from his mug.

"She's as furious with me for letting you stay here as she is with you for giving Luke that information. She doesn't tell me anything, Ging."

But that wasn't true. Beau told Jackie things. The new sonogram hanging on the refrigerator was proof. It'd been physically painful when he'd walked into the kitchen to make Jackie's morning coffee and saw it there.

Ginger's heart had fallen. He'd kept himself going on the basis of that appointment. She couldn't go through this pregnancy without him, so she'd have to forgive him by the appointment. Even if she stayed furious, and it took them weeks, months, years to rebuild their relationship, Beau would have to include him in this. It was the big one. They were going to find out the sex.

She must've canceled. She couldn't go through with it alone, but she's still too mad at me. That's okay. She needs more time. She'll reschedule and call me.

Then he saw it, held to the refrigerator by two ceramic magnets. Ginger had ripped it from the door, the magnets shattering on the kitchen tiles. He stared at it. It no longer resembled a jelly bean. He could see its head and the silhouette of its nose and lips. Its arms and legs. It looked like a person.

Ginger felt a sudden weakness in his legs, and he dropped into a chair at the table. He buried his face in his arms. Would he ever hold this child? Alive or dead? Or was Beau planning to drag him through a miserable divorce and cut him out? If she did permit him to be part of the child's life, what about her? Would he ever hold his wife again? Touch her hair? Kiss her temples and tell her how he adored her? Or would their only communication be snarky comments made through their lawyers?

God, isn't it enough that you took Dad? Why did you start this shit with Luke? Why did you take my home from me? And my wife and child? When will it fucking be enough?

But he knew the only thing he could blame God for was Jay. Everything else had been spurned by his own actions. And if given the option to go back before he'd given Luke the information to contact Tom DuBelle?

I'd do it again. I know I would. He'd struggled to restrain the tears. *I'd have always ended up in the same position.*

Jackie had found him heartbroken over the sonogram picture at her kitchen table that morning. He'd felt her hand on his back and heard the chair next to him pull out.

"I wasn't going to hang it. But you should know it's healthy."

"It?" Ginger felt a painful lump in his throat. "Didn't you find out what it is?"

"I don't know," Jackie said.

"You didn't?"

"She did. She just didn't tell me."

Ginger searched her face for deception. He didn't care if it destroyed the only relationship he had left; he'd force it from her if she knew. But she revealed nothing.

"If I knew, Ginger, even if she'd made me promise not to tell you, I would. That's possibly why she didn't."

He trusted her. Although she hadn't officially said it, he believed his mother-in-law had forgiven him. He knew she'd tell him. She did whatever she deemed right, whoever it might offend.

Jackie had made things easier, but he was still miserable. He missed Jay. He missed his wife. Occasionally, he missed Luke. The boy could be a douche bag, but he wasn't awful to have around. He pitched in at the funeral home when needed. He sang well and played the piano; in a house that could've been filled with death and sadness, he was comic relief. And he made Beau happy.

Beau had seethed during the initial days following Luke's disappearance, adamant that she didn't care if she ever saw or heard from him again, but when her fury cooled, worry set in. For her and Jackie.

Where was he? Why hadn't he called? Was he dead in a gutter somewhere? Beau had contacted the roommate he'd been living with in New York—the man hadn't seen or heard from Luke since he left to go home.

Jackie scoured the Internet, trying to locate a number to reach Tom DuBelle. She didn't want to call him, but she would. Unfortunately, she hadn't unearthed a trace, and for the life of her, Jackie couldn't remember any of Tom's associates to find *them* and form a link to Tom. She couldn't recall the name of his companion either—just that he had a big house.

"I hated Tom," Jackie had thrown up her hands after another unsuccessful search. "I still hate him. I purposefully tried to forget that man existed."

Ginger had stayed silent. It'd be risky to reveal that once again, he'd interfered. He felt he'd done the right thing and acted how Jay would've wanted, but he couldn't be sure how Beau and Jackie would view it. It wasn't fair that Jay had been there for he and Beau to pose questions to. Neither his mother-in-law nor his wife seemed inclined to provide Luke with answers, and he knew it wasn't only due to the boy's asinine behavior.

They don't know the answers. The realization had come to Ginger as he'd climbed the stairs at Jackie's command to ensure Luke took only his belongings and that he left the house in ten minutes. *You didn't like to talk about yourself, Dad. So aside from what they may have asked, they don't know. And if Luke has questions, there's only one person who can answer them.*

He'd stopped at the top of the staircase, knowing he was playing with fire.

Is that what you want? Give me a sign, Dad. Please.

Ginger expected to hear the voice that didn't sound like Jay but felt like him. The voice that sparked into his mind the night before Jay's funeral and told him he did not want to be saved. This was an important situation, and the voice would tell him what to do.

But the voice hadn't come. He'd watched Luke pack and tried to convey some comforting words, hoping his kindness would prompt the voice to make its desires known. There'd been only silence, and he'd run out of time. He'd made his own decision.

Luke had descended the staircase with the business card in hand. Still Ginger waited. Perhaps a feeling would validate if he'd done the right thing since it was over. If it was positive, great. He'd know Jay's wishes had been honored. If it was dark, he could tackle the boy and take back the card. But he'd felt nothing and had been left with only his own conviction.

Ginger had been terrified to tell Beau and Jackie that Luke was probably safe with Tom. Even if Jackie hated Tom, from Ginger's short but sympathetic conversation with the man, he hadn't sounded like the sort of person who'd turn Luke away. And they hadn't heard from Luke in two weeks. If he were dead in a gutter, someone would've noticed by now. Luke was likely holed up with Tom, being a dick and refusing to call. Or he might be in New York with the roommate, who could've lied.

Dad, I should've kept your phone instead of throwing it away. I could've called Tom myself and checked to make sure the boy was safe.

When he'd finally broken the secrecy, it was due to Beau. Ginger had woken to find her gone. She hadn't answered her phone. He'd driven to her parents' house, but she hadn't been there, so he'd sped to the funeral home, not knowing where else to search.

Her car had been outside, and he'd found her frantically rummaging through paperwork on the floor in the storage room. For a second, he'd scanned the shelf of white boxes—a hole was still present from the recent withdrawal. But her desperation had been about Luke.

"He said Tom knew about the baby. Dad must've kept in regular contact with him." Beau had pulled away from Ginger. She'd wiped her hand under her nose and tears had run down her cheeks as she'd frantically sorted a bank box of documents. "There's got to be some type of contact information here. I'll take anything!" She'd stopped and brought her hands to her face. "I'll snail mail that motherfucker! I need to know my brother is okay!"

That moment had been the last time he'd held his wife. He remembered how she felt in his arms—she'd shivered and clung to him, her fingers digging into his shirt. He could smell her hair as he dipped his head to kiss her brow, to whisper to her that it'd be okay. It was okay. Probably.

"You don't know that." Beau's words had stumbled out. "He could be anywhere. He could be dead. I know I was a bitch, but I didn't want him to leave forever. I didn't mean that. You don't know that he's okay."

"Not for certain. But I'm relatively sure."

And Ginger had then told her what he'd done. Immediately, she'd shoved him away.

"You did what? You did what!" Unshed tears hung in her eyes, and her mouth had been partially open. "You said you had no contact information for Tom DuBelle!"

"I didn't. Dad gave me his number on the business card, and I called him on Dad's phone, not mine. We threw his phone away, and I didn't have the business card when you asked me. I told you, 'I no longer have it.' I didn't. I don't."

"You didn't have it because you gave it to Luke! I told you to forget anything else you promised Dad about Tom DuBelle!" Beau had pointed her finger at him.

"Your dad didn't ask me to give Luke the information. I did that."

Ginger had kicked himself as soon as it left his lips. He should've blamed it on Jay and fallen back on his unquestionable fidelity to her father. By declaring the choice had nothing to do with Jay's wishes, and it was only *his* interpretation of what *he* imagined Jay would want—

"You had no right to do that! None!" Beau had gotten to her feet, her face red.

"But, sweetheart I—"

"Don't 'sweetheart' me! I'm not your sweetheart, Jacob! I am so fucking pissed at you!"

Ginger had felt a sense of relief. This was the same conversation they'd had at Jay's viewing when she'd learned he'd called Tom. She used his full first name. She'd been furious. She threatened to break his arm if he touched her. But he'd explained himself and been forgiven. So it would be okay.

"Let me explain, Beau." He stood as well.

"I've heard your explanation! You took matters into your own hands and made a judgment call that wasn't yours to make!"

"I think it's what Dad would've wanted. I—"

"You think so? You think he'd have wanted his son to fly cross-country into the waiting arms of a pretender? Of someone he never wanted us to know existed?" Beau's fists had been shaking. "He didn't want Luke to know anything!"

"But why?"

"You think you know him, you fucking tell me! Go ahead! Tell me!"

Ginger had nothing to say. He didn't know why Luke had been excluded. Jackie said the knowledge had been shared on a need to know basis, but she'd been assuming Jay hadn't told Beau. Had it been his immaturity? Had he judged that Luke couldn't handle it? Maybe he'd intended to but hadn't had the chance?

"That's right! You have no idea! I know you *think* you knew him, but he was *not* your father! He was mine! And he told *me* before anyone else! I'm the one most fit to make any decision as to what he'd have wanted!"

Having it spat in his face that Jay wasn't his father had hurt. However, her words had made him question which part of the situation offended her. She'd been saying things straight from Luke's self-absorbed playbook.

"Are you just upset you didn't get to call the shots?"

"It's completely inappropriate that you made that choice. How dare you! Without consulting me! Or my mom!"

"I thought I was doing the right thing." Ginger hadn't sounded as strong as he would've liked. But in the face of her rage, it'd been difficult to be confident.

"Oh, that's right!" Beau slapped her leg and gave an exaggerated look. "I forgot the mind meld between you and my dad. How could I forget that *you* know better than I would. *You* know better than my mom would. *You* know how he'd want *everything*."

"It wasn't my intention to—"

"Is it possible that, in all your *great* wisdom, you don't know what they say about intentions? It doesn't matter what you intended!"

Beau had turned her back after she'd finished shouting.

Yes, this is exactly how it happened before. She gets fired up, calms down, and we talk it through. She's also forgetting the main thing.

"But, Beau, you know Luke is probably safe. That's what's important, right?"

She turned around.

"*Probably* safe. *Probably*. For all your saving the day, the bottom line remains that we still don't know where he is, or if he's safe. But I'll tell you what I *do* know, Jacob." Beau clenched her jaw, and the tears returned. "You did *not* do the right thing. If you'd left it alone, Luke would never have found Tom DuBelle. He might've tried, but he'd have failed. He may have returned to New York, but eventually he would've come home and settled things with us. But if he is safe, because of you...because of you..."

She'd pointed at him again. "He's with that *other* man! You took Dad's only son away from him!" Beau had lowered her voice and narrowed her eyes at him. "You *betrayed* my father. And wherever he is, he'll *never* forgive you. And I'll *never* forgive you. I can't stand to be in the same fucking room with you."

She left before Ginger could stop her.

No, you could have. You could've run after her, wrapped your arms around her, and held her. You could have knelt at her feet, burying your face in her skirt, and begged for forgiveness. Openly declared yourself a poor excuse for a human being and you were wrong, even if you don't think so. You should've lied. Lied, and lied again. And held her. And never let her go.

But the next time Ginger had talked to her had also been the last time, when he'd parked outside their house, and she'd been waiting on the porch, a small suitcase at her feet.

"I want you to leave."

"Leave?"

"Oh, you can listen now? Yes, leave." Beau had kicked the suitcase down the steps.

"But—"

"I don't care to hear it. Just go. And don't go crawling to my mother. I've already told her what you did, and I wouldn't get within a mile of her if I were you."

"When can I come home?" Ginger picked up the suitcase.

"I'm shocked anything makes you think you would be coming back."

"But the baby?"

"You've done your part, haven't you?" She'd sneered at him.

Ginger had stared at her in disbelief. He loved her. Consummately. She was the mother of his child. How could this happen?

"What am I supposed to do?" He'd managed to stammer.

"I don't know." Beau had put her pointer finger to her cheek. "Let's see, what would my father do, Jacob? Why don't you psychically connect with him and ask? Not that you need to. You're so good at intuiting what he'd want."

She'd walked into their house and slammed the door.

☆☆☆

Lying on the roof of the van a month later, Ginger stared at the sky, and the stars became fuzzy although the sun had only just set. He wasn't sure anything or anyone could fix things between him and Beau. Jackie couldn't. Not that he knew if she'd tried, but he assumed she had. The baby couldn't fix things either. Beau wasn't intimidated at the prospect of raising it alone. And *he* couldn't fix things since she wouldn't talk to him. His calls had been unanswered, his voicemails unreturned. And the latch stayed fast whenever he'd gone to the house.

His thoughts went to Jay as they often did. His body was a yard away. Beneath hundreds of pounds of dirt, inside a concrete vault, and locked in the casket. What was left of him was so close. Rotting and coming apart but still close.

She'd listen to you. You'd tell her to give me a chance, and she would. You always fixed everything.

But now Ginger had no one. He was alone and waiting for a process server to hand him divorce papers.

He won't find me here. I can pretend I'm in my driveway, and any minute there'll be broom bristles in my face.

Ginger folded his left arm under his head. Yes, he'd dream that none of this awful—

The cell phone rang.

Ugh...

He shoved his hand into his pocket. Death found him wherever he was at whatever hour. It didn't respect his personal devastation. Beau having asked him to leave didn't stop people from dying.

Ginger put the phone to his ear. He didn't check if it was Beau anymore. It never was or would be again. He adopted the soothing voice that comforted the bereaved and answered. An automated recording gave the business name, and he only had to say his name.

"Good evening, this is Jake."

"Ging, it's Luke."

He pulled the phone away. Yes, it was Luke's number. They'd given up calling weeks ago; it always went to voicemail.

"Luke, where are you? Are you okay?"

Ginger clambered down the van's ladder. He remembered Jackie's prediction that if a call happened, it'd come in on Ginger's phone only. He had to keep Luke on the line until he could get to the house so Jackie could speak with him.

"I'm fine. I'm with Tom," Luke said. "How's Mom? How's Beau?"

He shook his head to keep back an emotion-choked voice and started the car. "Really worried about you. They've been calling every day. Several times a day. Didn't you get the calls?"

"I've had my phone off."

Fucking typical. You shut your phone off to play head games with two people who love you and have been beside themselves with worry. You're a self-centered douche bag.

"How are you?" Luke asked.

"I'm fine."

"I've been worried about you."

Ginger became suspicious. It was already odd that Luke would ask after his mother and sister. But to ask after *his* welfare and express concern over him? Without sarcasm? And hadn't he called him "Ging"? It'd been years since Luke had referred to him as anything but "Jake." What did he want?

"Why would you be worried about me?"

"Without Dad as a buffer, you have to handle their insanity solo. And one is pregnant to boot." Luke laughed. "I've been thinking of you being my whipping boy and imagining they've torn the flesh from your bones by now."

Ginger had to smile. However, he wouldn't be turned against his mother-in-law or his wife, even as part of a lighthearted joke.

"We've been worried about *you*." He pulled into his in-laws' driveway and cut the engine.

"I'm sorry. I've been busy."

"Too busy to make a quick call to Beau? To send her a text message to let her know you're safe?"

It was risky to criticize, as the boy never took feedback well. Luke could disconnect and never call back. But Ginger didn't know what else to say. He just had to get the phone to Jackie. He unlocked the front door and prayed for a glimmer of light anywhere.

There wasn't one.

"I know. I should've called." Luke hesitated. "I was afraid."

"Afraid?" He started up the staircase. It was also unusual for Luke to take accountability for any mistake or admit weakness. To anyone.

"Yes. That no one would answer."

Ginger stopped outside Jackie's bedroom. He spoke lightly so it wouldn't be taken as a reprimand. "Every time either of them picked up the phone, they were afraid of the same thing. And every time, no one answered. But they kept trying."

He heard Luke take a deep breath.

"I've let my fear and insecurity prevent me from doing a lot of things, Ging. And it's bad..." Luke's voice cracked. "And it's *especially* bad because what I do or don't do has an impact—"

The doorknob flew from Ginger's hand. Jackie stood in her nightgown and held her hand out for the phone. He placed it in her palm before he could hear what else Luke had to say.

His mother-in-law left the door open and walked to the chair by the nightstand.

Ginger remained in the hall and waited for her to scream at Luke. To demand to know where he was. Possibly to order him to come home directly, or to never come home at all. To lambast Tom DuBelle. To call Luke every name in the book. To ask why he'd left. Why had he said those terrible things? Why did he go to Tom? And why, for the love of God, why hadn't he called? Why hadn't he had the common fucking decency to pick up the phone and tell them he was safe? He was busy? He was afraid? Jackie wouldn't buy it. She was about to wipe the floor with him. She'd rip him to shreds.

But Jackie didn't try to talk. Ginger watched as she sunk into the chair, the phone to her ear, and her hand to her face. And she began to cry.

After only a few more seconds, Ginger went to the kitchen. While Jackie hadn't asked him to leave, it felt like eavesdropping, and whenever his mother-in-law finished, she'd appreciate coffee.

He listened to the machine pop as it heated the water. He was glad Luke was safe. Wouldn't Beau rather have him with Tom than dead? Would he come home? Ginger was now certain Luke would be welcomed back.

And if he did return, what did that mean for Ginger? And the relationship with Beau? If Luke hadn't changed and replaced Jay, alleviating Beau's fear, would she forgive him?

No, she'll say it's lucky that Luke is the same, but it doesn't excuse my actions.

He leaned back in a kitchen chair. She was too angry for it to be simple. He considered the sonogram hanging behind him on the refrigerator. For the kind of animosity fueling that type of cruelty, Luke returning unaffected after spending a month with Tom DuBelle wouldn't cut it.

And Ginger had a gut feeling that Luke being unchanged was too much to hope for. He sounded different. To ask how Ginger was? To be worried about him? True, both could be things the manipulative fuck was just saying, but to admit he'd been wrong? To hear a rebuke and not blow a gasket?

What are you asking Mom for? What do you want?

And he hated to bring it back to himself, but whatever damage Tom DuBelle had caused in a month, Ginger would be blamed for. Should he start packing his suitcase?

If he'd just thrown that fucking business card away instead of calling Tom in the first place. It wouldn't have brought Jay back, but every other crisis would've been avoided. And after he messed up once, to do it again? To pass Luke directly into Tom's hands for corruption? What had he been thinking?

But that's not fair. Really, there's no way to be sure that not calling Tom would've had better results. If Dad just dropped off the face of the earth, Tom may have come looking for him. So the way it played out was a somewhat controlled explosion. It could've been much worse. I'll tell Beau that if she ever speaks to me again. And above all, I was doing what Dad asked of me. I never let that man down. Ever.

And giving the contact information to Luke?

That was also the right thing to do. There's a reason Dad gave me Tom DuBelle's number. Mom or Beau wouldn't have called. He trusted me to do what I decided was necessary. I did have the authority to make that judgment call and do what I believed was best.

Jay had trusted him with Tom's information like other people trusted Jay with their dead. And he remembered how important this responsibility was to Jay. It wasn't a job; it was a calling. He didn't mark caskets and vaults up two and four hundred percent. He didn't coerce people into unnecessary things they couldn't afford. Money didn't matter, and as long as he could support his family, Jay was satisfied.

I didn't pay a dime for what he did for my grandmother. Nothing.

Not that Ginger had anything to give, but how many would've turned him away? Or if they hadn't, wouldn't have cared since there wasn't anything in it for them? They'd have insisted on cremation since it was cheaper. If they did agree to embalm, they would've whizzed through—potentially botching it with the speed or by using too much pressure. Stuffing her quickly, like she was a turkey instead of a person.

But Ginger had seen Jay care for his grandmother's body and treat her with dignity. With love—although he'd never known her. Jay had invited him to watch. And as frightening as the idea was, an eighteen-year-old Ginger put his faith in the stranger.

☆

He remembered following the gurney into the embalming room. Jay had unzipped the black bag, and Ginger helped lift the rigid body onto the table. His grandmother had been wearing her favorite dress, the one with orange flowers and lace at the sleeves and collar. Now it was ripped and stained with blood. Her chest had also been covered in the blood, and there were dark purple bruises on her skin. But it hadn't been as horrifying as he expected. It was evidence that the doctors had tried.

"You don't mind, do you?" Jay hit a few keys on a computer at the side of the room. Classical music filled the air, and Jay was at his side again, a hand on his shoulder. "I don't like to work in silence."

"I don't mind," Ginger replied.

"Have you ever seen a dead body?"

"No, sir."

"They aren't always beautiful, but listening to beautiful music helps."

Ginger hadn't cared what Jay listened to. There was still a dead body. There was still his grandmother, with her torn and gory clothing, her eyelids and mouth partially open. Music hadn't changed that.

Jay had removed his suit coat and folded his sleeve cuffs before he'd filled a shallow bowl with water and a clean-smelling liquid. He watched as Jay took a dampened cloth and delicately ran it over his grandmother's skin. He swept it over her face, shutting her eyes and turning her head so her mouth closed.

"In the Jewish community, there's a special group of people who care for the dead." He dipped his cloth back into the bowl and moved it down the old woman's arm. "The *chevra kadisha*. And the task they do is regarded as very admirable because the receiver is unable to return it. They call it a *chesed-shel-emet*—it's a good deed of truth."

"Are you Jewish?" Ginger asked.

"No. But I think about that sometimes. Giving with complete transparency and no motivation other than respect and love," Jay had said. "If people didn't worry as much about their personal payoff, or what others wanted them to do, if they tried to do more good deeds of truth, things would be better. Don't you think?"

"Yes, sir."

"Please, Jay is fine." He'd smiled and set down the clean hand. He then walked around the table and offered the cloth to Ginger. "Go ahead. It's not why you do it, but you'll feel better. I promise."

Notwithstanding his apprehension, Ginger had taken the cloth. He'd dipped it in the water and wrung it out, as Jay had done. Tentatively at first, he'd touched it to his grandmother's cold right arm. And he decided, as he washed the cloth over her skin, that Jay was correct. He'd felt better in performing an action with no motive save for showing love and honor.

☆

Ginger had felt the same way with each body he'd cared for, including Jay's. He'd remembered this conversation when Jay had been on the table. He had been filling the same bowl with the same antiseptic. And the same opera music had been playing from the speakers in the corner.

He was still anxious for Jackie to finish her conversation with Luke and come downstairs, but this memory gave him strength.

It's all trust. All good deeds of truth. That's what I was doing when I gave Luke that business card. It was the right thing. Dad wouldn't fault me, and I shouldn't blame myself either.

When he heard a door open and close somewhere in the house, he went to the cupboard to retrieve Jackie's mug. But on turning around, it wasn't his mother-in-law in the doorway.

Beau. Ginger dropped the mug, and it broke into dozens of fragments.

The crash brought her attention directly to him.

"Beau." The word had to twist its way through a jagged metal-edged maze. Seeing her was a mix of emotions. Awful pain, but also joy. Ginger wanted to wrap her in his arms. They ached to hold her close.

He took only two steps before she scowled and left the room.

"Damn it, Mom." Beau whipped around, and he noticed the phone to her ear. "You're always in the kitchen swilling your poison. Where are you?"

No! No! No!

Ginger wouldn't let this happen. He'd do what he should've done initially in the storage room.

He pushed over the table chairs and ran after her. She was climbing the stairs to Jackie's room, and he caught her arm as she stepped onto the landing.

"Beau, talk to me, please." He took her wrist with his other hand. It felt thinner. Had she not been eating?

"Get off me." She tried to pull her arm away.

Ginger refused. He examined her face. Her eyes looked tired. Her hair was longer. And she was starting to show. How could she have changed this much in a month?

"No. Talk to me. Mom can wait."

"I'm talking to Mom *and* Luke. Now let me go."

"I can't. You have to talk to me." It was dramatic, but Ginger fell to his knees and cradled her hand to his cheek. "Please, don't go."

She held the cell phone to her shoulder to mute the microphone and looked down on him with impatience.

But it's not hatred. It's not disgust. I can handle impatience.

"I need to finish this conversation, Jacob. If you wait up until I'm done, I'll talk to you. But you need to let me go right now, or it's no deal."

He released her instantly, and Beau stalked into her mother's room, snapping the door shut behind her.

Ginger decided it'd be safest to stay approximately where he was. He sat on the top step, leaned his back to the railing, and put his feet to the wall, creating a barrier. It was uncomfortable, with his knees bent and only half his body on the step, but Beau wouldn't be able to pass. The only way she could leave the house without taking the staircase would be to jump from the window. And she didn't hate him that much. At least he hoped she didn't.

Hours later, Ginger woke with his cheek on the landing, and his legs stretched over three steps. Someone could've picked out footholds in the four steps he was sprawled across to sneak away. Someone small and nimble like Beau.

Oh God, she's escaped! My one shot and I blew it! He sat up and nearly fell backward.

"Ging, calm down."

Contrary to any likelihood, there she was. Crouched on the landing with her hand on his shoulder. Waking him gently, and not using his full name.

"The agreement was that you'd wait up. This is twice that you should be glad I don't keep all my promises."

"What promises?"

"I said that if you had any further involvement with Tom DuBelle, I'd kill you. Or I *strongly* implied that I'd kill you. And you're still alive." Beau took her hand from his shoulder, and he noticed she was still wearing her wedding ring. That was a good sign.

"Barely."

"Luke is safe, but he won't be coming home for a while."

"Why not?"

"He's dying." Beau shook her head as his eyes widened. "No, not Luke. Tom. But save the shock. Luke is staying with him until he goes. He's taking care of him."

"That boy can't handle himself. How can he take care of a terminally ill person?" It was ridiculous. At the first sign of anything too difficult or that clashed with what Luke wanted to do, he'd be out the door.

"I know. But apparently he's been doing it for the past month. He goes with Tom to the doctor, makes sure he takes his medication, and keeps him company."

"How sick is he? To have traveled here a month ago and suddenly need full-time care?"

"Pancreatic cancer. He had six months to live when he was here. And he doesn't need a caregiver yet, but he will. Luke wants to be that person."

"Why?" Ginger wanted to slap his hands in front of his mouth. He thought about throwing himself down the stairs. Here it came. Beau's fear spoken aloud to become truth—Luke now regarded Tom as his real father. Ginger didn't have to launch himself down the stairs. She would shove him.

"He believes it's what Dad would want him to do." She curled onto her knees. "Apparently, you and Luke are able to determine with one hundred percent accuracy what Dad would've wanted."

"He made mistakes, but he was a good man. And it's not hard to imagine what a good man would do in any given situation; it's just not easy to carry it out." Ginger eyed her hand, flat on the landing. "He has no other reason?"

"No, and I believe him. He truthfully wants to be there for this person who meant so much to Dad." Beau leaned on her right hand and placed her left to her stomach. "They've apparently kept in regular contact for years. Dad's viewing wasn't the first time Tom has been here. That man saw me graduate high school. He was at our wedding. He saw Luke perform. He has our pictures on his piano."

Ginger wasn't sure how to read her. She seemed neither upset nor happy.

"How do you feel about that?"

"I don't know. When Luke told me Tom has been essentially stalking us for years, I was furious. I mean, Dad was here through everything. Not just the fun, 'proud of your kid' times. What right did Tom have to invade special, happy moments?" Beau spoke in an even voice, and Ginger marveled at how incensed she must've been to now be so tired. "Where was he when I was seven years old and still wetting the bed? It wasn't Tom washing the sheets and consoling me. Or when I had my first crush and heartache? Where was Tom DuBelle when I lost our baby?"

A bolt of electricity blasted through Ginger's brain.

That's why you were angry and wanted to pretend he hadn't existed. Why you were so cruel. You blame yourself. And is that what's spawned the coldness to linger? You haven't been the same—Beau was looking at him, so he filed away the insight and nodded.

She checked behind her shoulder. "At one point, Mom excused herself to the bathroom. And Luke said to me, 'Tom loved Dad very much.'"

"What does that mean?"

"I guess it means that he didn't want to stay away, but he felt he had to."

"Did Dad love him back?"

"Not the way he loved Mom. But he still deeply cared for this man."
Beau said. "And Luke intends to take care of him until he dies."

"I'm sorry, but that doesn't sound like Luke. It's too..." Ginger
couldn't think of any words that wouldn't make the boy seem like a dick.

"*Chesed-shel-emet*?"

She smiled at him. God, he loved this woman. She'd split him apart,
but he loved her. Ginger put his hand over hers.

"I asked Luke right off, 'What do you think of Tom DuBelle?'" Beau
didn't pull away, but Ginger bristled, waiting for the answer. "And he
said, 'He's not Dad, but he's a good man.'"

"Is that okay with you?"

"I think I can handle that. There was only one Dad, and no one can
take his place. But there can be many good men." She withdrew her hand
and patted his cheek. "You're a good man, Ging. You did what you
thought was best, and with no selfish motivation. That makes it the right
thing. Do you know who told me that?"

He shook his head, feeling he couldn't speak. He just wanted to be
still—the relief was starting to sink in.

"Luke. He said he wouldn't be able to care for Tom if Dad hadn't
taught him that being a good man is doing these good deeds of truth. He
was adamant that's what you'd done, so I shouldn't blame you for it. And
he's right."

Ginger could've cried, but he felt he'd been strained to his limits. He
only hung on her words, the emotion combusting and filling his chest.

"I treated you like Luke treated us. Only I don't have a noble excuse
for not talking to you for a month, or for any of my actions lately. I can't
give a reason, but I'm sorry."

"It's all forgiven." He took her hand from his cheek and brought it to
his lips. "Absolutely forgiven."

"There's another thing as well. I know what you did."

Ginger felt his face drain of color. But she was pushing her fingers
through his hair, so whatever he'd done now couldn't be that horrible.

"Baby, I may not have gone to mortuary school, but I grew up in my
father's funeral home. I've seen hundreds, possibly thousands of bodies
in caskets. And people put all kinds of things in there with them. Letters,
books, beer cans... It's an insult to my experience that you thought you
could hide something in Dad's casket without me noticing." Her hand

moved to his temple. "When you order the headstone, I want you to put the name you gave him on there too. And I'm sorry I—"

Ginger scrunched higher on the step and wrapped his arms around her. He put his face to Beau's shoulder and summoned the strength to cry one last time.

Chapter Seventeen

Williamsport, Pennsylvania
October 2038

His family waited at his parents' house to welcome him home, but Luke decided to make a detour. They'd disapprove, chiefly Beau, who was anxious for him to meet his new nephew. And Jackie would give him an earful, but the reproofs no longer seemed like scolding a child. She didn't talk to him with the affection Jay had, but her criticisms now came with an underlying layer of respect. When his mother said "You're being a stupid jackass, Luke," he felt she meant "You're being a stupid jackass, Luke," *right now.* He could be a stupid jackass. But he wasn't *always* a stupid jackass. No one laughed at him anymore. And no one referred to him as a boy.

He wanted to visit his father's grave before anyone could volunteer to go with him or "happen" to show up.

When he pulled the car aside on the gravel road, Luke cut the engine and sat motionless. He didn't know that there was anything specific he wanted to say to Jay. He felt he'd made peace with his father. That had been part of what he'd been doing the past eight months. Yet there he was, parked in the cemetery.

"I want to be alone for a minute," he said aloud. "I'll be back."

Luke got out of the car and walked to Jay's grave. The grass still wasn't fully grown in, but the headstone was there, which made the spot seem more official. It was a blue pearl granite upright, and the concrete base was wide enough to accommodate three permanent planters. Beau had placed a red geranium in the space on the right and a white geranium in the middle. Jay hadn't necessarily liked geraniums, and his first nephew hadn't lived long enough to like anything, but the flowers were a nice touch.

He'd been astounded to learn how Ginger had lied about putting the child's ashes with their aunt's body, and instead, hid them until he snuck the white box into Jay's casket.

Eight months ago, I would've loved to exploit that. To goad Beau into wondering what else he was lying about and keeping from her.

But he no longer saw Ginger as a looming threat and vulture who'd stolen his family.

Perhaps they'd been invisible to each other—five strangers passing routinely in the street. He saw them every day; he recognized them, but he hadn't *noticed* much about them.

Six months ago, the invisible theory struck him as he'd flipped through a photo album in Tom DuBelle's Salt Lake City condo. He'd glanced through pictures of himself with his parents, with Beau, with other relatives, and he'd wondered.

How did I not notice that Beau was moving on without me? She was growing up, and I was still a boy? How did I not realize that the digs Mom makes and her tough exterior is a front for her own insecurity? And Ginger never tried to take my place. He went out of his way to make sure he didn't infringe upon me.

Photo after photo showed Luke next to Jay, never Ginger. He always stepped away to let Luke be with his father, though Luke knew he'd craved Jay's attention.

Was that the first time you had your picture taken with Dad and without me? Luke had been looking at one of Beau and Ginger's wedding photos.

The bride and groom in the middle, with Jackie and Jay framing them. Previously, this pose would've been offensive. While the album was one of many filled with pictures of Luke and his father, he'd have honed in on this "evidence" of his exclusion.

And I would've been welcome in that picture too. At the time, he'd been fighting with the person running the stage during the reception. The man had been insisting Luke didn't need the spotlight on him while he sang during the couple's first dance. This was unthinkable, insulting, appalling, and absurd.

Luke felt a flush creep over his cheeks. *I guess my unreasonableness had its occasional advantages. That was a nice picture.*

He moved through several more sections until he came to a page that contained photographs from the opening night of his last performance. There was one backstage with the five of them.

Our last picture as a family. Luke traced his finger across a photo of him and Beau, of him and his parents, him and Jackie, and last, just him and Jay. *And this was my last picture with you...of you.*

There were no others of Jay before his death. The last visual record of him was a photograph with his arm around his son. His father's hand was on his shoulder, his body slightly turned, pushing him forward. And from Jay's expression it was perfectly, abundantly evident—

How did I miss that you really were proud of me?

"Ohhhh Gawwwwd, here come the water works."

Luke glanced up from the album. Tom had been sorting through documents at his dining room table for the past several minutes, but now he slipped the pen he'd been using behind his ear and grinned.

"You have your sister send that book to try to get *me* upset, and it's you who bawls all over it."

"I didn't have her send it to get you upset. I thought you might like to see more pictures."

"I did. Thank you." Tom waited for an explanation to account for the two tears.

"How could I live with someone, be around someone..." Luke fumbled. "How could I live for twenty-six years—"

"You're twenty-seven. Your birthday was two days ago."

Luke had forgotten. Was that why his mother and sister had called him? He'd been busy that day. Tom had had a doctor's appointment, and he never felt well after those.

"I was going to mention it," Tom said. He was good at knowing what Luke was thinking. "I tried to hint to you. But I figured you didn't want to think about it. Maybe you were starting to have a midlife crisis. You're one year closer to death."

"You're morbid."

"I'm allowed to be. But it suits me better if you just forgot. If *you* were having a midlife crisis, do you have any idea what that'd say about *me*?"

Tom volleyed between being preoccupied with his impending death and pretending he'd live another fifty years. Luke didn't know why he did this, and it often put him in the difficult position of how to best respond. He'd never tried to understand a person so much. Painstakingly uncovering someone's current mood and thought process with no benefit to himself was new. And then, whatever Tom was feeling, to adjust his own emotions—to go with it, whether he felt like it or not. Luke wasn't used to this. But it wasn't about him. It was about making Tom comfortable.

They smiled at each other.

"You'd still be wrong if you'd said twenty-seven though. You spent the last year in New York. Technically, you should call it twenty-five years. But I suppose the exact number isn't the main idea. I'm able to grasp the concept of 'long time.' Go on."

"How do you spend so long with someone but not know them?"

"Are we having this talk again?" Tom put his chin in his hand. "I don't know how many more ways to explain that you did know him."

"It's not that." Luke stared down at his palms. "How did I ignore... How did I not know that he was proud of me?"

"You really want me to answer that question?"

"I wouldn't ask if I didn't want an answer."

"Luke, you had your head so far up your own ass it's a miracle you could see to walk." Tom stretched his arms behind his head. "That's the good thing about being proud of someone. It's *nice* if the other person knows, but it's not *necessary*. Your acknowledgment of his pride in you was unimportant. He still felt that way."

Tom knew an awful lot about this. And as much as his sentiments were applicable to Jay, Luke knew he was also referring to himself. Though he'd made it clear that he was unwilling to share details of his life, Tom unintentionally disclosed quite a bit.

It hadn't been much at first, but the information leaked out in the context and under the guise of Jay. Luke had to treat what Tom said as if he were looking at it through a pair of 3-D glasses. He had to close one eye to see Jay in blue and the other to see Tom in red. Because Tom made statements that moved with the truth of both together.

"It's time for your meds." Luke had checked his watch and put the album aside.

"It's nice to pass on pearls of wisdom and have them cherished. I'm telling you, one of these mornings you're going to wake up and there'll be a line of people out the door, waiting for me to impart my knowledge."

"I thought you weren't a yogi on a Himalayan mountaintop?" Luke stopped and threw Tom a grin over his shoulder.

"I'm not. Yet. But you might want to start building me a temple instead of wailing over picture books. I need somewhere to receive my disciples."

"An altar for goat sacrifices in your honor?"

"Don't be an idiot, Luke." Tom had said to his back. "There aren't any fucking goats around here. I'm perfectly amenable to accepting chickens and small rodents."

The memory made Luke smile as he stood beside his father's grave. Beau struggled with how Luke could hold Jay so strongly as his real father but at the same time forge a deep bond with Tom. He'd tried to explain, but while his reasons satisfied her worries that he'd replaced their father, she still hadn't wanted a relationship with Tom. But that'd been okay.

She doesn't understand. You were the reason for everything. If it hadn't been for you, I couldn't have stayed with Tom. And if it hadn't been for Tom, I never would have known you, he decided as he looked at Jay's headstone.

Though it played a part, he wasn't exclusively referring to his father's "dark" secret. Luke felt better knowing more about Jay's past. From Tom's retelling of Jay's experiences, he'd been able to piece together why his father had done certain things. Why he acted like he had. Why he'd been able to tell Beau the truth, but it'd been so difficult to consider telling Luke.

Since I knew you were keeping a secret, all I focused on was myself. What was wrong with me that you excluded me? That you didn't trust me like you trusted everyone else? But it had nothing to do with me. It was always you.

Like most of Luke's inspirations, this one hadn't occurred with convenient immediacy. It'd taken him a while to ask Tom again why his father hadn't told him about being transgendered. He'd been scared of the answer. But when he had assembled the courage to ask, he not only understood, but the truth hadn't made him feel inferior or less loved. And that level of perception wouldn't have been possible without the foundation built with Tom.

For the first few days after Tom had given permission for Luke to stay temporarily, he'd been driven to get information. Besides Tom being the only willing resource to tell him about his father's history, the feeling that he should stay remained.

Luke noticed right away that Tom liked to talk about two things—playing the piano and Jay. He'd been cautious regarding the piano, since it verged on breaking Tom's rule about discussing himself. But when it came to Jay, there'd been no limit. Tom loved to talk about Jay. And Luke calculated that if he could keep Tom talking, he'd continue to be interested in having Luke around.

So before he became certain that Tom wouldn't retract his offer, Luke prompted him constantly to tell him anything he could think of about his father. It hadn't mattered if the stories seemed insignificant. Luke wanted to know it all. And one of the first things he'd asked was to see the real high school yearbook.

☆☆☆

"Yeah, I don't think so."

"Why not?"

"What do you need to see pictures for?" Tom had moved the fall over the piano keyboard and turned. "Jay destroyed any pictures so you couldn't see them if you did discover it. And he wouldn't have shown your sister pictures. He didn't have any."

Tom told him when Meecie died, Jay had taken the photo albums she kept locked in her trunk—and he'd burned them.

"I was on the phone with him when he did it. His mother's body wasn't even cold, and he was in the backyard squirting lighter fluid on those pictures. He didn't want you to see how he used to look."

"I don't think that's true."

"What makes you say that, smart ass? He *forged* his yearbook so you wouldn't discover it," Tom said. "He paid someone to edit out the other picture. And he *retook* his senior photo. Down to the last detail. He was twenty-five in that picture, if not *older*."

"But that's exactly why. Because he didn't redo it to the last detail."

Luke hadn't revealed to anyone the full story of how he'd established that the yearbook was false. He told Tom about the class ring and the cryptic message Jay had given when Luke was a boy. In Jay's perfectly woven tapestry, one small thread had been left exposed to be pulled and used to disentangle his past.

"I just think he expected if I did pick up on it, he'd still be here to tell me."

Luke didn't know if Tom agreed, but he'd conceded that Jay was a meticulous person. And he *had* gone to great lengths in recreating that yearbook photo. He wouldn't have included a detail like wearing a ring he hadn't owned in 2005 if he hadn't meant to.

Tom left to get the real yearbook.

"And is that true? The date?" Luke called after him. He'd removed Jay's class ring to show Tom the engraved date under the band, and he now spun it on the dining room table.

"Is that a true date? I believe that yes, there was a twenty-four-hour time period given the distinction 'February 18th, 2007.'" Tom's voice answered from the hallway.

"No, is that the day he purchased the ring? Or is there other significance?"

Tom reappeared, carrying not one book, but three.

"That's very good." He set the books on the table and took a seat beside Luke. "I don't know when he bought the ring, but February 18th, 2007 was the day Jay started hormone replacement therapy. He took his first shot that day. I was there. He was terrified of needles, and I offered to do it for him, but he refused. He wanted to take that step himself."

Luke nodded for Tom to go on.

"Besides being scared of the needle itself, beginning hormones was the point of no return. Starting testosterone is a permanent choice. He could've recanted at any time until then—changed his name back, reclaimed the damaged relationships. But he pushed aside the fear, the 'doubts and demons.'" Tom smiled. "He rolled up his sleeve, and he did it. On his own. He never wanted to forget that feeling. It was one of the most pivotal, important moments of his life. I'd have been surprised if he recorded any other date inside that ring."

Tom took the familiar plaid 2005 yearbook from the stack.

"Most people associate hormones with emotional teenagers and Viagra. You'll appreciate what naturally flows through your veins when you see what power it has." He pushed the book to Luke. "See if you can find him."

Instead of feeling excitement and anticipation, either for getting his way or to see the real pictures, Luke felt nervous. He'd been on the verge of meeting a different side of the man who'd raised him. The side of the man who hadn't been raised as a man himself and had spent approximately eighteen years with everyone seeing him as a girl.

First Luke flipped to the index and ran his finger along the list of last names beginning with "K."

"Your dad changed his first, middle, and last names. You won't find anything in the index."

This had been news to Luke. Jay had had a different last name from Meecie, but Luke assumed Jay had kept his father's last name after his mother remarried.

"Why would he change his last name? That has nothing to do with gender."

"His dad was a dick and wanted nothing to do with him."

"Dad said our grandfather went to war when Dad was in high school and never came back. He said he was a hero."

Tom laughed. "And lightning didn't strike him when he told you that? What a fucking lie. You want to know where your grandfather went when your dad was in high school? He went to Thailand and married another woman. He left your grandmother after she lost her job and couldn't support him anymore."

And Tom told him how the "happy" family of four—Meecie, "the dick," and their two children—went to church one Sunday morning. Jay's father made sure all their good Mormon friends and neighbors saw this perfect quartet. But he left halfway through the service. And when they'd come home, he was gone.

"That was another important part of your dad's life, Luke. He knew he was a young man trapped inside the wrong body. And he'd been about to tell them because he needed help," Tom said.

"But when that motherfucker abandoned them, he knew his mother wouldn't be able to bear it. As a result, he embraced the mask to preserve what remained of his family. He tried to love it and be the pretty, popular girl his mother wanted. But that's in these." He patted the other two books. "What you have in front of you is *after* he decided that everyone, including his mother, could go fuck themselves and their expectations."

So Jay changed everything. Not just his appearance and his name, but he'd reinvented the identity of anyone who didn't fit with the life he wanted.

"'You can't repeat the past' my ass," Luke said.

"Ah, but you're forgetting the close: 'boats against the current, borne back *ceaselessly* into the past.'" Tom motioned to the book Luke had closed as he'd been talking. "Go ahead."

It'd been with a moderate amount of unease that Luke flipped to the section of 2005 senior photos and scanned the face of every girl in a red dowdy gown for a glimmer of his father. Not that he doubted Tom, but he scanned the page containing the "K" names with extra scrutiny. But on the fourth page in, on the second row, in Jay's place in the forged book was another boy.

He searched for several minutes until he reached the end. And there'd been no familiar face.

"He'd be very pleased by that." Tom passed him another plaid bound volume. "You'll have more luck with this, and I'll give you a hint this time—turn to the first page of the junior section."

Luke had been unsure. He saw that, as in the 2005 book, the photos of every class except for seniors were in black-and-white. They were also significantly smaller. Though it hadn't yielded anything in the other book, his strategy was hunting for his father's light-colored eyes in every face. How would he recognize those in a gray-toned thumbnail? But he followed Tom's advice and flipped to the first page of juniors. Immediately he drew back his hand in shock.

"Oh, my God," Luke said, and Tom laughed again.

It was Beau. Or virtually Beau. Her eyes, her heart-shaped face. The long, dark hair that fell over her shoulders as she gave a saucy smile to the camera. She was sitting on the grass, her knees pulled to her chest and her arms hanging loosely over them. She wore a navy blue and red letterman sweater. And in another picture in the middle of the page, she was with four other teenagers in the same sweater. She looked like the rest of them. But this wasn't any other teenage girl—this was his father.

The caption showed a different name with no similarity to "Jay." A name in a crazy font next to the individual picture. A name in small crisp type under the group picture. A name on the felt patch sewn to the girl's letterman sweater.

"I told you. Jay didn't do any extracurriculars his senior year. But when he was trying to forget about who he really was..." Tom leaned away, hooking an arm over the back of his chair. "Your dad could teach you a lot about putting on a good show. See for yourself before I blow your mind."

Luke turned to the index to find his father's original name. There were a dozen page numbers indicating a photo. Jay had been involved in things Luke hadn't known he had an interest in. Not that his participation in an activity was a sign of interest. He hadn't been interested in staying with that identity. Yet there he was. In every picture, he seemed to be enjoying himself. He'd been a beautiful, popular teenage girl, the kind that other girls envied. And he did seem happy.

"That's how good of a mask it was. He was miserable. Believe me. Or rather, let me prove it to you." Tom took the book and opened the back cover. A sheet of stiff cardstock attached to the cover created a pocket.

Tom reached into it but waited to withdraw its contents. He looked at Luke.

"You love to have the spotlight on you, singing and dancing and everyone cheering. But what if you could never leave the stage? What if you were forced to stay there? To keep performing. To keep playing a character? However much the people praised and admired you, I guarantee eventually that spotlight would burn you alive."

Luke nodded as if he understood.

"This is the pièce de résistance. This was the night. *This was the moment*, if you like. He'd finally decided that it was enough. He launched himself off that stage without knowing where he'd land, or caring if anyone would catch him."

Tom removed two photographs and placed them side by side in front of Luke.

Both pictures had the same girl, but they were different from the yearbook photos. Appearance-wise, she'd been completely done up. Her dark hair was curled and styled—partially pinned with a glittering barrette. Her skin and makeup were perfect. She wore a long, pink formal dress that flared out at the sides from the tulle underneath. A necklace rested on the ivory triangle of her chest; there were diamonds in her ears, and a corsage on her wrist, but...

This is a boy in a dress.

There was so much discomfort in the rigid posture, in the face, especially in the eyes. The girl throughout the yearbook was so similar to Beau that he could've pretended it was her. But in this picture, if he only considered the pained, wretched expression of the eyes, this was his father. That was the look Jay had during the fight, and when Luke refused to forgive him before he walked across the parking lot to his death. It was the look of being trapped and not knowing what to do.

"Remember how proud he was of you at your final performance?" Tom asked. "That's how proud his mother was of him on that day. She didn't force him to do any of this, even if her instability made him feel otherwise. But this was the end for him. When Jay saw himself this way, he knew he couldn't take anymore."

"*You* don't look unhappy."

"I wasn't."

In the second picture, Tom held Jay's hand and beamed. He didn't resemble a carefree teenager. On the contrary, he looked like he had many cares, but they were all under his control. Whatever he may have been juggling was in perfect balance. And as Tom's hallucination came to him, Luke wondered if maybe all the cares weren't in the palm of his hand. Perhaps everything Tom valued was standing next to him in that picture.

"Tom, did you love my father?" Luke asked.

It took Tom a few moments to respond, but when he had, his answer had been as revealing as the length of time it took him to construct it. "Irrelevant, and in violation of rule number two. Next question, please."

Luke never directly asked Tom again. He hadn't felt he needed to. He knew the answer, not from the stories Tom told, but from the way he told them. This man had a profound and unreciprocated love for Jay. Both before his transition and after. *That* had been irrelevant to him.

But only for Tom had Jay's transformation been immaterial. When Jay had turned eighteen and been able to start fixing his situation, all his other relationships changed.

"Your grandfather had moved back to the States with his new wife, but he wanted nothing to do with Jay. He refused to accept him."

Tom told Luke about this a few weeks after the yearbooks. They'd been on his balcony late one evening. He repeatedly reminded Luke that it wasn't necessary to stay up with him when he couldn't sleep, but Luke still had. He'd been freezing, since it was always cold at two in the morning, but Tom had been fine with only his sweater.

"That's why he changed his full name, not just the first two. That fucker was unwilling to accept Jay as his son? Your dad was fine with it," Tom said. "Well, not *fine*. But he decided that his father wasn't worth much grief."

"Did he have a reason for picking 'Jay'?" Luke had drawn his legs up on the patio chair and wrapped his arms around his knees.

"I'd think that would be obvious. Shortly after prom, your dad was assigned to read a book in English class. About the self-created man." Tom gave Luke a shrewd look that said he shouldn't need to say more.

His parents were voracious readers, and there were many books in their library. But three rows on one shelf were dedicated to seventy-five motley copies of the same title. Luke had never questioned or wondered if there was any significance to this collection. After all, a beer company had the same name as one of his uncles, and the man decorated his house with their merchandise.

"In a lot of ways, he felt he was a self-created man. Everything he knew about how to be a man, how to be a father, how to be a decent human being, he'd read in a book. As far as he was concerned, he'd never had a father. The best thing that sperm donor ever did for Jay was to have a horrible, agonizing death."

Luke stared at Tom in confusion. For a man in the midst of a "horrible, agonizing death," he had little empathy. Death was death. Everyone had to surrender, so they were all equal in it, asshole and saint alike.

Luke had learned this from Jay, who took the utmost care with whoever happened to be on his embalming table. And even though he hadn't wanted to do it himself, Luke admired Jay's ability to not only see past the blood, or manner of death, but he could go beyond the person if he needed to. Everyone deserved decency and kindness.

The suicide in the garage was the most disgusting thing. But the one I remember most and that encapsulated him was also a suicide.

He remembered how the young man shot up with heroin, locked himself in a bathroom, and blew his head off. It'd only been because Ginger was in Pittsburgh taking his final exams that Luke accompanied Jay on the pickup.

He'd seen plenty of gore, though the scrambled-egg-man had been yet to come. A part of the man's skull had been on the bathroom counter. His blood coated the walls and floor. Bits of his brain dangled from the ceiling like dust caught in a cobweb.

Luke had been thankful to leave that horror room, but as they wheeled the stretcher out, the dead man's wife blocked their path. She had a baby on her shoulder, and her eyes were crusty from crying. She motioned to the massacre.

"What am I supposed to do with it?"

"I'm sorry, ma'am. We only take care of the body," Jay had said.

Thank you, God.

"Please." She sniffled. "I can't clean my husband's brains from the walls. I can't! I'll pay you. Please."

"I apologize, but this is all we can do."

Not for a million dollars, lady. Not for a million fucking dollars.

And they'd left her there. They drove the body to the funeral home and slid the bag in the refrigeration unit. But Jay had stopped Luke on his way into the house. His father had handled the messy end, but he'd still felt disgusting and couldn't get the smell of hot metal and blood from his nose.

"Don't shower yet. But change your clothes."

"For what?"

"We're going back." Jay looked at him as if it'd been apparent.

"But you said we just take care of the body, that we can't do anymore," Luke had protested.

"And that's true. That's outside the services a funeral director will perform. That's why we're going back, not as professionals, but as human beings caring for one of our own who's suffered a devastating loss. Now change your clothes."

When they'd returned to the home, the woman had been sobbing on the bathroom floor with a bloody sponge in her hand as the baby wailed in a crib. They took over the grisly task while the widow comforted her child. Jay had refused to accept any kind of compensation.

That's how I ended up cleaning brain matter out of a ceiling corner with a toothbrush at the age of thirteen. And when I realized that even if I didn't want to be my father, I wanted people to think of me like how they thought of him—as a good man.

Back on the patio, Luke thought of Tom, perfectly comfortable in his chair. He couldn't imagine Jay would condone Tom's statement that the most valuable thing Jay's father had done for his son was to die in pain.

"What makes you say that?" Luke asked.

"Because it's true. That's the only reason you're here today, Luke. The death of his father was what enabled Jay to become a father himself."

Tom proceeded to answer a question Luke hadn't thought to ask. How had Jay financially been able to afford not only the expense of starting a family in this way, but to live in Utah, unemployed for a year?

It had been due to his grandfather's death at the hands of the nursing home and the large settlement from the neglect lawsuit.

"Bed sores," Tom said. "Stage IV when someone caught it, but it was too late. Sepsis and so forth."

"Wasn't Dad checking on him? Wasn't anyone checking on him? How could that have possibly happened?"

"He refused to see Jay. They hadn't seen each other in years. And why would anyone check on him? He was a miserable bastard who drove his wife away and treated people like shit his entire life. When you're a dickhead to everyone, can you expect people to give a rat's ass if *you're* a little uncomfortable?" Tom laced his fingers behind his head.

"Sepsis isn't 'a little uncomfortable.'"

"Call it 'suffering for the greater good.' The only positive thing Jay ever said to me about his father was that he finally came through by providing the means to get what he'd always wanted—you."

Something Tom had communicated often over the past eight months was that throughout his life, Jay had had a fervent desire to be a father.

☆☆☆

"He always wanted you," Tom lay in bed with his eyes closed.

It hadn't been a good day.

"When we were kids playing all kinds of shitty games, we didn't know there was such a thing as literally being born in the wrong body. We'd play house and he'd insist he was the dad. Even when he was corrected, he was adamant. Someone told him, 'You can still hold the baby if you're the mom.' But that wasn't good enough. That wasn't *it*."

Luke sat silently in a chair next to the bed, his hand touching his arm so Tom would know he was there.

"When he first moved to Pennsylvania, he worked part time at a toy store along with his other job. He loved it at first. He brought home carloads of toys and collected them in the attic with clothes and blankets he'd been stockpiling for years. It was all okay when there was still hope he and your mom would be able to afford it someday." Tom shifted in the bed and resumed talking.

"But it finally dawned on him that it was never going to happen. Your mom's siblings and everyone else our age started popping out the kids. Jay was so upset. He had to quit that job because he couldn't stand to be around children, to look at children. Every one of them was a slap in the face, a reminder. He became reclusive. There were days he couldn't leave the house."

"He couldn't just be happy for other people?" Luke asked.

"It's hard to be happy for people who take for granted what they have. He'd call me and sob over the phone. And when I say 'sob,' that's what I mean. It wasn't light, pitiful 'I wanted a pony for my birthday' weeping. It was like he'd already had you, but you'd died. Just this intense, inconsolable grief. People who let their children run naked and dirty in the street could have them. People who worked constantly and never spent a minute with them; *they* could have them. Mormon mothers who had children could have six fucking more. And he couldn't have one. Not one."

"Adoption? Fostering?"

"You had to have the green." Tom opened one eye. "There are those who feed their children cat food, who can't put clothes on their backs, and they keep reproducing—no application, no background check, not a motherfucking thing. That killed him. So be grateful your grandfather died half-rotten in a nursing home. If that hadn't happened, not being able to have you would've driven him mad. It might have literally killed him." He closed his eyes again. "Jay told me once that you were so real, he could hear you playing right outside the window. But when he went to find you, you were always gone."

Luke hadn't been able to visualize Jay not being in complete control. He'd been the voice of reason, of sanity. How else could he have been a funeral director? How else could he live surrounded by sadness on a daily basis? If he'd been so unstable, how did he continuously collect the pieces?

"*You* were his dream, his 'green light.'" Tom curled his middle and pointer fingers twice without raising his hands. "Once he had you, he'd accomplished everything he set out to do and had everything he ever wanted. That's the man you knew. And it shouldn't be the least bit confusing to you that if a person is deprived of their passion, of their purpose in life..." His voice rose. "Then there *is* no stability. And there might as well be no life either."

By this time, Luke had become skilled at shutting one eye to see Jay's blue and the other to see Tom's red. Yes, some of this last statement was Jay, but it was humming with Tom. And it struck him then that Tom might want to commit suicide. Because it was bad. Though Tom didn't complain, he also hadn't gotten out of bed that morning to play his piano.

"Tom." Luke placed two pills into his hand. He had an appointment the next day, and Luke would press the oncologist about new meds. Or stronger doses to control the pain and nausea so Tom could have his piano. Luke hadn't believed he could stand to either help Tom do it, or walk in on the deed having already been done. It wasn't the principle of suicide. It was the man. Tom wasn't his father, but by then Luke loved him and wasn't ready to lose him.

As things typically do before they get worse though, they became better. Even in the last months there'd been a sprinkling of good days.

Luke remembered waking one morning to the music.

He'd walked down the hallway as he had the first day, and Tom had been playing the piano. He was frailer, his complexion more pale and sickly, but it'd still been him. Luke didn't hover in the doorway, listening and thinking, as he had the first time. He wasn't the same person who'd walked through the door six months previously.

Luke sat on the bench next to him. Tom hadn't looked over, but an unhurried smile spread across his face. He began to play the song Luke had been singing when Tom had taken the photograph now framed on the piano.

"He did see himself in you," Tom said, his fingers gliding over the keys. "He told me, when he saw you on that stage performing this song, he saw himself: the times in his life that pushed him to take action, to do more, to be more, and then the moments when he carried those things out." He chuckled. "And I said to him that one of those instances was damn near exact what you, in the role, were doing."

Tom was referring to the hormone replacement therapy portion of Jay's transition. They'd talked about this several times because it had been so important to Jay. The majority of his identity as a transgender man had been sealed and forgotten—the name change finalized, every document updated and the old destroyed, new relationships built—but the testosterone had persisted. He could never forget his past as a result of the compulsory injections.

For twenty-five years, under his children's noses, Jay had taken his shot every ten days. Somewhere in the house he and his sister grew up in, there were syringes and vials. Twenty-five years—913 shots. Luke could've walked in on him at any time.

"He'd have told you he was diabetic," Tom said when Luke mentioned this possibility. "Would you have believed him?"

Luke hadn't had to think it over. The more time he spent with Tom, the easier it became to be real with himself.

"Yes, I would have."

"You'd have been *that* stupid?"

Luke also hadn't had to consider his response. "No. I just wouldn't have given a shit enough to question. The needle wasn't in my ass, so why would I have cared?"

And they both smiled. If that had been the truth then, it wasn't any longer.

So Luke had no questions about Tom's reference. He was satisfied to just be with him. Happy that Tom felt like playing anything. Sitting on the bench was an improvement over the last few days. There'd been a hospital visit, and another procedure to keep things stable and buy a little more time, only it was never—

"In a way, you were right and wrong." Tom lifted his fingers from the keyboard and turned to Luke. "He did want you to be him. To a certain extent, he was trying to recapture how he wished he could've been. If you'd known about him, about his past, you would've spoiled that and what success he had in sculpting the life he wanted. He wanted to be a father and to have a son who didn't struggle like he did. He wanted to be a parent like he never had. Telling you would compromise that. And that's why he didn't. It had nothing to do with you."

They regarded each other for several seconds before Tom broke the eye contact. And when the "Intermezzo" flowed from the body of the grand, Tom returned to a topic Luke increasingly felt was less important.

"I'll tell you about this other time, when your dad was seven—"

"Tom." Luke had placed his hand on Tom's arm. "I don't want to talk about Dad anymore. I want you to tell me about you."

"Rule—"

"Fuck the rule. Listen, I know why you made the rule. You don't want me to lose sight that *he is my father,* and not *you.* You're protecting him. I understand. Trust me, that's not an issue. But I still want to know you. I want to hear what you have to say about *you.*"

Tom tugged at the collar of his shirt with his left hand.

"A large part of everything about me has been your father."

"I know that. And I'm okay with it." Luke smiled. "I love my mom. She and my dad did love each other. But I can still love my parents and be sorry things didn't work out for you. I'm sorry he didn't feel the same way about you, Tom. I truly am."

Tom had never displayed any emotion. Not as he heard the increasingly grim news from the doctors, or as they kept doing test after test, futile procedure after procedure. Even when the occasional sentimental thing happened. Even when he knew it was over and held Luke's hand for the last time.

This moment had been the only time when Luke had seen Tom become upset. Tears streamed down his cheeks, and his body shook from pent-up angst. Later, after Tom confessed to trying to convince Jay to stay with him twenty-eight years ago, Luke realized he'd been the first, apart from Jay, to acknowledge Tom's feelings.

He wasn't sure if their story had ended the right way, or not. Tom genuinely loved Jay. Maybe it could've worked out. Luke and Beau could've been raised happily by two fathers. How would it have been with Tom instead of Jackie? To have Tom drive them to school, tuck them into bed at night, feel their foreheads and cheeks when they had fevers. Luke didn't believe Tom would've been a poor father. Jay could have still had his funeral home, and Tom might have settled down to teach music. Tom, rather than Meecie, could've taught him and Beau how to play the piano.

Luke pictured sitting next to Tom on the piano bench as a little boy and being shown more than form, more than mechanics...but art. When Tom played Liszt, when he played "Paganini Etude No. 5," his hands moved like butterflies. The left perched over the right, playing with his wrists crossed and picking up his left hand with periodic grand gestures. He would've instilled a passion for music in his children. Tom would have sat next to his son and shown him how to pour over the keyboard like rain. It could've been a good childhood.

But what'd happened hadn't been bad. He loved his mother. For all Jackie's biting comments, tough love, and occasionally cold behavior, she was part of what had shaped Luke into the man he was. Who would he have been without her? Tom had been wrong in what he'd said to Jay in the cemetery. Jackie did love him and Beau. It wasn't the same love as his father or as Tom might've given them. But when Jackie heard his voice on the phone after a month of silence and worry, she hadn't yelled. She hadn't criticized. She'd cried for minutes on end. Jackie loved her children.

It was still unfortunate for Tom. He'd stayed with a person he could scarcely tolerate, living to play the piano and talk to Jay frequently. To hear about the children and life, to reminisce over their youth. To just listen to the sound of his voice and pretend Jay wasn't two thousand miles away with a life Tom could never be part of. He'd refused to progress and had only himself to blame, but it was still unfortunate.

I'm here now though, Luke thought as he hugged Tom. *And I won't leave you. I'll be brave enough to stay.*

When Tom pulled away, he forced a laugh. "You're a lousy kid. A real fucking piece of shit."

"I know. But I'm not stupid." Luke tipped his head toward the keyboard. "Tell me about the best place you ever performed."

"Ha, is there a question that could open a bigger can of worms?" Tom started to play livelier than Luke had heard in a while. "Have you ever been to Spain? Jesus fucking Christ. The venues are fabulous, but the food? The steaks? A-fucking-mazing."

As much as Luke had learned about Jay, as close as he now felt to the man his father had been, his favorite moments over the past eight months had been in the last two. Tom had opened up to him, and while things had continued their downward progression, Luke believed Tom had been happy. And he hadn't worried about Tom killing himself.

Luke scuffed the cemetery grass with his shoe before he walked back to the car. He circled to the passenger side and took a mahogany box from the front seat. It had picture frames on all four sides, each one filled. As he returned to Jay's grave with the box in his hands, Luke's eyes filled with tears.

"That's great. Seriously. You can put it on your mantle and turn it every day, so no one will ever know who's in there. It'll drive people crazy," Tom had commented when Luke found the urn online. And when it came, Tom selected the four pictures.

He wanted one side to have the picture he'd taken at Luke's final performance. Another side was to be the portrait Beau and Ginger had sent of them and their baby. The third held a picture of Tom and Jay twenty-eight years ago, a hand on each other's shoulders and wide grins on their faces. And the final spot showed a photo of Tom with Luke.

The picture had been taken on the piano bench, with the other photographs in the background. Luke held the camera in front of them, and they both smiled though they knew why they were taking it.

"I look like shit, but you can keep that one to the back," Tom said.

"You don't look like shit."

"Don't waste lies on a dying man. Lying to me about how well I look isn't worth burning in hell."

"I don't believe in hell."

"You don't? Okay. Lie to me." Tom shrugged.

Luke had laughed as well. Originally. But he couldn't laugh now. He stood at his father's grave holding the urn and let the tears fall down his cheeks.

You did look so sick. And there was nothing I could do. You kept getting sicker and sicker. And I know you were trying, that you didn't want to die, and it's not your fault, but there was nothing I could do.

He remembered the last time Tom had been in the hospital. By then, only Luke played the piano. Tom rested on the couch and listened, an arrangement he'd taken to with unexpected ease.

"It's okay. A musician uses the same parts of their brain whether they're *actually* playing or *thinking* about playing. So I'll let you do the hard work."

"Okay, Tom."

"I don't mess up as often as you do though. You make a lot more mistakes."

"I know." Luke played only octaves when they talked. He couldn't carry on conversations while playing a nonstop soundtrack in his head like Tom. He needed concentration and sheet music.

"You should practice more. Practice makes perfect."

"Already been said, yogi. Already been said."

"That's *master* yogi to you. Now shut the fuck up and play more than scales."

The last time Tom had gone into the hospital had been because he lost consciousness. He'd been leaving the room when he blacked out. Although he came around, Luke insisted they go.

He drove Tom to the emergency room and completed the paperwork while Tom was being seen. Although he'd attended the doctor's appointments since arriving and had taken charge of tracking Tom's medication and keeping records of the various tests and procedures, he'd never done the paperwork. In listing an emergency contact, he knew to put himself. But in the "relationship" field, he hesitated.

If I don't and it comes down to the wire, what if they won't let me see him? He'd watched too many medical dramas where everyone except family was kicked out of the room. What if Tom couldn't speak for himself to voice wanting Luke there? He'd promised not to refer to him that way, but Luke had also sworn not to leave. Not to leave or be forced to leave. So he'd written the three letters in the box and slipped the document over the counter.

Luke had been relieved for two reasons. First, there'd been no soap opera where medical staff tried to force him from Tom's room. And second, when the nurse had let the listed relationship slip, Tom hadn't flown off the handle.

Luke had spoken in whispers with the doctors outside the room. Yes, he knew his *father* was dying, and there wasn't anything they could do but make him comfortable. It'd be easier if they admitted his *father* in order to keep him on an IV of stronger pain medication. He didn't have much longer. Chances were that he'd take his *father* and either be back at the hospital shortly, or he'd slip into a coma at home. But it was his choice. And he should discuss it with his *father* first.

"Privately," Luke said. If Tom heard them, he'd hit the roof.

"Of course."

And cue the nurse who bounced into the room to adjust the morphine: "Mr. DuBelle, your son is here to see you."

Goddamn, motherfucker.

"What?" Tom had been resting, but his eyes opened wide.

"I said, 'Your son is here to see you.'"

You stupid, fucking bitch.

"Leave." Luke turned to the nurse and glared at her. "I said I wanted to talk to him privately. Privately! Get out!"

She rushed out as if he'd lit the cuffs of her scrubs on fire. When the door closed behind her, Luke perched on the edge of the chair at Tom's bedside and took his hand.

"Tom, I'm sorry. I'm so sorry. But if I hadn't put it on your intake form, I was worried they wouldn't let me see you if something happened. I'm sorry."

He'd been heavily medicated, but Luke still expected Tom to be livid. His hand would shoot out like a viper, grasp him by the collar, and jerk him close. He'd yell, swear at him, and command Luke from his sight before pushing him backward in disgust. Tom's original rules had been demolished, and this was *the* cardinal sin.

But Tom closed his eyes.

"I'm not your father. You had a father. But−" Tom paused, possibly to gain control as his voice wavered. "−over the past few months, you've been *like* a son to me. *Like* a son." He reopened his eyes and turned to Luke, giving a weak smile. "So, even if I could kill you, I might, under the circumstances, reconsider."

That was a good way to put it. Going back to the first important truth−if Tom was okay, so was he. Tom had been *like* a father to him. And as he was reminded by the beeping machines, he was also on the verge of having to be okay with losing him.

"Before you become a blubbering mess, I need to own up to one more thing. Something important." Tom proved again his aptitude for reading Luke's thoughts.

"Of course." Luke pressed his hand and tried to focus on whatever vital thing Tom wanted to impart.

"I know I probably don't need to tell you, but what I said the night you showed up at my condo? About putting no more thought into you than five minutes with a bad porno mag? I lied."

"I know you did."

"It was a great porno mag."

As he had on the first night he spent with Tom, Luke buried his face in his folded arms at Tom's bedside. But instead of sobbing, he laughed. And when he felt the hand ruffling his hair, he hadn't pretended it was Jay. He was glad it was Tom.

"You really are a mess, you know? Save your keening for when I no longer require you to entertain me." Tom chuckled, but his voice became solemn once Luke looked at him. "In all seriousness, I thought of you often. You and your sister. What things could've been, and what they really were. I was proud of you and loved you though you weren't mine to be proud of or to love."

In a way, Luke wished it'd been left at the joke. He felt like a hand grasped his throat, and his stomach was grinding into knots. He couldn't speak. How could he possibly respond with anything as—

"Don't bother. I prefer to have the last word. I don't say things to hear responses. I speak because I like the sound of my own voice. That's where you get it from." Tom winked. "So, what's the plan?"

Glad for a momentary reprieve, Luke had proceeded to repeat the options the doctors had given. Tom could have a room at the hospital, or he could go home. They could make him more comfortable at the hospital, but it was up to him.

"Where do *you* want me to go?"

Luke hadn't understood why Tom asked this. He wasn't the person dying, and he'd assured Tom that whatever his choice, he wasn't going anywhere.

"What would be easiest for you, Luke?"

Easiest for him? To not have Tom die. To have Jesus Christ appear at the foot of the bed and, in touching Tom's body, rip this awful disease away. To walk out the doors with him, return to the condo, and hear him play his piano long into the night. *That* would've been easiest. But with divine intervention not on the table per the norm...

If Tom stayed at the hospital, there'd be a team of medical professionals to help Luke care for him. Tom wouldn't be alone, and neither would Luke. If they went home, there'd come a moment when Tom would be gone. And he could handle messes, medications, and vigils. He felt he was even ready to go through another night like the first, with Tom hallucinating. But he didn't know if he could stand to be alone. If Tom died at the hospital, there'd be a nurse or someone he could embrace and cry on. If he died at home, Luke would have no one. Did Tom know he was scared of that? Not of his dead body, but of the silent rooms? Yes, the hospital would be easiest.

But he'd seen in Tom's face that, though he'd be willing to do whatever Luke preferred, he wanted to go home.

"I think we should go home," Luke said. "How will your disciples find you here, yogi? I didn't hang a note on the door."

"That's right. You're a very irresponsible young man." Tom gave a deep sigh.

Luke was sure this wasn't the first he'd been called a man, but if it'd been said to him prior, it hadn't been true. So he liked to think of this as the first *real* time.

"I'll let them know we're going."

"Tell them we're taking this drip with us; it's fantastic."

"Tom." He stood in the doorway, unable to forget what Tom had said. He couldn't leave without a response. Facing a difficult situation with bravery was part of no longer being a little boy. "If I'd known, I—"

"Would have sent me a mug and a tie every year? What do I need twenty-seven mugs for? And I don't wear ties. Don't beat yourself up about things you had no awareness of and that don't matter anymore."

"I wouldn't have sent you stupid shit. I just—"

"If we're talking high quality merch, maybe you should beat yourself up about it."

"Please." It may've been the manner in which Luke made the simple request—the end of the word choked back as he fought to stay collected. He was confident there'd be no interruption. "You're right, I did have a father, but you're still special to me. And I do love you." He scrubbed his hand over his face. "I just wish I had more time with you."

Luke considered walking out of the room. End the scene in a drama-filled, heart-wrenching moment. But this wasn't Broadway, and he wasn't just reading lines.

"You've given me a lot over the past few months, and I thank you for that." He didn't have to look at Tom again to know that he wasn't alone in battling emotion. Purposefully, he stared at the door jamb.

"Is there anything else I can do for you?"

"Yes." Silence passed until Luke relented and met Tom's eyes. "We can swing by the fro-yo place on the way home."

Tom smiled and settled back into his pillows.

Luke left the room and held it together until he reached the nurse's station. He broke down as he relayed that he'd be taking his father home to die.

As he'd promised himself eight months prior, Luke stayed with Tom until it was over. He set up a bed next to the piano and played for him as well as he could, though his mistakes became more frequent, compounding until it was just noise. Tom hadn't seemed to care. For a while, he pressed his hand against the frame to feel the vibrations from the casing as Luke played.

But there came a point when Luke hadn't been able to play further. And it was around the time when Tom hadn't seemed to be listening anymore. Luke pulled a chair to the bed and held Tom's hand.

He'd been terrified for the end to come, but Luke tried to give himself courage by comparing this with Jay's death. Jay's had been the only other death he'd witnessed, and it had been terrible. Holding someone's hand as they slipped away had to be better than cradling a ruptured head in your lap. Wasn't that true? It had to be.

It wasn't. He would've rather had Tom get mowed up by a Honda Civic like his father, or commit suicide as he'd planned months ago. It'd been horrible to sit by his side and wait for the inevitable. He'd meditated on a thousand things he should've said to Jay when he'd been dying, a thousand things he'd say if he had another chance. But now he had nothing. As Tom's list had escaped him twenty-eight years earlier, Luke's list failed him now. Such moments couldn't be planned. He didn't know what to say.

So he didn't say. He sang. In a quiet voice, he sang what he'd sung when Tom had seen him on stage. With one hand, he stroked his hair. The other he kept clasped in Tom's hand in the exact position it had been in the last time he'd opened his eyes. And he whispered the song over and over. It broke repeatedly with the lumps in his throat and the pauses he had to take because the tears were too much when Tom's breaths became ragged. Over and over and over. Until Tom's breaths hadn't come at all.

And then Luke had been alone.

He was just as alone now, holding the urn and looking at his father's grave. A house full of his family waited to welcome him back, but he still felt alone. As alone as Jay may have felt when he knew he was trapped on a stage in a performance he wasn't meant for? As alone as Tom had been when Jay rejected him? When Ginger had spent a month waiting for divorce papers? When Jackie and Beau had spent the same month worrying he was dead in a gutter? Maybe.

Luke realized that everyone felt alone sometimes. The awareness was nothing fancy. Nothing multifaceted or clever like the yogi would have appreciated. But it was true. Everyone felt alone. And the reverse was also true. Everyone also felt like the world revolved around them sometimes.

But neither place is a good home. Neither is a true home. You have to battle to the middle ground. To be happy with yourself, but striving for better.

Luke had initially planned to scatter Tom's ashes over Jay's grave, but now faced with that moment of action, he didn't feel right about it. He sighed and tilted his head from side to side, trying to arrive at what Tom would want. What his father would want.

Even if I'm not the center of the universe, though, I still matter. And I don't want to dump you here like a cigarette tray.

So he took the urn back to the car and sat it in the front seat. He would keep Tom with him until the right place came along. If it came along. Until then, he'd place the urn on the mantle of his apartment in New York. And he'd turn it so there was a new picture facing the room every day, just to keep people guessing who was in there.

About the Author

James Stryker is a Central Pennsylvania author who enjoys writing speculative and literary fiction. Themes in his work focus toward diversity in the LGBTQ spectrum and the voice of underrepresented or misunderstood viewpoints. His debut novel, *Assimilation*, was released in 2016.

James shares a residence with a pack of pugs, who continue to disagree about the ratio of treats to writing. Despite his day job and writing projects, James is never too busy to connect with readers or other writers. He welcomes you to check out his website, follow him on social media, or drop a line to his email.

Facebook: https://www.facebook.com/JamesScottStryker
Twitter: http://www.twitter.com/JStryker21
Website: http://www.jamesstryker.com/
Email: jstryker21@gmail.com

Coming Soon from James Stryker

The Simplicity of Being Normal

Excerpt

"Amanda Michelle! I won't tolerate that mouth of yours a second longer! Get out!"

"Or what? You'll hit me? Repeat performance sixteen years later. Go ahead!"

If there was one positive thing to be said of his mother, it was that she avoided violence. While her own mother had often resorted to physical punishment, Scarlet had never put a hand on Stevie. And she'd only hit Sam once, which was how she learned her lesson.

"Amanda was maybe one. Barely walking. I can't remember what she did, but I hit her so hard that she flew across the room. That's when I decided to keep my temper in check. I just send them away when I'm angry now."

Scarlet recited this story often when child discipline surfaced in adult conversation. She was proud of herself. Proud that it only took one incident of hitting a toddler with enough force to knock her across the room to realize that violence wasn't a good idea. She never understood why she received strange looks when she finished this charming anecdote of her parental prowess.

Because you should be ashamed *that you struck an innocent baby. That you hurt your child,* Sam would think when Scarlet told it, and people gave him the confused looks he often received when his mother opened her mouth. *You should want to bury that secret instead of continuing to get off on it more than a decade later. The last thing you should feel is pride.*

But sometimes he'd rather have a slap to the face than the emotional abuse Scarlet dealt. Bruises healed. The damage from seventeen years of being blamed for every negative circumstance? The constant feeling of rejection? The thousands of times when something or someone else was of more importance than him? His father. Stevie. The boyfriends. Work. The fucking *Golden Girls*.

I'll never get over it. Even when I'm free of you. Even when I'm free of Amanda. Sam stared Scarlet down and waited for her to respond. *You're a cancer to me. I'll cut you out. But I'll always have the scar.*

"Get out, Amanda! Get out!"

"Oh, I'm going." He lowered his voice and stepped into the hall. "But so should you. That's all I came to tell you. You should check into a hotel for a few days. It's not sanitary. And that's not even my opinion—it's the disaster crew's recommendation. You could get sick."

"This is *my* house, young lady. I won't be told what to do by you or anyone else."

It was the most below-the-belt thing he could be called, and his skin was smoldering. Sam didn't believe he was capable of laying a hand to anyone, especially a woman. But he needed to leave before he said something he'd regret. Like yelling in her face at the top of his lungs. Like using every profane word he could think of until her ears bled. Like divulging his secret when she had some power over him.

"Well, I'm not staying here."

"As long as it's out of my sight, I don't care where you go." She'd turned away. "But Stevie and I are staying here. I'm not going to pay for a hotel room because the basement is dirty."

"You know what else lives in their own shit? Pigs. It's too bad Gary's condo doesn't allow farm animals, or you could stay with him."

Scarlet spun around and slammed the door in his face without another word.

www.ingramcontent.com/pod-product-compliance
Lightning Source LLC
Chambersburg PA
CBHW022013170626
46808CB00001B/387